Falconburg Divided
Book 1 of the Falconburg Trilogy

Sarah J. Waldock

©Sarah J. Waldock 2017
ISBN 1546532757
ISBN-13 978-1546532750

Dedication & Acknowledgement

Thank you, Syltermermaid and Farconville,
Renderosity & Daz Studio for enabling my artwork.

Other books by Sarah Waldock

Sarah writes predominantly Regency Romances:

The Brandon Scandals Series
- The Hasty Proposal
- The Reprobate's Redemption
- The Advertised Bride
- The Wandering Widow

The Charity School Series
- Elinor's Endowment
- Ophelia's Opportunity
- Abigail's Adventure
- Marianne's Misanthrope
- Emma's Education/Grace's Gift
- Anne's Achievement

One off Regencies
- Vanities and Vexations [Jane Austen sequel]
- Cousin Prudence [Jane Austen sequel]
- Friends and Fortunes
- None so Blind
- The Unwilling Viscount
- Belles and Bucs [short stories]

The Georgian Gambles series
- The Valiant Viscount [formerly The Pugilist Peer]

Other
- William Price and the 'Thrush', naval adventure and Jane Austen tribute
- 100 years of Cat Days: 365 anecdotes

Sarah also writes historical mysteries

Regency period 'Jane, Bow Street Consultant 'series, a Jane Austen tribute
- Death of a Fop
- Jane and the Bow Street Runner [3 novellas]
- Jane and the Opera Dancer
- Jane and the Christmas Masquerades [2 novellas]
- Jane and the Hidden Hoard
- Jane and the Burning Question [wip]

'Felicia and Robin' series set in the Renaissance
- Poison for a Poison Tongue
- The Mary Rose Mystery
- Died True Blue
- Frauds, Fools and Fairies
- The Bishop of Brangling
- The Hazard Chase
- Heretics, Hatreds and Histories
- The Midsummer Mysteries
- The Colour of Murder
- Falsehood most Foul

Children's stories
- Tabitha Tabs the Farm kitten
- A School for Ordinary Princesses [sequel to Frances Hodgson Burnett's 'A Little Princess.]

Non-Fiction
- Writing Regency Romances by dice

Fantasy

Falconburg Divided [book 1 of the Falconburg brothers series]

Falconburg Rising [book 2 of the Falconburg brothers series, WIP]

Falconburg Ascendant [book 3 of the Falconburg brothers series, WIP]

Sarah Waldock grew up in Suffolk and still resides there, in charge of a husband, and under the ownership of sundry cats. All Sarah's cats are rescue cats and many of them have special needs. They like to help her write and may be found engaging in such helpful pastimes as turning the screen display upside-down, or typing random messages in kittycode into her computer.

Sarah claims to be an artist who writes. Her degree is in art, and she got her best marks writing essays for it. She writes largely historical novels, in order to retain some hold on sanity in an increasingly insane world. There are some writers who claim to write because they have some control over their fictional worlds, but Sarah admits to being thoroughly bullied by her characters who do their own thing and often refuse to comply with her ideas. It makes life more interesting, and she enjoys the surprises they spring on her. Her characters' surprises are usually less messy [and much less noisy] than the surprises her cats spring.

Sarah has tried most of the crafts and avocations which she mentions in her books, on the principle that it is easier to write about what you know. She does not ride horses, since the Good Lord in his mercy saw fit to invent Gottleib Daimler to save her from that experience; and she has not tried blacksmithing. She would like to wave cheerily at anyone in any security services who wonder about middle aged women who read up about making gunpowder and poisonous plants.

Sarah would like to note that any typos remaining in the text after several betas, an editor and proofreader have been over it are caused by the well-known phenomenon of *cat-induced editing syndrome* from the help engendered by busy little bottoms on the keyboard.

This is her excuse and you are stuck with it.

You may find out more about Sarah at her blog site, at:
http://sarahs-history-place.blogspot.co.uk/

Chapter 1

A single candle flame flickered feebly past the high turret window; and was suddenly paled into invisibility as a bolt of lightning ripped across the storm-black sky outside. For an instant the castle stood outlined luridly against the angry sky; then all was profoundly black. Almost immediately a crash of thunder shook the very stones of the keep and the little candle flame guttered apologetically in the draughty corridor.

"Don't go out on me," muttered a low voice.

The hand of the cloaked and cowled owner of the voice sheltered the flame, coaxing it into bolder life. The stairs were steep and treacherous; it would not do to negotiate them without any light. Gradually the flame lengthened and strengthened; and the figure heaved a subdued sigh of relief, careful not to breathe too hard on the insubstantial light. The way was lit; and the candle flame bobbed as it was carried downstairs, round the twisting turret stairway into the richly decorated rooms below. Feebly its light fell on painted pilasters and gaudy tapestries designed to make the main living quarters more comfortable and draught-free than the little room where it had begun its journey. As the flame danced in the airflow in the larger rooms, lightning again shredded the sky, bringing the colours into brief, stark clarity. Again came the sharp detonation of thunder, terrifyingly loud to the fugitive whose ears were straining to hear sound of imminent discovery. It was just in time that the thunder's angry grumble receded to permit the sound of footsteps to echo hollowly along the main corridor; and the gleam of a torch preceded the guards as they approached. Quickly the candle was blown out; the way would be easier from here anyway. The cloaked figure stepped nimbly into an alcove behind a tapestry, listening as the guards came closer, chatting idly. Their talk revealed that they had no qualms that anything was amiss, for the talk was inconsequential: though the bawdy story recounted in great detail by one of them brought a blush unbidden to the face of the fugitive.

Again the night was torn and shaken by the storm and one of the guards shuddered

"I hate this," he declared. His companion shrugged.

"So does everyone else." He said philosophically. "At least you can guarantee that for the first time you've been on night watch everyone else in the castle is also awake."

The first laughed a little shakily. Storms

frightened him.

"Except Hugh the vintner." He attempted a feeble joke. "Nothing short of Ragnarok – uh, I mean Armageddon – would waken him. I wonder how the Lady Annis is coping up so near the sky in her turret?"

The other had shot him a reproving look at his pagan lapse, but answered the man's question.

"I'll wager Lady Annis doesn't turn a hair. That young 'un has nerves of steel. Besides, she'll be all right. She doesn't have to go outside as we do to check the stable block. And 'tis no good putting it off by askin' impertinent questions and droolin' over the thought of the young mistress sleepin' you craven whoreson, so move."

They moved off, the other expostulating over his companion's intimations about his thoughts and went reluctantly out of the postern and into the stables. Still the fugitive waited, though in the confined space it seemed that a frightened heartbeat could rival the thunder for noise. After what seemed an age, the guards returned, grumbling gently about the driving rain; and went back the way they had come. The fugitive pulled a face. Rain was all that was needed!

Presently a dark figure was slipping out of the postern. Carefully the wet and slippery steps into the stable yard were negotiated, by the fitful light of a cloud-tossed moon; and the figure slid thankfully into the warmth and dryness of the stables. The horses stirred slightly at the sound of the stable door and the horse Rowan whickered gently as he caught a familiar scent; and was hushed. A concealed pack was retrieved from where it had been hidden earlier. Quickly, efficiently, slender hands saddled and bridled the horse and led him out. The outer postern was unguarded; the path to it was too precipitate for any that did not know its pitfalls intimately. The fugitive did know it, had climbed it countless times; and within half an hour was safely down on the flat, the horse Rowan following trustingly. On the flat Rowan was mounted; and the rider skilfully picked a path that would avoid most of the village that sprawled at the castle's foot. Once beyond habitation, the rider reined in the horse and looked back. The hood fell back as the lightning flashed, revealing the pale gold aureole of Lady Annis' hair and her serious blue eyes dark in her pale face. She smiled once, grimly, resettled the pack she had prepared; and rode off, turning her back on the castle where she had grown up.

Dawn found Annis sheltering in the Great

Woodland in the hollow trunk of an ancient oak. Rowan whickered deep horsey disapproval as the leaves of the gnarled old tree shook in the morning breeze and gave up droplets of water they had shielded so well from the forest floor during the storm.

Annis emerged from her shelter and stretched out the kinks of an uncomfortable night. She unhitched her unhappy horse.

"Come now, Rowan, let us find a stream for a morning drink. You will feel better for that, and some soft grass." She soothed the young stallion. Rowan showed her the whites of his eyes to give her to understand that midnight jaunts in the rain were not things of which he approved; but Annis merely laughed at him and patted his neck. "Now it is light I shall rub you down well," she told him; "As soon as we have found a good place to see to our thirst."

Annis led the beast to a clearing where soft grass carpeted the bank of a laughing brook, swelled by the storm rain. Tentative shafts of early sunlight quested their way into this little hollow, warming the wet grass and bringing it steaming into a light mist that swirled thicker about their feet as they passed through it. Spiders' webs sparkled with diamond drops of water strung on their silken threads. Birds sang with gay celebration of a new bright dawn; it looked like being a fine late summer's day. Annis watered Rowan and settled him to graze after a rub down with a blanket from her pack.

"There now, I imagine you are glad to have lugged the extra weight for this, mmm?" She laughed. Rowan gave her a sideways look. "I almost think you understand at least half what I say to you." She added. "Though I'm sure someone would say it heresy to even suggest it in fun. Now, have some breakfast and stop looking hard done by. You are fat and lazy anyway." She left the horse to his own devices as she breakfasted for herself on some of the oatcakes she had brought, sitting in her petticoats with her cloak and dress laid over a thorn bush in the sun to dry. She must wait too until the sun had risen enough to dry vegetation; for there were herbs in abundance in this woodland for the gathering. Annis planned to pay her lonely way through the world by pedalling herbs and simples, for she was skilled in the use of herbal medicines.

Sun-warmed and feeling free, Annis sought herbs that thrived in the wooded environment. Shady nooks were filled with violets, none in bloom, but with an abundance of leaves, good for coughs. Comfrey, such a versatile herb, grew on well-drained hillocks under smaller trees, loving partial shade; it was rather late in the year for the best of the leaves, a little early for the root: but Annis shrugged and made the best of it. Back down near the stream she found angelica for indigestion, and willow, the bark of which would make such a good painkiller and combat fever. Blackberry grew abundantly everywhere as did nettle for rheumatism and dandelion for bladder trouble. She had to search for eyebright, stealing the goodness from the ground-hugging plants it colonised slyly underground by suckers; yet so useful that it seemed wrong to think of it merely as a parasite. She felt lucky to find a clearing filled with feverfew, still in flower with its raggy white daisy flowers. Feverfew was rarely out of flower save in the winter months, there were usually a few flower heads right through the autumn. Annis chose leaves from those plants that were not in flower, for they would be stronger in effect, not having to go to the effort of reproduction. Headache sufferers would be glad of a tea made from them! She had put on a simple gown of unbleached wool, that it matter little if she damaged it on thorns or stain it from the picking of her herbs; and she might have passed as a peasant wench.

Annis was so engrossed in her labours, selecting the best leaves, that she did not hear the men entering the clearing.

It was the sound of a harsh, grating voice

that made the girl whip round as it broke the stillness in the glade.

"See, Pierce, a pretty wench. Jus' a-waitin' for ussen, wouldn' you say?"

The speaker was a hefty man with heavy jowls and greasy hair. He was dressed well enough, but there was a suggestion about his clothes of unkemptness; and Annis could smell the stale sweat on his body as he moved. His companion was little better, though his armour-clad jerkin at least seemed well cared for. Both men had serviceable looking weapons. Annis thought to herself 'mercenaries' and felt slightly sick.

The two men advanced on Annis. The girl's heart was pounding; but she stood her ground. Running would be nothing but an exercise in futility; they could easily outrun her – and they stood between her and Rowan. Unseen, however, by her would-be attackers Annis held the big knife she had been using to hack back brambles. She kept it held relaxed at her side, hidden in the folds of her gown, forcing herself to breathe deeply and easily. Now the unwomanly lessons in warcraft she had pestered out of Will the Steward would show their usefulness. Still as she could make herself, Annis stood until the first was reaching out to her, chuckling.

"Look like she'm a willin' wench too!" He crowed, his hand on the front of Annis' robe.

He bent forward towards her, and Annis tried not to blench as she smelled the foulness of his breath. Her training told her dryly that he should have chewed on liquorice and cloves; and she firmly dismissed the thought, concentrating on what had to be done.

The man screamed, once, a scream that ended on a horrid gargle as she struck; struck the way Will had showed her as she played at being a warrior in the happy days before her father returned. She had got it wrong; her knowledge of anatomy told her where the heart should be, but somehow the resistance of the body to the knife caused the blade to deflect. He should have been dead instantly; and was not. Annis stared in horror as her assailant sat down, his hands clasped to the sticky red ooze from his side, a surprised look on his face. He looked up at her reproachfully, opening his mouth to speak; but a red froth came instead of words and with awful slowness he rolled over to one side and lay still.

Waves of nausea roiled through Annis and she faltered. The other villain, the one called Pierce, recovered his wits first and leaped at her, drawing his sword. He called out, summoning companions.

"Hey, fellas, there's a wench here an' she's gutted Solly!" He cried, holding his sword threateningly. Annis acted instinctively as the blade came close, swinging up her own short weapon to knock his away.

The man was heavier, better trained, the veteran of many battles. There should only have been one outcome. But suddenly the man dropped the point of his sword, stepping out of range of the girl's knife as he did so, keeping half a watch on her but mostly staring behind her, a look of fear lurking at the back of his eyes. It might be a trick; but Annis knew she had to look over her shoulder.

Besides, the thud of hoofbeats on the short turf told her that they had been joined by another; and Annis wondered in sudden terror whether her father had discovered her absence and come to find her. If he had, she would never have another opportunity to escape! She turned slowly, unwillingly; and heaved a sigh of relief that she knew not the newcomer.

A man on horseback had entered the clearing. The first impression Annis had was of black: his horse was black, he was garbed entirely in black, even his hands on the bridle wore soft black leather gloves. A closer look revealed the glint of steel; and his curiously wrought helmet was dark metal but looked very serviceable. The helmet was wrought to resemble a bird of prey, the eye on one side filled with some magical glass which looked like a mirror, the other side showing enough of his features to intimidate with a scowl.

Annis quailed inwardly.

Everyone had heard stories about Gyrfalon the Warlord, despoiler and spawn – so they said – of the Devil. Here on the northern marches of Alegothia, King Engilbert's writ did not run; such law as there was came from the martial might of the individual barons and brigand lords. And both barons and brigand lords thought twice before tangling with Gyrfalon, said to once have been a nobleman, and now the most feared and ruthless brigand lord of them all.

Annis, as a healer, had little time for superstition: but she knew this was a man to be feared. The better, therefore, not to show it. This might just be as bad as falling into the hands of her father or his men.

Annis spread her skirts in a curtsey and forced a polite smile.

"Lord Gyrfalon," she murmured. "I am …. charmed to make your acquaintance."

His visible eyebrow raised in supercilious surprise at her cultured accents; with her torn bodice bespattered with the blood of her dead assailant her attempts at civility seemed incongruous. The corner of his mouth twitched with rare amusement at the girl's boldness.

"How flattering to be recognised," he mused. His voice, though quiet, was redolent with the menace of the sound of a steel blade drawn from its sheath. "But you have the advantage of me, girl. I do not like that. What is your name?"

He checked his black horse as it tossed its head impatiently; Annis noted that muscles like steel held the mettlesome beast with seeming effortless grace. She swallowed but kept her chin up.

"My name is Lady Annis Haldane of Highkeep, daughter of its custodian, Lord Peter Haldane," she answered him fair. "I do apologise, my lord, for not being dressed suitably to receive an illustrious visitor; you see I was not expecting you."

Gyrfalon stared at this conventional inanity and gave her a suspicious look. Annis knew her dimple was popping in and out as she contained an incongruous mirth over her ridiculous comment; and the warlord noticed. The eyebrow went up again and he scowled, unsure how to take such deliberate flippancy. He dismounted, throwing the rein to an underling who stood close by the horse's head to hold it still. He strode over to Annis.

"And what," purred the black garbed figure, "is the lady Annis Haldane of Highkeep doing abroad at this hour of the morning and unattended?"

Annis swallowed again, bit her lip and dropped her gaze. Her chin was raised roughly by Gyrfalon's riding crop. He stared at her thoughtfully.

"Riding to meet a lover?" He queried. She snorted derisively. The eyebrow twitched upward. "Well as you say, you are not dressed for that anyway ... A runaway then?" He asked softly, and read the truth in her defiant eyes. "Well well! To run implies cowardice – which I despise – but your spirited stance against poor Solly gives that the lie. And," a sneer flashed briefly across the bronzed face, "You know my name but show little outward fear. A paradox."

Annis sniffed.

"To judge by stereotype is orthodoxy; which will leave many a paradox; and a fine pair o'doxies they be," she could not resist the word play even in a potentially desperate situation. "If you will but take your whip from my throat, my lord, I might just feel civil enough to answer your question," she added tartly.

The corner of his mouth twitched at the impudence of her first comment; and at the second he stared.

"Do you rebuke me?" He asked, amazed.

"If the rebuke is meet, accept it," she snapped, looking down her small straight nose. His assumption that such tactics would intimidate her irritated her beyond the fear engendered by his reputation.

There was a gasp from those men who had joined Gyrfalon in the grove. Gyrfalon glowered for a moment; then threw back his head and laughed, withdrawing the whip from under the girl's chin and thrusting it back in his belt.

"Just a snip of a girl," he roared, "but with more balls than the lot of you!"

"Excuse me, my lord," interrupted Annis, "whilst that may have been intended for a backhanded compliment, may I say I have never before been accused of possessing male accoutrements."

Her comment amused the warlord.

"You are no blushing violet, either," he remarked. "So, what am I to do with you, Lady Annis of Highkeep? Mayhap your loving father Lord Peter will pay well for your safe return?"

Annis shrugged.

"T'is a moot point, Lord Gyrfalon," she said carefully. "I may be some use to him as an instrument of alliance. It is, after all, apparently the lot of a woman to be bought and sold for the commodity of a small and insignificant region of flesh, be that many times for a street whore or as a singular transaction if she be a lady." She considered briefly with a frown. "Though the price is higher in the latter case, the rent might in normal circumstances be expected to cover the use of more internal organs for nine month periods." Her voice held scarcely concealed bitterness over these prospects.

Gyrfalon grinned maliciously.

"So do we have a loving bridegroom who might also pay for his pretty bride, do we?" he asked

Annis swallowed.

"My Lord Gyrfalon," she spoke carefully and with what she fondly hoped was dignity, "I am a skilled herbalist and healer. As such I could be of more use to you and your men than the small amount of gold you might extract from either my father or his choice of husband for me. They would seek aid from the Church first for my ...betrothed has ... cronies," she chose the word with care, "high in the Church." Her young voice was filled with scorn.

He paused, surprised.

"You sound as though you scorn the Church – yet you wear a crucifix." He accused, gazing upon her cross with loathing.

"I believe in God, my lord," she answered him evenly. "But I also know that corruption gnaws deep at the roots of the Church, filling those venal churchmen who seek only power and advancement with the temptations of peculation and chicanery. Such creatures as Lord Marfey are hypocrites who use their supposed devotions to bribe the corruptible into turning a blind eye to any perfidy!" Her voice rang clear in condemnation. "I had rather marry the Devil himself; who is at least an honest villain!" She finished, shocking herself at her own temerity.

Gyrfalon's laugh rang out again.

"And am I an honest villain too, then, girl?" He asked, still chuckling.

She regarded him thoughtfully.

"If the stories are true," she said carefully, "I'd say, if nothing else, you have, um, more balls than most of them."

There was a moment's stunned silence; then the warlord shook with silent laughter.

"Why, I do believe you might be the most amusing hostage I have ever held," he said. "I will indeed hold you ransom; but I may yet decide to double cross your father and keep you and the money both!"

He turned from her, his cloak swirling behind him as he vaulted lightly into his saddle; and made an imperious sign that she should mount Rowan and ride with his company. Annis remounted easily.

"Pass me my bag, fellow," she said to one of the soldiers.

He goggled.

"My Lord?" he asked Gyrfalon.

"What be in it?" the warlord demanded.

"Certain herbs that I planned to make into common simples to peddle," said Annis, "as it be a waste to leave here after mine efforts; that may also give proof to my words that I be a competent healer, and be used to aid your men. You have not felt it necessary to take my knife; there is nothing dangerous in my bag not even herbs that may be poison in large quantity. I had not yet gathered monkshood for a rub against rheumatism though an I work for you I would suggest you permit me to do so in the future. In the pack on my saddle are but my clothes which I will be needing."

"Hand her the bag," said Gyrfalon. "We shall see how good a healer she be."

So it was that Annis found herself riding back to Gyrfalon's castle. He had not had her tied; there was a sufficiency of men to make it obviously futile to attempt an escape. It was a fine day for a ride, and under other circumstances might have been enjoyable. Annis however was wondering whether she was out of the frying pan and into the fire; or whether this new development might somehow come out to her advantage. One thing she regretted was that her father would learn her direction and would be bound to act – one way or another.

It was not a far ride to the castle; the wood stood on the borders of the lands of Lord

Gyrfalon and Peter Haldane and made a rather uncertain boundary. They emerged from the woods not far from the warlord's castle, that it was said he had taken by force from its previous occupant who had been hanged from the walls. Annis knew not whether such were true or not; but she had heard no good tales of the previous occupant as a lord, though she had nothing against him save that he was a harsh taskmaster and accounted a hard man; as many a lord of the northern marches might be for the uncertainty of the living with the wild northern barons beyond them and brigandage rife across the country. She looked up at her new dwelling place with some interest.

The warlord's castle rose, gaunt and mournful, a sheer black crag piercing the mist that rose sullenly from the marsh that lay on three sides of the keep. Towers thrust aggressively upwards, darkening the rich cerulean blue of the late afternoon sky by their ominous presence. Ravens croaking on the embrasures made the vision almost too melodramatic.

Annis felt a gurgle of merriment rising, and could not entirely suppress it. Her laugh escaped as a snort and a gurgle.

Gyrfalon rounded on her.

"What is so funny?" He demanded.

Annis bit the inside of her mouth to bring herself under control; but her eyes still danced.

"I am sorry, my lord," she managed "But it is so....so....*suitable*!" And she dissolved again into gurgles of mirth. "So very much what one should expect as the castle of a bold bad baron!"

Gyrfalon's mouth twitched.

"I thought so when I took it from its previous owner," he said dryly. Annis hiccoughed once or twice and brought her laughter under control.

When they reached the village which sprawled untidily at the foot of the castle, Annis' amusement was wiped from her face. Dispirited peasants worked fearfully, leaping out of the way of the cavalcade as Gyrfalon and his men rode through the rude collection of huts; and their lacklustre eyes were cast down for fear of giving offence to any of the armed men. Annis drew her brows together in disapproval. This was fearful submission, not respect. She would have to do something. The girl noted that at least the village church had been left standing; a poor enough building, made of wattle and daub like the houses and barns, but still possessing its bell and proudly erect crucifix on the small steeple. Presumably Gyrfalon had left this as a sop to keep the peasants working; it was one thing at least. And she need not fear that a country priest would be tarred with the same brush as some of the cynical city ecclesiasts. Annis determined that she would do all she could to help the unfortunate peasants here.

The cavalcade swept on across the bridge that spanned the moat which was in truth merely a continuation of the marshy mere into which the castle's natural rocky foundation thrust. Within the outer walls, it was less forbidding: the courtyard was full of bustle and life. The keep was a large squat building, hunched sullenly against the rear wall. Around the walls were the customary wattle and daub outbuildings, between which people moved on their daily tasks. Gyrfalon looked around and picked out a leather clad warrior, beckoning imperiously. As the warrior approached, Annis saw that it was a woman, battle-hardened and competent looking, her blondish hair cut as short as a man's. Gyrfalon spoke.

"Elissa. This here," he swept his hand towards Annis, "is the Lady Annis. She is to be permitted free range of the castle and its environs,"

"Free range, Lord Gyrfalon?" Elissa queried, surprised. He grinned.

"You think I grow soft in my old age?" He

asked jocularly. Elissa swallowed and shook her head rapidly.

"Just clarifying, my lord," she said hastily.

He laughed harshly.

"It is my whim that she have free range," he repeated. "I rely on you to see to all her wants and needs, Elissa, and protect her from unnecessary insults. Oh," he added, smiling mirthlessly, "and kill her if she tries to escape."

The woman bowed her head.

"Yes, Lord Gyrfalon," she acquiesced.

Gyrfalon rode forward, leaving Annis face to face with the female warrior, who was appraising her, evidently not delighted at the prospects of seeing to the needs of some gentlewoman. It was quite plain that she expected the girl to require something between a wetnurse and a tiring maid. Annis smiled coolly.

"Pleased to make your acquaintance, Elissa," she said firmly. "My primary needs after I have settled into my involuntary accommodation will be your aid in maintaining my fitness – and lessons in swordplay. My skills are indeed basic; and it will aid towards making the protection part of your duties less onerous. I presume I am to go with you this time and not see to mine own horse."

She dismounted as Elissa blinked; and looked around for a stablehand. Gyrfalon was unashamedly listening; and Elissa turned to him.

"My lord, is this girl for real?" She asked bluntly. Gyrfalon gave Annis a quizzical look.

"She knows the rudiments of swordplay," he told the astonished warrior. "She killed Solly when he would have – amused himself – with her. If it amuses you to bring her on I shall not prohibit it. It may," he added dryly, "keep her out of trouble. Be careful, Elissa – I suspect our hostage has a propensity for being trouble."

Elissa re-avaluated the young girl. A ghost of a smile touched Annis' lips.

"Lord Gyrfalon is quite correct in some ways," she remarked. "Except that I never go looking for trouble. It just crops up unawares like a cheeky stablehand."

Gyrfalon's good eye glinted.

"Be wary, wench," he said softly. "I believe you just compared me to a cheeky stablehand."

Annis blinked.

"I was not," she said, looking down her nose, "at the time necessarily thinking of you, lord Gyrfalon, as trouble. Actually, right now you are more in the nature of a good angel." She smiled brightly at him.

"By all the devils in hell, girl, you know how to turn an insult!" Gyrfalon roared.

Annis let her gaze become limpid, though

her heart hammered at the temerity of the risks she was taking in playing such games with him.

"You will not want me then, lord, to put you in my prayers?" Her dimple twitched in and out despite her apprehension. Dangerous the game might be, playing word games: but it was fun, sheer fun! At last she had met one who appreciated her dry understated wit, recognising it for what it was, one who could appreciate irony and deliberate choices of words! Besides, her games seemed to please him; and Annis knew well that her only chance lay in pleasing the volatile warlord. She scorned to take the path of appeasement and grovelling; and had she but known it, to do so would have earned nothing but contempt, as indeed would gentle womanly compliance and civility. As it was he grunted a half laugh.

"I would fain prefer curses to prayers and blessings, girl. And when you have visited the turret room that shall be your prison, you will come to my apartment. Let us see what healing skills you really have." His mouth sneered as he swung down from his horse, handing the rein to an underling as he strode away.

Chapter 2

Annis wondered whether being assigned a turret room might be a good omen; for her chosen chamber in her erstwhile home had been high in a turret. The room to which she was taken differed little from her previous home; it was sparse, but Annis herself was an austere little person and saw no lack in the very basic furnishings with which she was provided. The view from the window across the marsh was decoration enough to her mind; the bleak beauty of God's creation, constantly enlivened by the abundant wildlife that the rich if sometimes noisome waters supported. As she watched there was a vivid flash of turquoise blue that was a kingfisher diving; and a heron flapped lazily by.

That she had passed Gyrfalon's apartments on the way up Annis knew, for Elissa had indicated the warlord's door; Annis judged that he held a room two floors below hers as well perhaps as a room or rooms within the body of the keep. She had not long until she might test her surmise; Elissa gave her enough time to lay down her pack and see to the more pressing of her bodily discomforts at the garderobe and quickly change into an untorn gown before hustling her back down the precipitate winding stairs. Annis felt happier however; not being in need of emptying her bladder was heartening and so was a clean gown, a soft woad-dyed blue gown of linsey-woolsey. The linen-wool mix was suitable for the warm day though she had warmer gowns too; if only that she might sell the odd gown if she was down on her luck. This gown was finer in cut too to the unbleached workaday gown, and had bands of blue and gold-coloured damasked silk binding the neck and bodice, and laid in stripes down the seams and in a broad band of purflage about an inch above the hem. It looked well on her, and Annis knew it. Elissa gave her a look of some brief envy for the fineness of the gown – she was female enough to admire beautiful clothes though she had chosen a warrior's path – ere she knocked on the heavy oaken door and nodded to the girl.

"I'll wait out here – to see you back or to bury your carcase," she told Annis laconically. Annis gave her a curt nod and went in.

Gyrfalon's room was as sparsely furnished as Annis' turret. It indeed occupied the situation the girl had surmised, but the circular turret opened through an arch into a big square room with a large window onto the courtyard and arrow slits in the curved wall that had an angle to overlook the side gate. In the far corner a bed stood, heaped with furs; a huge oaken table dominated the centre of the main part of the room. There were a few chests stood by the walls, mostly iron bound with intricate locks; and a great high backed chair across which the warlord had thrown his cloak. There was as yet no fire in the wide grate and no hangings to keep out the draught that would come with winter. The only spot of colour was in the maps lying on the table, weighted down under smooth river stones.

Gyrfalon looked up as Annis came in and his one eye glinted unkindly.

"Ah, healer." His voice was dangerously soft and held a note of sarcasm. "I would like your opinion of this."

With a sudden movement the warlord had removed his steel helm to display the dreadful ravaged mess that had been the left side of his face. The eye stared lifeless, sightless, whitely dull within a seething mass of livid scars; some weeping, some raw and angry, all repellent in their obvious agony.

Whatever reaction Gyrfalon had anticipated of Annis it was not the one he got.

"Sit." She instructed him sharply. "How can I make an examination when my eyes are no higher than your solar plexus?"

The logic was undeniable; and he sat, scowling. It had given Annis the second or two she needed to adjust to the horror of his wounds – not that she had felt any urge to recoil as perhaps many would, but to come to terms with the enormity of the wounds that could not fail to sicken by their extent. She approached her patient; and Gyrfalon's jaw tightened in disapproval as she took his chin to turn his ravaged face to the light. She frowned thoughtfully.

"Well?" He asked, harshly.

The girl stepped back and looked him squarely in the face.

"It is my opinion," she told him tartly, "that you should take whoever has been treating your face and hang him."

Gyrfalon blinked.

That was not what he had expected to hear; indeed that the fragile looking girl should make so ruthless a suggestion was enough to catch his interest anew. But she might easily say anything.

"Indeed?" His voice was heavy with sarcasm. "You could do better?"

"Assuredly," she said. "So far as I can determine, the sole treatment has been to sear away feeling rather than to attempt any kind of cure. It smells of witchery; and poor witchery at that."

"You are so sure, girl," he growled. "Yet there is no cure! The wound is cursed. Only witchery brings relief to such a wound."

"Nonsense!" she snapped. "If there is a curse, it could mean that it is not entirely curable; and a wicked curse it must truly be, too," she added "But it can surely be eased. You will not see immediate results – it will be several days before any ointments I prepare have any noticeable results – but undoubtedly I can ease the pain and maybe have at least something of a curative effect." She gave him a direct look. "You will have to give me an escort to collect specific herbs; and give orders that I am to have use of your stillroom, and that my pestle and mortar and other tools be not disturbed or used by any other, it will be" she smiled brightly "a challenging task."

He scowled again.

"And if I feel no relief in two or three days – shall I then hang you?" he growled.

She held his gaze.

"I would give it the seven days round," she suggested. "And then if you feel no relief, by all means hang me." Her voice was steady and calm; and it impressed him despite himself. Then her irrepressible dimple showed again. "But by then," she added "It should be feeling so much better that it even starts to mend your famous temper too."

He moved fast, and had her by the throat.

"Just watch my famous temper, my girl," he hissed. "I could break your neck where you stand."

Annis stood unmoving, scorning to let instinct drive her hands to his in fruitless struggle. He released her, and she stumbled; fought with her balance; and regained her stance, regarding him with her big solemn indigo eyes. They held no fear, nor even reproach; only, if anything, compassion. A shaft of late afternoon sun flashed on her gold crucifix, and Gyrfalon swore.

"By the powers of Hell, girl, how do I know you do not intend to use your potions to do more harm?" He spoke through gritted teeth. She looked down her nose scornfully.

"I am a healer. If I ever want to kill you I will wait until I am adept at sword and come front on, not in a coward's attack through skin-absorbed poisons. It is true that if I am lucky enough to find Mandrake, the preparations may cause you to feel detached for a while after I put it on, and maybe have vivid dreams at night, for it has side effects of hallucinations. I will not be using it in quantity, however, because of the risk of impaired judgement. If you mistrust me, either continue to be in pain, or send one with me that has herb lore. There is bound to be a village wise woman even if you have none in the rag tag and bobtail you field."

He ignored the insult to his men, the possibilities in what she had said previously striking him.

"It is possible then to kill with herbs through the skin?" He asked incredulously. She nodded.

"Eminently so – though it is more the mineral poisons than herbs that can be so used. But a man can be driven insane through dreams and visions – with mandrake, for one if the dose and the preparation is right. Enough to drive him to suicide. I know the means in order to counteract such poisons, but a true healer does not deal in such things; and I will not brew you potions to thus dispose of your enemies."

It pleased Lord Gyrfalon again to be amused at her temerity; and he barked a laugh before he dismissed her. And as he re-donned his helmet it occurred to him that not once had she either flinched or stared in horror at the ruin of his face; but looked at him as though it were still whole. Superficially the girl might bear a passing resemblance to his dead Alys; but there were depths to this one as yet unfathomable. And she feared him not.

What a son she would have made!

"He didn't kill you then," Elissa commented, as the girl emerged. Annis sniffed.

"I am neither important enough, nor insignificant enough for him to kill me. He may be a warlord with an insalubrious reputation – but he is a pragmatist. Else he had not remained a warlord long."

"My, you're cold blooded," marvelled Elissa.

Annis shrugged.

"I, too, am a pragmatist," she said. "My situation is not ideal, but it is an improvement on what might have been. And I intend to make the best of it. Meantime, he's going to arrange me an escort; I expect you'll be along. I have herbs to collect, and you never know what riff-raff you might meet in the woodlands."

She raised her voice slightly at the last comment, hearing the warlord's door opening, knowing he would know that the comment was aimed at him. She was rewarded by hearing a snort of appreciative amusement; Gyrfalon evidently enjoyed verbal fencing as much as she did. After all, she reflected, the rabble he had collected were scarcely a prepossessing bunch. He had even less scope for intelligent conversation than she had had since old Father Simeon had died last year. Father Tobias, his replacement, had been devout, dour, scantily educated and a dead bore. And it was so tedious to make a joke and either find it went over people's heads, or left them taking her seriously when she spoke in jest.

Annis rode out next morning with half a dozen armed men as well as Elissa. She had spent a fairly comfortable night, sleeping deeply as only the young can to catch up on her busy night the night before. The day was fine as it had been the day before and she had high hopes of finding everything she needed. Carefully she sought out the herbs she needed; more comfrey, the best leaves she could find; oak bark, for open wounds; plantain for the neutralisation of infection; sage too for its manifold healing properties; St John's wort, that great healer. By the stream she took willow bark for pain relief, then searched for borage in a dry clearing and eyebright nearby. Finally she smiled to herself as she recognised the leaves of the mandrake plant..

"Our final stop." She told her escort as she dismounted. "Mandrake."

There was a stir amongst the men. One of them even crossed himself. Superstitious awe showed in all their faces.

"You b'aint pullin' that right now, be you?" Asked one fearfully.

"Naturally," her tone was cool. "What would be the good of seeking it out and then leaving it?"

He shuffled, uncomfortable.

"But the safeguards ...." he began. She looked at him scornfully.

"You don't really believe that it screams when it is pulled?" She asked incredulously, referring to the superstition that mandrake pulled would scream loud enough to drive a man insane. He flushed.

"You mean it don't?" He asked. "Is that because it ain't midnight on a full moon? Don't that make it less effective?"

Annis sighed.

"The phase of the moon has nothing to do with the efficacy of any herb. Some herbs yield better effects at certain times of the year – the comfrey leaves are a little old and tough, for example. And the time of day may be important to prevent leaves being either damp, or dried right out. But there is no magic involved," she added, "However, at least you ask. What is your name?"

"T'is Kai, my lady."

"Then, Kai, if you are interested, you may assist me in the stillroom and I shall instruct you in the use of herbs." She smiled. "But you must never use mandrake until you are experienced; not for any magic, but because it can be a powerful poison if used carelessly."

"Lord Gyrfalon won't like you using a poison," he warned her. She laughed.

"All medicines are poison," she told him. "It is a matter of degree. Too much of anything can kill you. It's just that too much mandrake is a really small amount. Do not fear for your lord; I have used mandrake before and I know what I am doing. Now, help me pull it."

Kai swallowed and came forward to help her, taking his courage in both hands. The others retreated, two going so far as to ride out of earshot. Annis snorted.

"Lord Gyrfalon will know of such cowardice, be assured," Elissa said, as much to prevent the others from fleeing as anything else.

"She's got a crucifix," one of the other men, a big blond man, pointed out.

"So?" Elissa sneered. "If the thing screams, 'twill not prevent her hearing. And if the crucifix stops it screaming, why then you are safe too."

Annis rolled up her eyes, took off her cross and handed it to the fearful man.

"Do you hold it then if it makes you feel better," she said. Then she rolled up her sleeves and started to pull the roots she required. Kai grinned in honest relief as the first came up noiselessly; and helped her with a will to obtain a couple of other young roots. Annis examined them.

"Why," she said gaily "This one looks like my father's chaplain – I should call it Tobias."

"Will you do magic on him, lady?" Asked the blond one.

"Don't be so ridiculous," snapped Annis.

"Haven't I told you there is no magic involved? I made a joke, merely. I wish no ill on poor Father Tobias; nor have I any power to do so. And I'll have my cross back please." She took it as he meekly handed it back and slipped it back around her neck.

Not long after, Annis was busy pounding herbs with the help of Kai, and singing to herself. She was unaware how many people looked at her askance, since she was largely singing hymns; but no-one commented. At last she was satisfied, and filled several jars, sealing them with beeswax. She was still humming one of her favourite Lauds when she ran up the stairs with one of the jars to knock upon Gyrfalon's door and let herself in.

The warlord regarded her with disfavour.

"Do you have to sing that rubbish?" He grumbled brusquely.

Annis treated him to one of her brightest smiles.

"Yes," she said.

"What did you want?" he demanded.

"I have your ointment. Will you try it right away, my lord?"

He grunted.

"Why not?" he said; and removed his helmet.

Annis smeared a generous amount of her

concoction onto the livid wreck of a face, smoothing it in with the intense concentration that seemed to aid healing, though she knew not why. Perhaps there was witchery in it; but if so, it was unconsciously used, for Annis accounted herself far too practical to have need of any supernatural means. Her young hands, cool and gentle, soothed the searing heat; and the warlord gave vent to a long sigh.

"Aaaahhh yes, girl, I do believe you might know what you are doing." It had not been paining him as badly as sometimes or he would not have been in a good enough mood to let her try; but pain him it always did. Annis smiled thinly and replied to his comment.

"I were a fool indeed to boast unduly to a man not noted for his patience or forbearance," she remarked with some asperity. "I may see you as something of a saviour right now, but that does not mean I think you might be a plaster saint willing to overlook transgressions."

He grunted.

"I have been told by others that the task is beyond them," he said.

She stepped back and met his eye steadily.

"I have never promised you a cure," she said. "Remember that. I know I can bring relief. But I can understand that there would be those who would tell you that the task is impossible from the outset rather than face your wrath if they tried and failed. Your temper, my lord, is legendary in its ferocity. It scares people off from attempting difficult tasks lest you punish failure. Which be counterproductive from your point of view."

He scowled.

"I have found that fear can be a motivator. But tell me girl! Why are you not afraid lest you fail?"

She regarded him calmly.

"I really have nothing to lose." She said simply. "And besides, I always was a fool for a stiff challenge." She did not think it meet to add that pointing out the needs of his demesne was also a challenge she had set herself.

"You must fear your bridegroom very much if staying with me is to be preferred," his voice was mocking. "And he must be truly repulsive if you can look upon this face unmoved."

"I am not unmoved, my lord Gyrfalon. I am angered that anyone should set such a wicked terrible curse as to prevent such a painful wound from healing. As to my bridegroom – well, as to his physical form, he suffers from the self inflicted wound of overindulgence; for his face is swollen with too much food and drink, and his body with not enough exercise. Moreover, one day I shall tell you why it makes me laugh to hear you

37

described as evil when I have seen the results of the real thing. You, from what I have heard, are merely ruthless and vicious. It is my thought that you pull about you masks of 'Gyrfalon the wicked warlord' – pause for tinny fanfare played on ill-tuned trumpets – in a loud and flamboyant way in the same way that you mask your face. It is," she said sweetly, "often the way with the overly sensitive. I have finished for today," she added, gathering up her jar.

Gyrfalon spluttered.

"Overly sensitive??!!" he bellowed. "I have flayed men alive without flinching!"

"An exotic, if rather useless skill," she commented, firmly schooling her features. "But the hurt is soul-deep, else you would not care enough to hide it. And the melodramatic stories do not all sit with one practical enough to achieve what you have achieved in taking this castle, especially with the rabble with whom you ride."

He caught her by the throat.

"And what do you know about hurts soul-deep, girl?" he hissed.

Again, her eyes held compassion, not fear.

"Not, my lord, I think as much as you," she said quietly. "And it is not something I am qualified to heal."

He thrust her away.

"Go away and stop your silly prating," he

snarled. "Your mandrake juice leaves me light headed. Get out."

Annis left, shutting the door quietly after her, a thoughtful look on her youthful face, her big eyes smoky blue as they reflected her ponderings. Something or someone had hurt the warlord and he was rampaging like a wild beast in pain, avenging himself on the whole world. She would have to find out more; for her feelings were, she felt certain, correct in feeling that Gyrfalon had more to him than just a vicious mercenary commander.

Annis set herself to exploring the castle; so that she knew her way about. Elissa tagged along, half amused at Annis' youthful explorations, half bored.

Annis asked question of how Gyrfalon had taken the castle and that pleased Elissa to answer, for she was proud of her lord's prowess as a warrior; and he had managed to goad the previous lord into making a sally, that had been duly met while a second force – which Elissa had been a part of – skirted the force that rode out, Gyrfalon having tricked them into coming right forward, and rode like demons into the courtyard to take the gatehouse unawares and have control of the castle gate.

It was a simple but devastatingly clever trick; and Annis nodded approval.

She might approve less that all the defenders had then been slain; but she acknowledged that to have those within the castle who swore false fealty in order to avenge their erstwhile lord, or to have armed trained men turned loose outside were both risky that the warlord had little choice; and opined such.

Elissa nodded.

"Well you're no sentimental fool," she said.

"Myself I think I'd have turned them out and told them my men would patrol and would hang any that they saw," said Annis. "Without a leader they'd be inadequate to the task of retaking the castle. But with a small and rather motley band – the group you were with seeming the exception rather than the rule – I can see he'd not take that risk."

Elissa shrugged. She knew that they were a motley band, whom the warlord was licking harshly into shape with drills and practise. Hence the forest patrol he had himself been leading; and from what she had heard of Pierce and Solly wandering off on their own, Solly had in dying got out of the punishment enacted on Pierce for disobedience who had been flogged for it and was like to die of the same.

Annis did not know of this or she would have made salves for Pierce's back; but Gyrfalon had not troubled to tell her.

So instead she enjoyed herself in the exploring; and came upon chests in some upper chamber filled with lavender-scented cloths.

"Are these the clothes of the previous lord?" she asked curiously. Elissa shrugged.

"I suppose so," she said "My lord does not bother with any cloth save black; he will not have shown an interest."

"Will he mind, do you think, an I occupy myself between sword practise with sewing on such?" asked Annis.

Elissa shrugged.

"Why not ask him?" she said.

"I shall," said Annis and ran off lightly to knock on Gyrfalon's door while Elissa sighed to herself.

"What do you want?" demanded Gyrfalon.

"My lord, I have found discarded chests of clothing belonging, Elissa thinks, to the previous occupant; may I occupy myself sewing and using such fabrics as I find?"

He shrugged.

"I care not what you do with them; make what you will of them," he said indifferently.

"*Thank* you my lord!" said Annis.

Elissa was to curse somewhat at being involved in getting the chests up to Annis' turret room; but she could not help exclaiming with Annis over some of the beautiful fabrics.

"Gowns galore for both of us" said Annis happily, startling the woman warrior. "And these ones that have just been stuffed in for being worn, torn and rubbed, why then, that we may use in decoration, in the making of hangings to make the room warmer for the winter, and patched onto old blankets to give another layer as quilts."

"None of this 'we'," said Elissa "I don't sew."

"No matter; I do" said Annis cheerfully "And well too; oh my, there be *furs* in this chest!"

"No!" Elissa came to look.

"Fine ones as well as common coney," said Annis happily, "And look at this sable; I be certain I saw a black brocade in one of those chests, I might make Lord Gyrfalon a sable-lined robe as a Christmas gift. I should think he'd like that, don't you?"

"You're insane," said Elissa. "Yes he probably would; if you still be here at Christmas."

"Don't be so negative," said Annis "Once I persuade him I am more use to him as a healer than a hostage I be sure he'll like to keep me."

"Girl are you truly mad?" demanded Elissa "Nice young girls flee from Gyrfalon's very name; they don't ask to *stay* with him!"

"Well you chose service with him, did you

not?" said Annis, unanswerably.

Elissa grunted and chose not to answer what she could not without getting bogged down in the difference between a sell-sword who was not acceptable to many lords for the fact of being a woman and a lady of gentle birth that this silly chit seemed not to be aware of.

Between sword practice and the brewing of simples therefore Annis sewed contentedly. And Elissa sighed in wonderment and left her to it, whilst covertly admiring the clever way garments took shape beneath Annis' nimble fingers.

Chapter 3

The next few days saw the establishment of a routine. Morning and evening Annis applied her lotion to Gyrfalon's face; and in the morning before her visit to the warlord she took lessons in sword from Elissa. The other sell-swords in Gyrfalon's motley band were inclined to make game of the slight, young girl, and insult her; and since she wore breeches and a tunic as the most practical garb, some felt she might yet be easy, conveniently forgetting her stand against Solly in the forest, and attempted to handle her indelicately. Elissa fought one verbal tormentor; and when one man laid his hand on her pert little breast, Annis deliberately plucked the knife from his own belt and transfixed the offending member. The man howled with pain and rage: and his friends began to advance upon the girl, hands going to knives and menace in their faces. She dropped into a defensive stance with her sword, Elissa behind her, and prepared to fight. Once again she found trouble forestalled by Gyrfalon as his harsh mocking laugh rang out.

"The girl has taught you an object lesson I shall not have to, Ralph," he said, striding over. "She is a hostage; and she is no value deflowered before she can be returned to her bridegroom." He ignored the scowl Annis gave him. "I do," he purred silkily "so dislike my orders being disobeyed. I do trust it will not happen again?"

There were frightened murmurs of assent from the men. Gyrfalon's disciplinary measures for disobedience were inclined towards the rather final. The warlord smiled grimly.

"Good," he said. "Girl, you are getting competent, but I note that Elissa is teaching you her own bad habits. I will take over your training myself." In truth, Gyrfalon had been impressed by the girl's tenacity and instincts and felt her a potentially worthy pupil. He had seen few enough with the swordsman's instincts since he had trained his brother Falk as a boy. It would prove interesting.

Never one to waste time, Gyrfalon looked appraisingly at Annis.

"We will begin today I think," he said, "as your lesson with Elissa was cut short."

Annis nodded and buckled her sword back on. Gyrfalon gave a brief nod of approval that she wasted no words; not out of fear of denying him – he believed she would speak up soon enough an she disagreed with him – but because there was no need to speak.

The watching men had retreated somewhat; but as they were not dismissed outright, they remained to watch the fun. Gyrfalon was worth watching for his prowess at any time; and the men had seen those of their fellows who though they could best the warlord given painful and punishing lessons for their contumely. Besides, the linen tunic that Annis wore clung to her slender body where sweat had dampened it and it was a view the men enjoyed for its own sake; though Annis herself was unaware of the effect and the impact that it had.

Gyrfalon noticed it too; but said nothing. The garb the girl had chosen was practical to fight in, and his men had been warned not to pursue the lustful thoughts the sight would arouse in them. The chit would just have to put up with the lewd looks that would inevitably be cast her way at the soft curves of her trim figure.

The warlord set aside his cloak and surcoat for the exercise; well developed muscles rippled under the sleeveless leather vest beneath, a reminder of his panther-like speed and strength. Annis noted a white scar running across his chest beneath the lacing of the vest and wondered what story lay behind so grievous looking a wound. Her healer's eye approved his physical condition and was impressed with what she saw. There was not an ounce of surplus flesh on him and the tautness of the muscles on his flat belly showed his dedication to keeping himself fit. It was, reflected Annis, an attractive trait.

His voice broke harshly into her reverie.

"Do you know how to watch the belly muscles to see when your opponent signals that he is about to strike in his own body's betrayal of him – and why?" he asked.

She nodded briefly.

"Some men will change their expression; others shift their grip. But all flood the lungs with air and it creates a ripple" she said.

He nodded, well pleased.

"A more useful catechism for you to learn than any the church teach; though later I will show you how a man in the peak of fitness do *not* do that; that he may increase his lung capacity enough that he have enough air without drawing in more than a normal breath," he said.

"And I presume you do such that make it harder for me?" she said wryly.

"When I fight for real; for your training I will try to remember to let my belly muscles speak to you – to give you *some* chance to defend," it was half a jeer. "Now, on your guard!"

Fighting with Gyrfalon was both more wearing and more rewarding than with Will Steward or Elissa; and soon Annis ached in muscles she scarcely knew she possessed. Yet by punishing the weak points in her guard he showed her graphically how an expert could kill her over and over. Soon she was so tired her breath came in sobbing gasps and she could hardly raise the sword's point; and he slapped her flanks with the flat of his blade.

"Enough," he said harshly "You have stopped learning. We must needs work also on your stamina – if you still wish to be a worthy swordsman," there was half a sneer there, and Annis' eyes narrowed.

"You will *not* put me off, my lord," she managed, breathlessly. "I will gain the stamina and skill to prove myself to you."

He raised an eyebrow.

"I thought you learned for to please yourself," he said. "What does mine opinion matter?"

"I do so learn for myself; and for mine own protection. But," her chin went up in defiance, "I will teach you not to sneer at mine efforts. One day, my lord, I will be ready to slap *you* across the backside."

There was an appreciative gleam in his eye at her spirit, still there after a gruelling hour's work; and there were too subdued murmurs of approval and grudging admiration from those of his men who had suffered sword practice against the warlord.

"What, you'd not use your skill to run me through?" He asked mockingly.

She considered.

"That were gross ingratitude to a teacher, methinks," she returned. "Besides, although there were times just now that I heartily detested you, I think on the whole I quite like you."

He laughed, a harsh sound, containing as much self mockery as mirth and the men shuddered.

"Quite like me? Girl, did no one ever tell you that emotions concerning me involve fear, hatred, respect, loathing and at best dislike?"

She shrugged.

"It sound half hearted to only quite like you I suppose; but it comes with respect. And as to emotions, Lord Gyrfalon, why methinks I go mine own road. I do not like or dislike to order or the command or even recommendation of others. And though I may fear consequences and actions, I would scorn to fear any man; for we all feed maggots one day. And *none* shall make me fear to order; I be too stubborn" and she drew her brows together.

"Indeed!" His brow rose; and he stepped a deceptively small slight step to seize her by the throat in his hands, pressing until she felt the bruises come, and her blood pounded in her head leaving her giddy.

"Do you now feel fear of me?" he asked.

Annis whispered perforce; but her voice was even.

"No fear, my lord; only pain."

It was true; common sense told her that he

would be unlikely to kill a potentially valuable hostage on a whim; and moreover her deep faith led her to believe that she would go straight to Heaven. Indeed, a passing thought of pity touched her that she had a certainty of salvation that the warlord did not; that his own fear of death made him wish to frighten others. And perchance something else that made his sense of self-worth less than it should be, deep down; that he must needs dominate.

Gyrfalon released his grip on her and stared.

"Can it be that you Christian women *wish* death?" he wondered.

She shook her head, scorning to wince as it hurt, resisting the urge to touch her bruised throat.

"Oh no, not at all," she sad emphatically. "Indeed, to die now would be very inconvenient and would make me all irritable so I shouldn't enjoy Heaven as much as I ought until I got over such grumps. Just because I do not fear death does not mean I will not do my best to avoid it you know! I enjoy life very much at the moment; I have every reason to live to continue enjoying it, for apart from such occasional megrims of yours you have been a most excellent host to me!"

"Megrims?" he enquired waspishly.

She smiled sunnily.

"Well, I can think of no other way to describe your odd starts of wanting to be frightening," she said. "It does not trouble me, you need not fear on that ground, and do not in anywise spoil mine enjoyment of your company."

Gyrfalon glared at her and turned on his heel to swing away, picking up his surcoat and cloak on his way back to his room.

"Are you *trying* to make him kill you, little fool?" Said Elissa. "You *don't* talk to Lord Gyrfalon like that; he's far too bad tempered. *Megrims*, indeed!"

Annis beamed on the female warrior.

"He'll just have to get used to being aggressively liked, won't he?" she said.

Elissa muttered something unrepeatable to herself.

Annis was outside her understanding.

Later Annis came to Gyrfalon's room to apply her salve and found him uncommunicative. Cheerfully she embarked upon a monologue about the havoc worked in the kitchens by a large water rat so agile that several men had tripped and injured themselves in their clumsy attempts to catch it.

"And then do you know what happened?" she chuckled.

"I neither know nor care," Gyrfalon snapped, "Cease your prattling girl!" and then he refused to speak further. Annis laughed unconcerned.

"You are being a crosspatch!" she said merrily "And I hope that wondering what became of that rat will haunt your thoughts all day! Can it be that you seriously believe that it be possible that one day I shall be able to break your guard and spank your fundament? 'tis an ambition methinks that will take many years of practise; that I am well willing to put in if you will teach me but it also assumes that you will not learn new skills in the meantime; for no man ever stops learning."

She elicited no response; but at least he showed no rage, and she held her tongue. Instinct told her – and Annis relied heavily on instinct – that confidences could not be easily forced with this complex, enigmaic man.

Gyrfalon stood it for about an hour after Annis had left then sent for a pot boy and demanded peremptorily if the water rat in the kitchens had been dealt with suitably.

He was goggled at briefly in awe at his omniscience.

"Oh my lord it were wholly nimble!" said the boy "Half the servants did fall over tryin' to catch it and then it knocked a pot right over it and tried to run off, that the pot scuttled on little legs and we all fell about laughing it looked so comical, my lord and then cook he put the spit through it."

"I hope he cleaned the spit before roasting anything for me," said Gyrfalon dryly. "Very well boy, you may return to your nether regions and get on with your duties; and if the pot that fell on the rat has not been scrubbed do that on your return."

The boy tugged his forelock and fled thankfully, glad to have survived an encounter in person with the warlord.

Gyrfalon pulled a wry face. There was a crude humour to the situation; and it would have probably been funnier as described by Annis. Well, now he knew. And was served for his ill humour with the chit that he had a cruder and less well crafted telling of the incident than she would have managed.

Well she need not think that she could make him laugh for the trying.

And one might see how much she was laughing after several more practices.

The next day Annis came prepared for the punishment she knew she would take from the warlord in sword practice; for he was quite relentless. Again he told her roughly that she had ceased to learn as she tired and dismissed her; but at least when she came to him to smooth on the salve he spoke to her of the practise.

"You are slow getting the sword up to parry," he said. "Your muscles are weak."

"Yes my lord; and I wondered if I might do some exercise in addition to sword practise to help strengthen them," she said. "But I am not sure what."

"Well you are a glutton for punishment" he grunted.

"I am pragmatic enough to recognise that one gains nothing without putting in the effort, aye, and the pain too, for the gain," retorted Annis. "I may hope that as my muscles develop the practise becomes less painful; until you increase the pressure you put on me as I am sure you will."

He laughed harshly.

"It will be the only way you will learn," he said. "Now why do I bother? You may be gone to your father's house ere you make a decent swordswoman."

"Or you could tell him to go away and keep me instead," said Annis. "I'm more use to you than I am to him; and you're more use to me than he is, though that hardly flatters you for I have no time for my father."

"You can exercise by lifting and lowering something heavy," said Gyrfalon, ignoring the last comment "A sword in each hand would do well; that when you have a sword held in both hands it be by comparison light."

Annis nodded.

"Very well; that exercise I shall do - twice a day?"

"Aye; morning and evening, twenty lifts to start with increasing one every day. And think not that I shall let you off practice for this."

"Such never crossed my mind," said Annis. It had not; she had assumed any exercise would be supplemental to her practice.

So Annis began exercises; and Elissa watched her amused but somehow impressed by the girl's stubborn will to succeed.

"You do realise, don't you, you silly wench that if you were being forced to take this level of pain it would be called torture beyond what your church would consider reasonable for a male prisoner, let alone a girl?" said Elissa.

Annis shrugged.

"You mean I'm a fool to care that he not sneer at my weakness and should sit back with my hands folded? That likes me not Elissa. And whether he laugh at me that he may make me take this pain or whether he do not, I will be the gainer in the end for learning and for being stronger."

"You will," Gyrfalon's silkily dangerous voice came disembodied first as he revealed himself by vaulting over the wall by which Annis stood to practise lifting. Elissa shuddered. He had such a trick of being where no-one expected him to be. "And I do not laugh at you girl. I am not displeased that you have the stubbornness to take the pain. The level of torture, is it. Elissa?"

"It might be so argued if she be returned to her father's halls, my lord," said Elissa, trying to sound calm.

"And I would be bothering to tell my idiot father for what reason?" said Annis scornfully "He has no need to know; then when I challenge him to a duel, if he does not die of an apoplectic fit from laughter as might yet happen then I shall more readily kill him. I have no complaint, my lord, of your treatment of me, nor of Elissa's protection."

"Good," said Gyrfalon. "Keep up the exercises; you may yet succeed as a fighter if you do" and then he was striding away.

"He *is* the devil himself popping up out of nowhere," said Elissa.

Annis laughed.

"I suspect he would but thank you for the compliment if he heard it," she said. "He has a quiet tread, that is all; a warrior born. Methinks there has seldom been his like."

"And plenty would thank your God for that," said Elissa dryly. Annis chuckled.

"And you his follower!" She laughed "You're supposed to be proud of his cat-like tread and status as a pre-eminent warrior aren't you?"

"Well yes, but he gives me the frights,"

admitted Elissa. "And the more when you, you crazy creature, will insist on baiting him."

"I don't think he likes milksops," said Annis meditatively. "Which were just as well; for methinks I'd find it hard to be one."

It was several days before Annis suddenly became aware that sword practice was hurting less. She had been rubbing the aching muscles, which had only performed the weight exercises by sheer will power sometimes, each night with a warming salve to prevent them from knotting. But suddenly they seemed to have learned how to keep up with the arduous exercises set by her grim master! She tossed back her tied-back hair, laughed up at him in sheer joy and attempted to press forward an attack where hitherto she had been forced to do little but defend.

For a moment her laughing eyes took him off guard; then he parried her assault, disarmed her and kicked her feet out from beneath her.

Annis pulled a rueful face and looked up at him from the ground.

"I did do better though, didn't I?" she asked.

"It were a reasonable attempt," he allowed. He reached a hand to her to pull her up. She took it; grinned wickedly at him as warning; and aimed a kick at his crotch. He leaped back swearing.

"Blast!" she said in chagrin "I thought that one might work."

Gyrfalon laughed.

"You little vixen!" he said with appreciation "Well you have the right attitude; you want to win and while you live you are not defeated. We'll make a swordsman of you yet."

Some of the men that had idle time on their hands were watching now as much to see the swordplay as to ogle Annis' body; and less were the scornful comments passed on her prowess. Annis had only had some basic training but she displayed a natural aptitude and retentive memory that pleased Gyrfalon. Only his half-brother, Falk, had learned so fast; his adoptive son, Buto, for all his willingness to please his adopted father, had possessed the soul of a bully boy, not a warrior. Gyrfalon's mouth pulled sideways as he helped her up one morning following her epiphany of skill. He remembered Buto still with pain. The boy had got himself killed by his own arrogance, by attacking a foe he was unequal to manage.

"You should have been born a boy," Gyrfalon said, half regretfully.

"Why indeed my lord, that were a waste," she countered.

"How so?" he demanded.

"Consider; as a girl I can be feminine and wear pretty things and learn womanly arts – but I may also, with your kind indulgence, put on boyish garb and learn the manly arts of war. Think you that a boy could so well put on petticoats? Why my lord," she dimpled at him "I fear such would not become you; and I fear you would not ply a needle so well as I do the sword, nor manage so graceful a curtsey!" And she curtseyed to him, blithely uncaring that she had no skirt to spread.

He snorted.

"And nor would I wish to" he said.

"Then truly it is as well that you are a man and I a woman – for we might then both be happy in what we are," she said.

"Yet a woman is ever a pawn. Does that not irk one of your spirit?"

She shrugged.

"A hit, my lord; for it irks me oft times. 'Tis why I took mine own fate into mine hands and fled my father's demesne. As to now, when I be your pawn, 'tis surely irrelevant what my sex be that it please Lord Gyrfalon to hold me; and be I never so male I would still have had to yield before you in the wood. Indeed, you might have been more inclined to kill me as trouble; for a wench is a bigger prize with which to bargain. Thus I come out the winner, at least as things stand. And yet as a wench, my father doth despise me; and may not pay, as may be the best outcome from my point of view. Whence I shall be free to be your healer with no obligations on your part to give me up" she shrugged "I live in great hope; though I suspect he will attempt passage of arms to retrieve me purely because I am a possession of his however much despised. We shall see," she added philosophically.

Gyrfalon shook his head in wonderment.

"You are a strange child," he said. And yet what she had said was valid; and it would have been a waste of her pale, almost ethereal beauty to have it laid upon a male face. Almost she was a parody of feminine pulchritude; delicate and dainty, tiny and pale, looking as thought the wind might blow her away like thistledown! Yet her eyes, blue as midnight, grey as steel, held a life and fire that suffused her whole body transforming her into a creature of fire and élan that any man should be glad to see in his offspring! Gyrfalon's mouth hardened. Peter Haldane was a fool not to appreciate his child; yet he, Gyrfalon, had no child to call his own, or train, or delight in the growing skills thereof.

"Does it displease you so much then?" Asked Annis, of his last comment, seeing his mouth harden.

He shrugged.

"No; why should I care?" he said carelessly

"I think your father a fool to lose you."

"I keep telling you he's a fool," said Annis.

"And I think I agree with you," grunted Gyrfalon. "But you are still a strange child."

The warlord also took to summoning Annis to his chamber for an hour in the evening to instruct her in the theory of warfare and combat; which took the form of him posing questions to her and correcting her fiercely when her answers displeased him and pushing the discussion further when she got it right.

He started with a question about mounted warriors.

"Which is it better to have, knights or foot soldiers?" he barked at her.

Annis considered.

"I don't think there's a definitive answer, my lord; surely that is dependant on circumstance?"

"Go on."

Annis considered.

"For a set piece battle knights are essential to provide the heavy troops; that may break a group of foot soldiers if the enemy have only such, and to provide balance and protection of the foot an the enemy have horse too. I think, though I'd not want to take mounted men on a long journey through country I did not know," she said.

"And why would that be? Horses can carry a lot more than men."

"But if there is insufficient forage, then the horses will die and the men have more equipment to carry than they realised; if you take fodder you have to know how much, for how long, and carts of such will slow you up. Also, horses take a lot of caring for; in enemy territory, the morning feeding and grooming of the horses and tending their feet is going to be an ideal time for an ambush- or so it seem to me. Unless there are military tricks around that?" she asked. "I would think on an extended journey horses will be more trouble than they be worth and I'd prefer to make my proud knights use their own little feet."

He laughed. The girl had very little reverence for knights in shining armour then!

"A good answer. Yes, on extended campaign, horses are more trouble than they be worth; and if a march be of greater duration than five days, men marching can get there faster for the time that must be expended on horses. Neglected horses die rapidly; to ride several horses to death for the speed to get an essential message through is one thing but to needlessly spend expensive assets is foolishness. It is wise to have a few mounted men; that may be used as scouts. Then there is more than one man to see to the needs of one horse, as may speed matters up; and they may too be guarded while being cared for. A leader too should ride that his troops can see him. On the whole I had rather had more footmen than a few horsemen."

"I would think mules and asses might be useful to carry equipment," said Annis, "being hardier and less delicate than horses and also able to go where horses cannot; in mountainous terrain for example."

He nodded.

"Another well made point. But then I can see that you would like asses; they have stubborn streak like yourself. Or is it their association with your God?"

Annis grinned.

"You learn to know me, my lord! Asses obey because they feel like it not because they are trained to it and I must say I like the independent spirit. I had not considered their relationship with Our Lord; but presumably he did not disapprove of independence."

Gyrfalon grunted.

"I thought it were supposed to show His humility that He rode a creature seen as low. And false humility is part of the stinking rites as a whole."

Annis shrugged.

"That too; that He is not a conqueror. How others behave in His name becomes them not but is nothing to do with it. What do you care? Leave religion out of it; we differ on that my lord; and so there is no point discussing it. We spoke of asses for their usefulness I thought."

He grunted.

"As you say; and for baggage train asses have their uses. Mountain campaigns are to be avoided where possible; that is if invading mountain country. Inevitably the defenders know their land best and may make devastating ambush."

"But one must surely cross mountains at times that need not be enemy territory; or at least not securely held," said Annis. "A pass considered hard to traverse might be lightly defended to preserve men; that a clever lord could send some men that know mountains to climb ahead covertly so they may watch as a larger body of men come that will draw out ambushers; and ambush them. We got off the subject of mounted troops here."

"We did, but you use your intellect, which is what I hope to instruct you in" he said "Aye; if one has the *right* troops one might do much. Drawing out ambushers is a good idea, though not always so easy as it sounds in the comfort of a castle. What is important is that you have no preconceived ideas, no conventional wisdom; that you think beyond the set piece battle, beyond the art of war laid down in the classics. Which is not to say such things are not valid; they are. But when a particular action calls forth an almost formalised response, if one does something different then one has the upper hand. Why?"

"Surprise?" suggested Annis.

"*Shouldst* have been a boy," he said. "Aye, surprise. By all the demons in hell, with your quickness, if you were my child I'd be proud to own you."

"There is much I do not know" said Annis "But if you will instruct me I will be glad to learn."

"Heh; and much of it common sense that you seem to possess in abundance," he was pleased to be in a good mood with her for not returning the conventional answers – or those he expected from an ignorant young girl – that horses meant better mobility.

"I believe I am on the whole quite pragmatic," said Annis. "And I am not generally like to loose my cool head when under pressure; for it seem to me that if one might rattle an enemy – by, say, doing the unexpected – one has half won, whether hand to hand with swords or in larger battle."

"Quite right child. Remember too that an angry opponent is oft times a defeated opponent; and that I speak as one with a hot temper who must strive not to let others know how to do so goad me. Only one man know me well enough to raise mine ire hot; but I can overcome that. You should be aware of your own weaknesses; that is why I needle you when we fight. You heed not insults to your God; or on your appearance; but methinks that you rise to me calling you feeble and puny and sneering at your ability."

Annis flushed.

"Aye; that is a fault," she said. "I suppose one is angered most by those things that one knows have much truth in them. What you say about God hurts him not; He can afford to laugh at it and so too will I; mine appearance is bound to be dishevelled when fighting; and I know I am good looking and if it is not a look you admire, that is your loss not mine. But I am weak and it irks me that I have not the stamina to match my will."

"You do your looks down," he said harshly. "Art not really whey faced that I have called you; and that you hast the wit to know. And you *are* weak. But shouldst learn not to let me taunt you."

"I try to rectify my weakness rather than getting angry; it is that I be overcome by frustration as I tire," said Annis. "But I will endeavour to do better. The frustrated, angry and ill-considered moves I make open me to your attacks. I would have done better, methinks, to feign greater weakness than I have, ere I tire; and fall perhaps to one knee to husband strength that I might then make a final attempt to kill mine opponent as he come to take me prisoner or whatever. That way too I would not compromise honour by yielding and then treacherously attacking."

"No man expects a woman to obey any code of honour," said Gyrfalon.

"No; but if I am a warrior I expect to behave by the code that warriors must follow as a code of mutual respect. Those that do not obey a code cannot expect to be treated according to it; it has nothing to do, really, with honour; but more to do with a pragmatic desire of all warriors to live to fight another day."

He stared.

"I had not looked on it in such light before," he admitted. "You really do think deeply! But be aware, girl, now I know your ideas of feigning weakness I shall be looking for it!"

"Oh of course!" Annis agreed "But I would not want to use my last strength to kill you; I should hope perchance to come close to wounding you, but you train me to fight others, over whom I shall feel no such qualms; and I wanted to know if you think it would work."

He nodded.

"I think it is one situation where your fragile feminine beauty might be in your favour; for no man would expect you to have the strength to find a last attack; nor the ability to think and be duplicitous when tired; nor the resolve; nor the iron will to wait helpless until the best opportunity present itself. It is a good solution that takes advantage of the strength you may extract from your weakness. As any warrior knows himself and knows how to make best of his strengths and minimise his weaknesses. To make a virtue of a weakness is a rare ability. I have trained only one other with the potential such as you possess."

Her face flooded with joy at his praise.

"Does that mean you've decided to keep me and bite your thumb at my father?" she asked hopefully.

"It means nothing," he said, his face closing. "I have still not decided. Now about your business girl!"

Annis curtseyed and left him; but she was pleased that she had pleased him. He was a harsh mentor; but he cared that she learned.

She left him for her self imposed tasks in sewing; for it was relaxing after what might be unsettling sessions with the warlord!

Chapter 4

After she had been in the warlord's castle for two weeks, Annis felt in need of spiritual renewal; and having kept track of the days by her Book of Days that she had brought with her rose early on Sunday morning. Elissa, disturbed, blinked sleepily. Annis had put on her best gown, which was well fulled wool, almost as soft as a velvet, in a dark rich indigo blue, embroidered at hem, cuff and neck with real gold thread in an intricate knotwork pattern that shimmered as it caught the light.

"What are you after now at this hour of the morning?" Elissa demanded irritably.

"Church," replied Annis succinctly.

"*Church*? Are you mad?" squawked Elissa, startled into being fully awake and sitting up scrubbing at her eyes. Annis shook her head, laughing at her.

"I want to attend early Mass," she said.

"The old ... Lord Gyrfalon'll have forty fits!" cried Elissa in lively horror.

Annis shrugged.

"His heart is strong. He will surely survive that calamity. Are you escorting me or not?"

She swept out looking every one of her few inches a great lady, leaving Elissa gawping and struggling hastily into her trousers to catch up with the girl. Church indeed! Really,

Elissa fumed to herself, this Lady Annis might have been less trouble had she been some cowed milksop of a gentlewoman who would not find new and innovative ways every day of irritating Lord Gyrfalon! Even if she, Elissa *had* had to wait on such a silly creature hand and foot!

Gyrfalon met Annis as she descended the narrow stair, Bible in hand.

"Where are *you* off to?" he demanded tartly.

"Church," Annis' voice was patient, as though explaining to a slow child for the umpteenth time.

He blinked.

"I forbid it," he growled.

"Then if I am a total prisoner, you may then brew your own balms," she snapped. "I am not asking you to go with me as my escort; nor am I intending to recite my catechism to you. I want to go to church; and if you stop me I can think of a dozen ways of showing my disapprobation that may get me punished by you but will still irritate you. Even if I am locked in my room I can still be in your ears all day reciting Bible stories and singing sacred songs out of the window until you capitulate."

"Until I – girl, has it not occurred to you that I am the one who makes terms to *you*?"

"My Lord Gyrfalon, I had understood that

we had accommodation between us that was to our mutual satisfaction; that I am given limited freedom for my healing, that I am douce in my behaviour in return for martial studies. I can withdraw goodwill as you will notice in the lack of salves almost as quickly as in my making of myself a great nuisance by being no help and a great hindrance. Like refraining from teaching your indifferent cook how to make better use of herbs and spices and how to be a bit more adventurous in his cooking; as you have surely noticed."

Gyrfalon blinked.

The cooking had improved. He was no gourmet to care much about what he ate save that it were wholesome; but the tastier dishes served of late had been welcome. He had given it no real thought but now he did the idea of returning to unappetising watery stews and meat burned on the outside and half raw within was not attractive.

"But you despise the church," he said baffled.

"I despise those who use the church, the venal rapacity of some high ranking churchmen. I have a mind, however, to hear the simple sermon of a country priest," she said firmly, thrusting forward her tiny delicate chin.

"Church!" his voice was filled with venom "Well then go – not for fear of your silly threats but because I promised you freedom in the environs of the castle. And I wish you joy of it!" he swept away ignoring her demure,

"Why, thank you my lord."

Elissa had caught up by now and came up behind her with a sniff.

"How do you get away with it?" she asked,

"Maybe he likes me," suggested Annis lightly. The female warrior snorted.

"He likes no-one," she asseverated.

The bell for Prime was starting to ring as the girls left the castle, to the surprise of the gate guard as Elissa told him,

"She have permission from the old man."

Annis had allowed plenty of time to argue with Gyrfalon as she thought she might have to; and was happy to have got away fairly quickly. The sun was still low in the sky; it were not so long since sunrise and dew lay heavy still on the ground, that had Annis hold her skirt well up to prevent the heavy woollen hem dragging in the wet, unaware that the gate guard was appreciating her neat ankles. She pulled her grey cloak up to cover her head to enter the church, wherein she had to endure the surprised stares of such villagers as chose to attend this early service. Work being forbidden on the Sabbath many peasants would attend more than one service for something to do but doubtless some took the opportunity, if they did not have stock to feed, to have a rare lie in. Most however would have been up long since to feed chickens and hogs if nothing else.

Work of course did not cover such; nor, thought Annis cynically, did it cover the preparation of food that was in all but great houses and castles the lot of the women. She headed for the screened pew of the castle family, genuflecting to the altar as she approached it. Elissa, behind her, did not.

The service began and Annis found it moving. However, soon the sermon was interrupted by the loud rhythmic snores of her companion. Annis tried an elbow in the ribs but to no avail. She stood and walked to the lectern.

"I prithee excuse me Father," she said, picking up the great Bible. It was something of a struggle to carry it back to the pew and heft it over her head; but her arms were strengthening under Gyrfalon's tutelage and her own exercises. And it was very satisfying to bring the great book down on Elissa's sleeping head. The woman woke with a startled yelp.

"Feel the weight of the Word of the Lord!" cried Annis wrathfully "If you must sleep, do it quietly, or outside, not grunting like a rutting pig!"

Elissa gaped at her; and there were one or two chuckles from the assembled peasantry. Annis looked scorn on her guard and went on,

"As a hostage I am sacred; and it is your duty to guard me, which task Lord Gyrfalon set you to do. Yet you sleep on such duty and in a place outside the castle; from whence I could escape, were I so minded, or from whence some rude impious person might attempt a counter strike to carry me off. Lord Gyrfalon has trusted you; is this how you mercenary rabble generally repay trust?" She left Elissa gaping, shamefaced and burning red with embarrassment, as she had not in many a long year; and returned the Bible to its customary place. "I apologise, Father," she said softly. "I was carried away by indignation."

The priest made the sign of the cross.

"Ego te absolvo, my daughter," he said "Righteous indignation has also been our Lord's speciality at need."

Annis smiled at him and returned to her pew; and the sermon concluded without further opposition.

After the service the priest, a man in his fifties, approached the girl.

"You are a hostage of Gyrfalon's, my lady?" He asked confirmation of her earlier words to Elissa. Annis nodded and the man's eyes softened in sympathy. "It must be difficult for you, daughter; at least he permits you to attend Mass. Will you wish the confessional?"

"I would if you are prepared to hear my sins," said Annis. "Bless me father, for I have sinned," she used the time honoured words and began her confession. She told him of her killing of Solly and the circumstances; that she had feared for her virtue. It was a relief to talk about it, and how horribly easy it had been to kill a man and how she regretted making the death slow for her lack of skill, that she had cut his belly not stabbed him in the heart. And as she spoke she felt a weight lift from her of having carried the horror to herself. The priest readily absolved her.

"And then you fell into the hands of that man's master; whom they say is the devil himself, my poor child," he said. "A hostage at the disposal of Gyrfalon – I cannot begin to imagine how hard that is for you."

Annis smiled at him in thanks for his kindness.

"I do thank you for your sympathy, Father, but truly my position is by no means insupportable," she explained quickly, unwilling to act a lie to the kindly priest in letting him think she be an object of pity. "I have a very great deal of freedom, for giving my parole, and Lord Gyrfalon has indeed shown me every courtesy that I have no plaint at all."

The priest blinked.

"Forgive me, my daughter, but that does not sound like the tales we have heard of Lord Gyrfalon when holding hostages."

Annis shrugged.

"Perchance it be that I have given promise not to escape and not irritate him. Well not too much," she amended.

Elissa interposed dryly

"What she means, priest, is that she is not a milksop that annoys him by tears and whining and is quite capable of holding her own in a slanging match with him. My Lord is enough impressed by her to give her much leeway," Elissa grinned at the thought of the taunts that Gyrfalon had used as part of the swordplay exercises, calling Annis a whey-faced brat with no strength; and Annis had retorted cheerfully that if she lacked strength she would have to use her superior youthful speed to kill an aged foe of at least thirty who would surely be either slow for his eld or make a mistake in senile dementia. And how Gyrfalon had laughed and called her a nasty tongued little virago in as close to an affectionate tone as Elissa had ever heard him use to any save Buto.

And perchance even more affectionate a tone than he had used to Buto, who was often enough a disappointment to his adoptive father.

The priest shook his head, not sure how to take the woman warrior and her deliberately mannish garb and stance. Annis took pity on him.

"I am able to make myself useful to Lord Gyrfalon with my skill as a herbalist," she told him. "He is pleased that I am able to treat him and his men when needful," she smiled "It gives me a position to bargain with, though Elissa puts it more picturesquely."

The priest made the sign of the cross

"Then may God be with you in that demon's den," he said softly. "And may he not go back on any such bargain as you have managed to make with him."

Elissa wondered on the way back to the castle what it was that gave Annis her charisma; for no other would dare so tease Gyrfalon, and though Annis had hit her and rebuked her in the church yet she felt herself no resentment, only chagrin at what had been, after all, a just criticism. Even as she took the odd blow from Gyrfalon himself for failing to perform to his stringent standards – rare for Elissa – without resenting him for it.

Fearing him that he lose his temper with her and kill her outright, yes; but not resenting a rebuke from a lord.

And she also wondered that Annis had not left her sleeping and crept away, as well she might have done. She decided not to ask the girl why she had not; the answer was probably something to do with the parole Annis considered herself to be under. Elissa respected her for keeping her parole, though she wondered why the girl might do so when none would expect her to do so..

Annis strode purposefully to the 'demon's den' and knocked purposefully and firmly, entering when she was so bid and dropping a polite curtsey to the warlord.

It always startled him, even after so many days and that was one reason Annis did it.

He took in her finery this time, having failed to notice it earlier, for the shock of her declared intent to attend a church service. She was beautiful; her hair loose as it was not when she practised swordplay nor when keeping it tied back to undertake her healing ministrations and it flowed like a ripple of pale golden water down her back, framing her piquant little face. That face was serene and the eyes soft from Annis' enjoyment of the Mass, yet by no means devoid of her fire; for in her determination there was a glow within the indigo orbs that were set off by the gown that matched them. The fabric was well cut and clung almost as closely to her gentle curves as did the sweat-soaked linen of her tunic and Gyrfalon wondered if there could possibly be a more beautiful woman in the world or one with as little consciousness of how breathtakingly lovely she was at the moment. He tried to conjure the vision of Alys to compare the two; and found it hard, for Annis was so vibrant a personality recalling his dead love was difficult. And that made him frown and speak brusquely.

"What?" he demanded "I'll not hear your catechism you know."

"I have a question to ask," she said quietly, ignoring the jibe."

He raised his eyebrows.

"Ask then; I may even answer it," it pleased him to sound whimsical.

She gave him a quick affectionate smile for his games, though in sooth she was in serious mood.

"Do you intend to hold this castle and its demesne or do you intend to be a second-rate warlord in charge of scum and rabble forever capable of no more than thievery and half-baked banditry?" she asked.

He stared outraged.

"I intend to hold it, thou insolent whelp!" he roared. "Thievery and half baked banditry? What say you, naughty wench? How dare you!"

She nodded as though satisfied, unmoved

by the bellow that made all the men within earshot cringe.

"So you will then be making sure to reassure your peasants and advise them that when my father's army comes – as assuredly it will come – that they will be brought within your walls here; and that you will pledge aid from your warriors in bringing the harvest in as is shortly due."

Gyrfalon stared at her.

"What?" he demanded.

She sighed and let him see her impatience.

"Knowing that contented peasants work better, you will wish them to feel secure that you will protect them without oppression and protect them from the rapacity of an outside army; which will encourage them to raise a greater harvest, especially as they too will be eating it themselves inside the castle. And you will then still have peasants left to plant in spring for the coming year's harvest; so you continue holding the land, not having to rely on banditry on the lands of others. It make sense after all."

"And you are an expert on land management and siege warfare?" he asked sarcastically.

She shrugged.

"I have had a hand in running my father's castle since I was nine years old; and made most of the decisions pertaining thereunto from my twelfth birthday until the old sot came home from the rear ranks of the Holy Wars whence he protected his skin and grabbed all the loot he could," she explained "Will the Steward guided mine hand but I have learned enough to run a castle even if my knowledge of siege craft be but scant. Doubtless you will feel that four years is little enough time, but it is a quarter of my life and I have been learning almost half my life. And you already know that I learn fast and remember lessons well and fully"

He glowered at her.

"I know the process of training a noble boy goes through – as your Will Steward seems to have treated you – well enough" he snapped "I too was trained to take my father's mantle – HAH!" he snorted "Well what you say does make sense; I do want my peasantry there for the spring. But," the corner of his mouth twisted, "I note that a good little Christian girl fresh from church does not mention my duty to the peasants or kindness and Christian charity."

"Feudality goes both ways," said Annis. "It was not a question of Christian charity but of good economic sense. Besides, you pride yourself on being amoral so appealing to your non-existent better nature would be a waste of time. However my sense of what is right is able to coincide with what is also good sense;

which is convenient. That way everyone can be satisfied – even the peasants."

He stared at her; then he laughed.

"I am glad to see that your devotion to that weakly religion has not robbed you of your wits. But be careful how you try to manipulate me, my girl!"

She twinkled at him.

"Oh I will, my lord," she told him; and later it occurred to him that she had not told him she would not manipulate him but only that she would take care of how she did it.

And he laughed again at the chit's temerity.

The reeve of the village came trembling before Lord Gyrfalon on the morrow; and left a relieved and happier man for the interview with the harsh featured warlord about the fate of the peasantry.

And the men were ordered out to aid with the harvest that there would be plenty of food for a siege and sent too to cut hazel to weave hurdles and use them to build rude shelters that might be plastered with mud for places to house the peasants and their livestock within the castle walls. And with the reassurance of Gyrfalon's avowed intent to protect his peasantry, the reeve felt able to bring to the warlord's attention to an incident that had occurred during the harvesting.

Annis was trotting along behind Gyrfalon as he inspected his men. She had an apron full of potions, physicks and salves for those who had approached her tentatively; and some for those who had not. The boy with the hacking cough was stunned to be presented with an old wine bottle full of medicine and tart but specific instructions as to how much to take and how often; and the grizzled warrior who had been concealing an ulcer on his leg for months blinked in amazement when Annis presented him with a salve and a cryptic

"You know where to put it."

She had too salves for the haemorrhoids of another, medicine for the man with worms and a warning to take no more than she had indicated if he wish to live himself, and a draught for the man with painful urinary stones and the pithy advice to keep drinking and pissing as much as possible. Gyrfalon found her treating of his men as though they were naughty little boys in the way she addressed them highly amusing; and that they pulled forelocks to her as though she were the lady of the hall and they her servants as well as his.

They had finished the rounds of the men when Gyrfalon's captain, whose name was Foregrim, approached. Annis had had little to do with him to date, save to tell him to chew on a clove for a painful tooth.

"My Lord," said Foregrim ,"The Reeve Bullard is here; with a girl. Will you see him?"

Gyrfalon frowned.

"Yes, very well; let him approach."

Annis caught up after advice to a man with a problem of constipation and stood by Gyrfalon as the reeve approached with a tearful young girl. Gyrfalon's mien was forbidding as always and Annis saw Bullard quail and almost change his mind. Swiftly she took the decision from him by stepping forward to the girl.

"Now, child, what it this? Tell me your name and all about your trouble," she asked matter-of-factly, putting an arm around the girl, who was much her own age. A fresh gale of tears ensued and haltingly the story emerged between much sobbing.

Gyrfalon's lip twitched amusement at Annis' use of the word 'child' to the girl and he looked at Bullard.

"A straight tale from you, reeve, if you please" he said "I do not intend to unravel the hysterics."

Bullard shuffled, then began.

"Raped she were, my lord, by one of your men. They was supposed to help with harvest as you ordered them, me lord; but this one was more interested in sowin' than reapin' an you take my meaning!"

"Indeed. And can you identify the man in question?" said Gyrfalon softly.

Bullard nodded.

"There was several witnesses, me lord; him didn't care; said you'd not care what a warrior of yours did with peasant scum. He is the one with half an ear missing."

Gyrfalon nodded and turned to Foregrim.

"Bring Barthol here. He is to be hanged," he said.

A ruffle went through the ranks and Gyrfalon raised his voice.

"You are my men. You are but a rabble but you *will* be an army and you may someday be warriors. An army has discipline and that means that you do not steal, murder or maim your own. This village is *my* village. By touching the girl without her consent and mine, then *my* property is damaged. Is that clear?"

It was clear.

The trembling Barthol was dragged before Gyrfalon. He attempted a sneer.

He also leered at the girl, whose name Annis had discovered was Avis, causing her to burst into fresh sobs of terror. He had been one that Elissa had fought on Annis' behalf and who was always there to leer at her when she fought. Annis had wondered before if she might have to kill him one day.

"A suggestion, my lord?" said Annis,

comforting Avis.

The warlord turned his gaze on her.

"Suggest," said Gyrfalon.

"It would be an object lesson to emasculate him instead," she said coldly. "That will not prevent him from working but will prevent him from repeating the offence and will provide an example."

There was a gasp of sheer horror through the ranks of Gyrfalon's men.

Gyrfalon regarded her thoughtfully.

"Emasculate him; and then hang him," he told Foregrim "You," he said to Annis, "can be considering why I have the fellow hanged as well. I will expect you to be able to tell me later if you would continue your training in holding a demesne." He turned to Barthol. "Anything to say?"

The man spat at him.

"'T'ain't right, a man need his recreation. Ain't that so cullies?" He called to the other soldiers, trying to rally them to action against Gyrfalon. "And we be more than you, my fine lord as can take the castle, and please ourselves with the fine wench you keep to yourself, that you even take her suggestions, ain't that so, my friends?" Gyrfalon gazed at him, his one eye hooded. There were some mutters in the ranks. Gyrfalon turned his gaze on the assembled soldiery; and such was his charisma that they froze.

"Recreation," he said, softly, though his voice carried to the furthest of his soldiers. "Recreation is implicit as a reward for labour. And you, Barthol, were not labouring at all but wasting time that could cost your fellows sufficient to eat in the coming winter. Your momentary rutting might have made the difference between holding the castle and having to surrender it to a siege. But you are not the only offender. You have all grown lazy," he scowled upon the assembled men. "When," he voice raised, "*when* you are an army worthy of the name you shall have recreation. An army with a reputation attracts the female followers you crave. Until then you have *no* recreation. You have me instead," he added with black humour. "And excess energy obviously needs exercise to work it off. In your companies you will all undertake twenty mile route marches daily as part of your patrols. That will do as a start. Now get on with the execution."

The mutterings turned now against the man Barthol whose defiance had given the whole army punishment; and there were no protests as sentence was carried out, though there was a collective groan as the quick blade of Foregrim sliced off the man's parts. The hanging was a quick and quiet affair.

"That was mildly nervous for a moment," Annis remarked to Elissa. "Barthol might have whipped the men up to act rashly, forgetting that they only be as well off as they are for the leadership of a great man like Gyrfalon. I was wondering if we might have to fight in earnest against the fools."

"And it never occur to you that I might have joined with my comrades?" asked Elissa.

Annis looked surprised.

"Never," she said. "I credit you with too much good sense to be swayed by the spurious maunderings of a man seeking a way out from being hung. Whether it is because you are a woman or just sensible I am not sure. But you are no fool, and it would have been messy, half for and half against Gyrfalon. And hard to tell friend from foe. Did that fellow actually imply that Lord Gyrfalon is being sufficiently injudicious as to damage the value of a virgin hostage?"

"That was how I understood what he said," said Elissa dryly.

"Idiot," said Annis. "And how would such a short sighted fellow that could think only with his cods ever manage to hold a castle?"

"By believing, I should think, that having a loud voice and a lot of weaponry constituted being a leader," said Elissa. "I guess I'd rather follow you into battle, untried as you are; at least you have a grasp of reality and, more important, the things an army needs besides weapons."

"And does Lord Gyrfalon know that you too understand the value of supplies and procurement of food and clothing?" said Annis "Because if he does not, I shall tell him; that you should be promoted captain."

"He does now," said Gyrfalon's voice behind her as he came up silently. "Elissa I underestimate you; I shall watch you closely and see of mine own mind that you warrant a captaincy; I may take the odd suggestion from mine hostage but I think I'll not have her making my promotions for me. As to you, my girl, I trust that you have been considering as I told you to do; and when you have salved my face we will discuss that further."

"My lord," Annis curtseyed; and went for her salves.

Chapter 5

"So tell me girl, why did I hang him?" Gyrfalon asked.

Annis had been thinking deeply.

"Lest the resentment be deep enough for him to overcome fear and try to kill you or foment mutiny – as indeed he tried," she said.

Gyrfalon nodded.

"Understand, child, that such a punishment strikes deep into a man's being. It could destroy his mind. Even a supposedly celibate monk would be affected. Even I, who have no chance of attracting women," he concluded bitterly, sneering at himself and at Barthol for his assumption that he, Gyrfalon, would take an unwilling woman as the soldier had no hesitation in doing.

Annis, sidetracked, stared at him in bewilderment. Gyrfalon was in the habit of leaving his helmet off as the salve worked in when he would talk to her after her treatment and she scarcely noticed his ruined face.

"I think, my lord, you are oversensitive about your scars," she said. "I see no reason that they would be sufficient to be responsible for diminishing your appeal as a man."

He smiled a brief, twisted, bitter smile.

"You are determined to accuse me of over sensitivity!" he sneered "But I suspect you have merely become used to the hideous aspect of my face."

She shrugged.

"Maybe. It is not pretty; but is it not the point that I have got used to it? It can be got used to. It is not as though the scarring has touched your lips," she flushed rosy pink, "such as a woman be interested in; and your body is muscular and vigorous as is apparent when you strip your sleeves for my sword practice," the flush had deepened and Annis was annoyed at herself that her body behaved in so silly a way as to blush like a silly peasant wench.

Gyrfalon laughed mirthlessly.

"So you would be prepared to wed me then?" he asked scornfully, watching her for the recoil he anticipated at such an idea. But she regarded him steadily, ignoring the fresh wave of blood that mounted to her face.

"I don't see why not," she said. "You are a far preferable bridegroom to the one picked for me by my father; though I fear that scarce flatters you my lord. You claim wickedness; but compared to him you are a very stranger to the ways of evil. But if you wish to wed me I would lay certain conditions; that I may not demand but would ask of our good understanding so far."

"Conditions? You would wed me on conditions?" He was curious; cynical; but he had to ask. She nodded.

"Firstly I would wish to be married by a priest who has not been coerced – or at least," she amended, "only coerced a little bit; and I would expect to stand as junior partner to mine husband, taking a share in the running of his demesne, consulted by him. Not relegated to the position of producing a baby a year until I died of it; that I choose to use herbs to control when I might conceive and how often. Those are my conditions."

Somehow referring to a husband in the third person made her blush less than had she used second person to him.

"Is that all?" he stared. That she spoke of using herbs to inhibit conception meant she did not mean to impose any regulation on her husband about when he should lay with her surely! She smiled.

"It is sufficient. After all, if I were unsatisfied by my treatment, well then, a man would find his – recreation – hard to take if he were spending all his free time in the garderobe."

He laughed, delighted with her vindictive pronouncement.

"Little savage, I declare any man that would be your husband must be a brave man indeed – or a foolhardy one! But then, mistress I-have-it-all-under-control, what is so terrible about your betrothed that you think me almost sinless? Am I not condemned and vilified by the church?"

She sniffed.

"My lord hath too much honesty and personal integrity to make the correct bribes to the right high ranking churchman that he get preferment and his sins get overlooked and covered by indulgences," she told him cynically. "Lord Marfey does. As to his wickedness my lord," a shudder went through her body and he read horror in her smoky eyes, "though I be a skilled healer I could not save the life of a peasant girl some eleven summers old who was birthing his child; nor that of the babe. And he had been using that little girl for *three years*. I am small enough and slight enough that I may fit within his perverse desires, that he may imagine me younger than my years, at least enough that he hope to get an heir on me as he desires. But he is loathsome!" she shuddered again and moved close to the warlord as for protection. He laid a brief hand on her shoulder.

"An exotic pastime," commented Gyrfalon disgusted. "He is no man."

"Do you know what I would like?" said Annis, viciously.

"No; but somehow I expect that you are going to tell me," he said dryly.

"I would like," she said, her eyes flashing, "to perform an introduction between Marfey's tripes and the good fresh air. Rather slower than I did to Solly."

Gyrfalon laughed.

"Well at least I know your words are not merely vain and that you'd not chicken out of following them through. And perchance you may yet have the opportunity; it does not require a mighty slash to empty the guts into the lap."

She smiled at him, a brittle smile.

"A little cut and then kick him over backwards, perchance down a few steps," she mused. "I should think that everything ought to come tumbling out on the way down, shouldn't you?"

He looked at her with admiration.

"You really are a little virago, aren't you?"

"I've been hating him for as along as I knew what he was; and then even more since my dear father proposed an alliance with him," she said. "Women are often crueller than men you know when they learn to hate."

His face closed like a shutter and his hand went involuntarily to his left eye.

"Yes," he agreed flatly. "Cruel and faithless."

"Not all faithless," said Annis "Will you tell me of her?"

"Tell you? Why not?" he shrugged. He sat back in the big oaken chair and stared into the distance, his mouth twisted, not quite a sneer on it, not quite pain. Annis dropped onto the floor beside his chair and leaned against his leg. He did not notice for his thoughts were far away and a number of years distant. "My father held a castle on the Northern Marches" he began. "I grew up knowing it would fall to my lot to help defend the kingdom against the barbarian hordes. My mother died when I was small; I barely remember her. I grew up mothered by my father's troops," he paused a moment. "They were what an army should be. And such I *will* make my rabble. I may be prepared to show myself as bad as ever I have been painted and worse, but I'll be it with efficiency and not as some -what did you say, half baked bandit" he snorted "You know how to poke in barbed comments sharper than any sword girl. Anyway" he added harshly "When I was ten years old my father remarried; and I was ready enough to greet my stepmother doucely at first. But she would treat me like a baby, so we got off rather on the wrong foot; and my relationship with my father was less good for he accused me of jealousy and not trying to get on with my stepmother and would not listen to explanation, declaring that it was her good care for me that made her limit me from doing what I had been doing for years. Rowing myself, or riding out unattended, these things were too much for a boy of ten," he sneered.

"That a maid of ten ride out unattended, save on her father's own lands might be cause for concern but if you ask me she sounds a trifle touched in the upper works," said Annis scornfully.

He gave a brief bark of laughter.

"You are refreshing, my child….. anyway, she had a baby boy and then it was better for she virtually ignored me, lavishing all her maternal foolishness on the child. And when he got older he followed me about like a tantony pig and wanted to learn from me. It was…..flattering," he scowled. "I taught him all I could, though his idiot mother had impractical ideas on warfare. She accounted it against the laws of God for any reason, even protection; and she wanted her baby protected from anything nasty as though he were a maid child. He was quite seven ere he was breeched," he sniffed. "Anyway, for me life was fairly good; I was learning to lead men and my father needed me to deputise for him for his wounds received in battle and his eld were becoming too much for him as a leader of men in the cruel cold of the north. But he meantime arranged for me a betrothal with a daughter of a neighbour; and she was the prettiest little thing. Soft gold hair and big blue eyes and she hung on my stories of life in the marches with her little rosebud lips parted in excitement for my tales," he glared down at

Annis. "You have a look of her."

Annis threw back her head and gazed up at him, looking down her little nose.

"I have the look of myself, Lord Gyrfalon" she said curtly "I am mine own self and nobody's copy"

He gave a half smile and reached out a hand as if to touch her face, then withdrew it abruptly.

"You are an original" he admitted. "Well, to continue; years past as I waited for Alys to grow up; and I came home from a lull in the fighting, expecting praise from my father for repelling a stiff attack – I had done well and the men had performed superbly – and admiration from my little brother. I also expected to have time to get married." He clenched the arms of the chair with both hands. "I was wounded; half a burning house fell on me, so I came home unexpectedly, with a broken arm and a burned face and neck. And when I arrived, I came in on the wedding day of my sweetheart and betrothed who was then at dalliance with her new husband – my dear brother!" He spat the words from between clenched teeth. "I lost my temper – who would not? – and tried to kill him for such duplicity."

"Had he no explanation?"

"Only that he loved her and she loved him, and when a false rumour had reported my death, they found themselves free to marry. Without thinking to verify the rumour, mark you; and equally my father chose to believe the rumour, as I later found out, to bequeath the family birthright to my younger brother. A sword, made by the elves; which would have aided me greatly on the frontier. It was bound to our family, and our totem, the falcon, and the pommel a piece of amber from the far north, almost as big as a fist, which looks like a falcon's eye. Those bound to it may find many powers through it, including, it is rumoured, the ability to assume the form of a hawk or falcon at will. Though our blood might be too diluted for that power," he added wistfully. "And I confess I was in such a rage I demanded that Falk should fight me. I think," he said, softly, "Had I but cut him, my rage would have dissolved. But the wench threw herself between us."

Annis gasped.

"How stupid! Why if she feared for your brother, she had done better to have found a branch to sweep your feet from under you, or brain you with it!"

He laughed a harsh laugh.

"You are undoubtedly more of a prize to any man than my idiotic fiancée," he said. "Naturally, she was mortally wounded, and her dying words were a curse that the wound I had sustained would consume me with pain forever, and mar my face so all who saw me would know my evil. This wound," he touched the scar on his face. "So now you know. Now you know that I am cursed by a devout Christian wench and hunted by her equally devout lover, my noble upright brother; and you know now why I see this devout stance as no more than filthy canting hypocrisy and sickly words that have no depth!"

Annis laid her hand on his arm.

"Not so noble and upright if he deceived you" she said dryly "To fall in love cannot be helped – but he should have written to you, begged your pardon, and explained."

Gyrfalon snorted.

"He said he wanted to tell me face to face, man to man. *HAH!*"

"An idiot too then" said Annis.

"No, he is not stupid. Else I had been able to kill him long ago, despite the magic sword that should have been mine. No, he is just too noble to be true."

"Had he....with her?" asked Annis delicately.

"I doubt it," he sniffed. "Not outside of marriage; too improper."

"These noble types probably have difficulty finding it anyway," was Annis' verdict. "Anyone that boring deserves to be saddled with a milksop."

He stared; then laughed.

"You know far more than a young girl of noble birth should!" he said.

"We have horses. How can anyone miss figuring out what goes on?" she said prosaically "Stallions run around with it all on display in almost as foolish a display as some of your men. Besides, I am a healer; I have delivered babies since my years were first marked by double figures. To pretend ignorance is but coy foolishness." She frowned thoughtfully "If she was a maid the curse would be effective if folklore is to be believed. But,

'a curse that's laid by maiden pure
unblemished maiden then must cure'

as they say; so my lord we had better cancel any wedding arrangements until such time as I have sorted out your face; for I am a maiden as may be able so to do."

He gazed down at her, his expression unfathomable.

"We shall see," he said harshly.

Elissa waited outside the tower, perched on a buttress, eavesdropping on the conversation of the troops. Annis' suggestion that she should be a captain had given her furiously to think; and she had come to the conclusion that the reason Gyrfalon was such a good leader was that he know most of what was going on amongst his men; and knew their mood and how to play it. Consequently she listened to a group discussing the execution; and Annis' part in it.

"I heered her, plain as plain" one was saying "Ee-masculate 'im she say, cool as you please!"

"Ar, and her do look the sweetest, most harmless liddle thing too!" marvelled another.

"Sure, I'd not have laid a finger on her for fear o' lord Gyrfalon anyway," put in a third "But it's on her own account I'll be avoiding giving her any reason to take offence!"

Elissa chuckled quietly to herself.

"D'you reckon as he's swiving her like Barthol said he were?" the first voice asked.

"Ar, woud'n' be surprised," said the second. "Iff'n y' ask me they bloody deserve each other!"

There were sounds of assent; and Elissa smiled to herself. Although she could readily tell the men that Annis never stirred from the chamber across whose door Elissa now slept, it made her job of guarding the girl easier if the men thought she was the personal property of their warlord!

The old man, as they called him half fearfully, half in the odd affection a soldier has for his commander whatever they feel for him, had never showed any inclination to take a woman before. Or a boy or even an ass. Elissa had come across both of those inclinations. She wondered about Annis though. He was ... different ... in his treatment of the girl; that were half the same as the way he was wont to treat the ill-fated Buto and half ... something else. And what might happen an he decided he desired the chit Elissa was afraid to contemplate; for Annis were not one to take being disposed at the pleasure of others without retaliation. Elissa shuddered and hoped fervently that the warlord's interest was purely as to a potential adoptive daughter. Annis would surely never accept any such overtures from Gyrfalon, she thought!

With the further proof of Annis' ruthlessness there was increased interest in watching her lessons; and some degree of frank curiosity to see whether Gyrfalon would be soft with her, that would be proof that she was his mistress, it was argued. Some others thought it prudent to stay away from the practices; but enough were nosy.

Neither Gyrfalon nor Annis cared in the single-minded pursuit of gladiatorial excellence. Annis was now getting good enough that Gyrfalon delighted in pushing her further; and she delighted in trying to get under his guard, and in being able to sometimes block his attacks.

It chanced this morning that there had been autumnal rain overnight; that had been an unpleasantly penetrating rain and with the aid of the soldiery to get the harvest in the whole crop had been saved, to the delight of the villagers and the satisfaction of Gyrfalon who was consequently ready to enjoy himself in the exercise. The damp conditions could not quash his good spirits this morning, though mud was in everything and the squared cobbles of the castle courtyard were slick with wet and mud and untended lichens and weeds that Gyrfalon had not yet got around to having scraped off. Fighting was difficult; and Annis, hard pressed, set her foot awry upon a slippery flag and fell backwards with a yelp of surprise.

Panther-like, Gyrfalon sprang forward to punish the error; but mindful that he treated their practise bouts almost as seriously as real fights, the girl reached out blindly with her free hand; and seizing upon a struggling but optimistic clump of grass forcing its way between two flags she pulled it up bodily and flung it in the warlord's face. As she expected he fell back instinctively; and she rolled aside, thrusting her sword in his direction as she did so to discourage the lunge she expected.

Such viciousness in fighting did much to dispel the idea from the minds of some that the warlord took the girl to his bed; but the main interest was in the skill that was worth watching; and the tenacity of Annis who received spontaneous applause from several of the watchers.

The lunge from his sword did not materialise; and Annis felt her sword point catch and hold a moment. Gyrfalon grunted; then shook clear the last remaining remnants of the offending grass and mud. Then he was upon her, pinning her wrists down with his hands, his knee on her thigh to stop her kicking.

Annis went limp.

"I believe I must yield, my lord," she panted, gazing ruefully into a face only inches from hers, a savagely exultant tiger grin upon his countenance. Her eyes met his one eye and for a reason she could not account for her face was suffused with blood in a flush. Her breath came raggedly still from her exertion; and from the excitement of the fight; and a sudden joy in life and contentment filled her, that was scarcely to be believed when flattened in a muddy puddle beneath the weight of one's conqueror. Annis knew she was smiling at him.

He grinned savagely back at her.

"You wounded me, girl," there was chagrin in his voice; yet pride in his pupil. "Few but my brother can boast of that!"

Distress filled her smoke blue eyes briefly; but a rapid and practical glance at the wound showed that the blood flowed but sluggishly.

"I fear it was luck more than skill, my lord," she confessed "I thrust to keep you at bay as you taught me. I did not mean to rake you with the point."

He laughed.

"No matter; the thrust was correct, and the wound a fair one; that such a thrust will make if the attacker be dilatory and slow as I was. Your aim with it was accurate; I was but blind longer, , than you expected that slowed me."

She gasped, looking concerned again.

"My lord, I pray that I have not hurt your good eye?" she asked in consternation. He shook his head.

"No, you little wildcat. But it was a good try," he was appreciative.

Annis was still on the ground, still pinned by his weight; she may have yielded but he had not let her go yet. She was waiting to get her breath back and finding it difficult

"M- may I get up now?" She asked, finding it difficult to phrase the query in terms that had any shred of dignity left in them from her supine position. To her surprise her heart was still beating wildly, though she had been relaxed a while since; and though her present position lacked dignity, somehow that was unimportant and she asked because she felt she ought to.

Gyrfalon grinned wolfishly at her.

"Why certainly, my lady. Since you have yielded to me," and as swiftly as he had seized her he let her go, rising to his feet in one fluid movement. Annis loved to watch his grace in such movements; it always impressed her. He extended a hand to her; as he had not since she had used the same to attack him.

The difference was that she had yielded; and he knew she would abide by that. Annis was glad of his help on the slippery ground.

"I must needs dress your wound, my lord," she said, coming to her feet with almost as much grace thanks to his strong hand.

He gave her another wolfish grin.

"What, patch your handiwork?" he mocked gently.

She pulled a rueful face.

"I suppose it be something along those lines," she returned. "Come; it is not serious but we should not delay," she held out a hand to him to hasten; and dropped it as he strode past her.

"Shalt change into dry clothes first girl" he said "You are saturated from lying on your back half the morning and cold enough that any man be like to enjoy sight of your nipples as you might disapprove of. The wound will wait a few minutes."

Annis flushed darkly; and wondered in

passing if he had included himself in the description 'any man'. How like Gyrfalon to make the suggestion that she lazed by lying on her back! She gave a rueful grin.

She was halfway up the stairs to the tower when the innuendo hit her and her flush was even deeper!

Annis changed and stalked into Gyrfalon's room with salves. She was frowning.

"Well, it looks as though I be in for a bad time" said Gyrfalon.

"My Lord is pleased to make smutty jokes in front of his men," said Annis.

He took her chin.

"Did that hurt you? I meant it not so; art such an earthy little thing that I thought you would take it in good part."

She flushed.

"It took me half way up the stairs ere it dawned on me you meant not to chide me for supposed laziness; *that* is what hurts, mine own slowness," she said.

"Your honesty is remarkable," he said. "So you will not take issue if I say I be the only man to ever lay you on your back?"

She flushed but laughed.

"I do believe you are a bad man!" she said.

"I keep telling you that," he said.

"Why so you do!" she said. "Perchance I might believe it – a little. Sit, bad man; I must needs patch you up."

He sat; and Annis bathed and dressed the sword cut high on his chest, packing it with a healing cream consisting mainly of comfrey and bugle. Her other hand she rested lightly on his muscular chest to balance; reflecting on how well he kept himself in condition. Her eyes ran thoughtfully up to his face and rested there.

"What?" he asked, rather peremptorily.

She gave a half smile.

"I was thinking of your silly comments about your face the other day and was comparing you favourably to Lord Marfey, my lord," she admitted. "Though your face's beauty is marred you take such excellent care of yourself. Your muscles," her eyelashes fluttered to veil her eyes, "are quite good enough to teach anatomy from. Marfey has made himself unattractive as well as having an unattractive personality and a lecherous cruelty that make his face uglier for his soul being reflected in it than a dozen burns might; actually he'd be better looking for being burned and rendered down for lard," she added meditatively, "and the thought of touching his flesh is totally repulsive."

"Which mine is not?" his mouth twisted "I am not sure if your compliment is straightforward or backhanded – that I am in good shape for mine age. Were not one of the jibes you have thrown at me to do with mine senile decrepitude?"

She grinned and shrugged.

"Your age is hard to guess, my lord; I made but jibe as you have about me being whey faced. Anyone over thirty is decrepit, surely?" she twinkled at him.

He gave a bark of laughter.

"Thou minx! I am almost forty years old; and I would love to hear you tell my sainted brother that he be approaching decrepitude!"

Annis chuckled.

"Not having seen him I know not if he be so well cared for as you; who are a good example to the rest of us to stay fit, I imagine. There, that is done," she patted the last bit of dressing into place. "if you would care to put on your tunic I shall go down to the stillroom for a new jar of salve for your face."

She packed up her paraphernalia neatly and headed for the door; and turned to survey him again ere she went out. Gyrfalon muttered an oath as he pulled on his tunic, almost angrily; and Annis wondered if it were thoughts of his brother that had turned his mood so swiftly.

Gyrfalon scowled and she tripped lightly out. The chit could be so disturbing when she chose! No, such was unfair, it were not that she chose it. It was just that he could not fathom her.

When he had held her down earlier he could almost have imagined that she seemed….responsive to his touch. And she blushed readily … but she responded in so light a tone to his half serious jesting and now was so clinical in her treatment of him … and serve him right for an old fool that he should hope … decrepit at thirty forsooth!

Annis was well pleased with her own self control. Gyrfalon had a strange effect upon her feelings that disturbed her; and she was glad to take refuge in the clinical stance of a healer! She paused in the cool stillroom to get her rapid breathing under control and to let her hot face cool.

And by the time she returned to the warlord's chamber with the new pot of salve she had herself back under control.

Chapter 6

Annis dipped her fingers into the jar of salve and scooped out plenty to apply to Gyrfalon's face. She stood a moment, considering where to start, then with a sudden startled exclamation shook the stuff from her hand and started wiping it frantically.

"What is it?" Gyrfalon asked impatiently.

"My lord.... Oh Dear God, there is something in it; something that burns," Annis was washing her hands hurriedly in his wash bowl. "If I had not paused before putting it on your face while I assessed how it was healing it would have been too late ... look" she held out her hand to the warlord to demonstrate the small blisters all the way down the inside of her fingers. She shuddered and her teeth chattered suddenly in shock. "It would have been agony, Gyrfalon; almost unbearable on your raw skin!" her eyes were dark with horror.

Gyrfalon's face tightened.

"Is this an attack on me, girl – or on you? For if such a thing occurred, I might well have lashed out unthinkingly in mine agony and slain you by accident; for you are only a fragile creature I could break in half with a blow," he took her hand to look again on the blisters, as angry and red as if she had plunged her hand into fire.

She shook her head, considering his comment.

"I know not, my lord – but I imagine in some respects it comes to the same thing. If you killed me you would then be bereft of the pain relief. Excuse me, I want to get the other jar; I must find out if it, too, be contaminated. If it is not, I may then treat your face – and my hand," she sniffed hard and a tear of pain escaped one eye.

Gyrfalon rose in one rapid movement and emptied the water in the bowl down the garderobe, and poured more water from the ewer.

"Put it in that. I will have Elissa fetch the other jar. And," he caught a second tear on a surprisingly gentle finger "My hostage does not cry; not in front of any of my soldiery".

Annis nodded, sniffed hard again and did as she was told, shocked to the pit of her stomach both by the intensity of the pain itself and her imagination of the agony it would have caused an open burn.

Gyrfalon put his head round the door and issued instructions to Elissa who waited, as always, without.

It was not long before the rangy female warrior knocked and abruptly entered.

"I have had stuff on my finger all the way up the stairs, my lord," she said laconically. "I feel nothing untoward; a coolness perchance and a little numbness. And the wax seals were undisturbed too," she added.

"Excellent," Annis turned round from the bowl, patting her hand dry in a fold of her linsey-woolsey gown. Elissa grinned at the childish gesture; but she stopped grinning as she caught sight of the girl's blistered hand.

"What in thunder could do that?" she demanded, seizing Annis by the wrist to look closer.

"Giant hogweed; prepared in a certain way, and with a spell," the girl replied. "One avoids the very plant if possible – even brushing the leaves can give a nasty burn if the skin is then exposed to the sun's light. Whoever did this must have harvested it with gloves and might even so be blistered. Look closely, Elissa, among the men next time you are amongst them in case you see any similarly afflicted."

Elissa was dutifully studying the blisters.

"Why would any do this?" she asked bluntly "It would not kill, just make you infernally angry my lord."

Annis managed a shaky grin.

"Some might say, when he is in a bad mood, infernallier angrier," she said.

"Vixen," said Gyrfalon. "Yes Elissa; you are correct. And it seems to me that I might have been expected to have killed Annis for the same."

"Why? Even I don't find her that irritating," said Elissa. Annis made a face at her.

"It rather depends, I would have thought," said Annis dryly, "who it would most benefit in having me out of the way." She scooped out another handful; and waited despite Elissa's assurances. It might after all have been Elissa who was the culprit, though Annis did not think so. "I would have said that my single most effective feature is mine ability as a healer. Before I came you were, my lord Gyrfalon, dependant on one who, as I pointed out to you, seared feeling rather than curing. My skills deprive this party of a modicum of power over you."

Gyrfalon stared at her thoughtfully.

"The wizard is many miles from here; a three hour ride, at my estimation," he said.

"But does he have agents?" she asked.

"It is possible. We must consider what to do," he began to pace up and down.

Annis, to Elissa's horror, pushed him firmly into the chair and began working the new salve into his face. Elissa averted her gaze; the sight of it sickened her. Gyrfalon's good eye saw the motion and gave her a look of derisive amusement; a look that warmed as he flicked his eye back to Annis.

"If, my lord," suggested Annis, "you were

heard to give a terrible scream, then went flying off to the wizard, and had suitable back up following, you might then judge if he were expecting you and you and your guard might then kill him. And I, supposedly dead, could watch to see if any followed to claim reward."

"Someone might even slip out ahead of Lord Gyrfalon to apprise the wizard of his imminent approach," suggested Elissa. Annis nodded.

"It means a lot of watching, but you might yet find out your traitor, Gyrfalon" she said.

"No escort," he said firmly. "The wizard will know if I bring others; he has some means of knowing some of my thoughts. I must deal with him myself."

Annis caught Elissa's eye behind Gyrfalon's back, tapped an imaginary sword, and mimed holding reins. Elissa nodded briefly and Annis grinned, almost back to her old self now the lotion worked on her blisters as on Gyrfalon's face.

Unaware of their byplay behind him the warlord continued,

"When the ointment has soaked in we will put it into action. Elissa, you are responsible for Annis' safety while I am gone."

"I will keep her in my sight at all times and away from your troops until you return my lord," promised Elissa quite truthfully.

Gyrfalon resumed his helmet, to Elissa's

relief.

"And now to make a horrible scream" he said grimly.

"If you can't, I'll bite you if you like," volunteered Annis, twinkling at him. He stared at her and gave a half grin.

"Little vixen, I believe you would too," he said appreciatively. "There is, however, no need" he stood by the window that opened onto the courtyard, wider than the embrasure on the other side.

"*AAAAAAaaaaaaeeeeeeeegh*!"

He flung back his head and cried out; and Annis heard in the cry all the remembered suffering and all the frustrations he had nursed to himself for so long. Then he turned to the two women and grinned; and the grin was almost boyish and mischievous.

"That ought to do it," he said.

Already guards were pounding up the stairs. Annis cast herself artistically on the floor with her head on one side as though her neck were broken. As an afterthought she pulled up her skirt on one side to display one leg bare to above the knee. Gyrfalon gave her a nod of approval.

"Thorough," he approved. He opened the door and pushed past the guards, ignoring queries; and leaving the door open. Elissa appeared and after being sure the guards in front had seen Annis's apparently lifeless body pushed the door shut and barred it.

Annis sat up.

"Quick – see if any slip out of the postern," she said. "Fulke is on duty on the main gate at this time and he owes me for helping his rheumatism. He will tell us if any left that way."

Elissa nodded and went to the embrasure to peer out. Annis ran to the door to listen.

"The guards have gone," she reported.

"So too has a cloaked figure at the postern," said Elissa laconically. "And I hear Lord Gyrfalon's horse now."

"Let me pull on some dry breeches under my skirts at least," said Annis, "and get my sword." Her eyes sparkled as she opened the door and pelted up to the turret room to kick off slippers and pull on her second pair of breeches and kilted her gown up over her girdle that it hung no lower than her knees; and ran down again to meet Elissa as she buckled on her practise sword over the kilted gown that would hold it more securely.

"Ready? Good" approved Elissa "You don't hang about."

"He might yet need us," said Annis. "And I don't want to be too late to help him; he is too splendid to permit anything to happen to."

Elissa laughed as they went to the stables to saddle their horses.

"Funny child you are," she said. "You're

not supposed to admire your captor you know!"

"I shall if I like," said Annis, "and I still have hopes of serving him you know, officially!"

She felt shy suddenly of confessing to Elissa that she had made a kind of proposal of marriage to Gyrfalon; who had not said yet if he took it seriously or not, so she said nothing.

And she drew ahead on Rowan so Elissa would not see the colour that seemed so easily to come to her face these days.

Following Gyrfalon was not easy; the warlord had set a breakneck pace, adding verisimilitude to his supposed agony.

"Our spy will be hard pushed to get there first!" Annis called to Elissa. The older woman nodded and grinned.

"Methinks he'll make it naytheless," she called back chuckling. "For every time he remember who be on his heels he'll spur his horse on that he not fall into the hands of Gyrfalon in a state of, er, infernallier angrier."

Annis chuckled.

"What it is to have a reputation eh?" she said.

"Oh it be deserved," said Elissa dryly. "Just because he treats you as he was wont to treat his adoptive son you'll see evidence of his ruthlessness in the woods soon enough."

"What happened to his son?" asked Annis curiously.

Elissa shrugged.

"He overstepped his abilities – as usual – and tried to please his father in a clumsy and stupid way – as usual. He managed to antagonise my lord's enemy, Lord Falk, by slaughtering a village just as an example. Lord Falk was already displeased for my lord was holding an abbess hostage for church monies. Only unlike you, he had her closely confined."

"I expect she was douce and reasonable at him," said Annis sagely, "as would infuriate him methinks. What then of this Buto? He died?"

"Aye, you have Gyrfalon's measure," said Elissa. "Buto thought to decoy Lord Falk and kill him, by his brutality, but he was such a posturing little … fool that it was a foregone conclusion that Falk would cut him to pieces. Fortunately Buto did not trust any woman warrior, so I was not one of his bodyguard."

"Ah; another score against our lord's brother, even though it were Buto's own fault," said Annis, half to herself. "You didn't like Buto."

Elissa shrugged.

"He tried to please Gyrfalon but he had not an idea how to do it. He was as stupid as a stump and took violence as the only solution to a problem. Where Gyrfalon would purr low in threat and menace, Buto would bluster and shout and lose his temper. Art a better son to my lord by far."

Annis grinned.

"I'll take that as compliment," she laughed.

If he wanted to adopt her she would at least get to stay with him.

They soon saw the reminders of the warlord's ruthlessness that Elissa had spoken of as they found themselves in the dark woods; skeletons hung from nails in their wrists from trees. Annis shuddered slightly; then stopped as she reminded herself that from what gossip she had heard from the men, these fellows had been bandits who had fallen in with travellers by dressing as monks. To crucify them might be cruel; but it had a degree of appropriateness and well in keeping with Gyrfalon's black sense of humour.

The woods thickened as the light faded, making progress difficult; but there was a definite path and here and there twigs showed white to mark Gyrfalon's precipitate passage which had broken them off. The women picked their way more cautiously, trusting to the instincts of the horses until the moon rose high enough to shed a golden harvest light over the scene

"We'll be hard put to catch up" muttered

Elissa.

"He can't have ridden at that pace all the way," Annis countered prosaically. "Even Nightmare has his limitations, and Gyrfalon won't kill the best horse he's ever had," she added, referring to Gyrfalon's big black steed. "Besides, he'll have slowed up to give the spy time to get ahead."

Elissa nodded dubiously; then stood in the saddled, peering ahead.

"The forest is opening. Look, it is open moorland before us. And our horses are fresher for having to go slow earlier."

They urged their mounts into a ground eating canter; and Annis was glad that Rowan was a good natured steed that cared not that she held the reins with only one hand; for all the salve there was yet soreness in the one that was burned that reins would rub cruelly. And then the girl was pointing as her quick young eyes caught a glimpse of Gyrfalon, his cloak flowing out behind him, silhouetted briefly atop a rise ahead of them.

After another hour's riding in silence it became apparent that Gyrfalon was making for the high bluffs of a massive tor that rose threateningly like a natural castle from the moorland. The top was apparent from miles away, but the full size of the feature did not become evident until they breasted the final rise. It was breathtaking; and the view from the summit must be commanding: but the greater part of the tor itself lay hidden in the folded terrain. As they approached, watching Gyrfalon disappear into the shadows at the base of the tor, there seemed within that dark shadow a patch of even darker gloom; and as they stared, eyes fixed on it to recall the position, there was a green flare deep in the blackness.

"Witchery!" whispered Elissa, fearfully.

"Well we knew that anyway," said Annis, practically. "Remember, Elissa, they say that witches fear cold steel and we have two feet of that each."

"You have no nerves at all, girl," said Elissa disgustedly. Annis chuckled.

"Oh I have plenty of nerves; but I won't do myself, you or Gyrfalon any good by letting them rule me. At least we not have to climb to the top of that thing; for 'tis heights leave me shaking with illogical fear and I fear the fear that might make me freeze. Ready?" Elissa nodded, swallowing hard. If this chit could face it so could she. "Then forward," said Annis, urging Rowan on.

Gyrfalon had given the shadowy figure of the spy time to lead his horse into the cleft ahead of him. The flickering green light of the necromancer's arcane experiments lit the way eerily; and he hung back briefly, lest he be seen by the wizard's man too closely on his heels. He dared not wait too long; for who knew what means the wizard might have at his disposal for knowing who lay without! Gyrfalon hitched Nightmare to a rocky protection and strode in, leaving the stallion whickering discontent. Even Nightmare did not like this place much.

Annis and Elissa approached the tor as quickly as they might with caution. The horses flinched and tried to head away; they liked it not. But their riders were implacable; and hitched the sweating mounts near Nightmare. But not too close; the horse had as wicked a temper as its master. When he was unsettled, the big horse had a propensity to bite other horses, and the intelligent beast sensed the unnatural, and rolled his eyes at the approach of others, even those he knew well. Elissa drew blade; but it was Annis who entered first, grimly purposeful, determined to find and stand beside Gyrfalon.

The slit in the rock ran straight a short way, then turned and finally opened into a chamber. There was a conversation going on; and the voice that Annis first heard gave her the shivers up and down her spine.

"But my dear Gyrfalon," it said, in a

chiding whisper, that were almost androgynous in tone rather than being high pitched as such "My dear Gyrfalon, I *own* you. I really find I have to reprove you for seeking alternative aid. Only I can truly aid you. You will come to acknowledge this."

"I acknowledge only that you have lied, that you have set your creatures to cause me harm such as to prompt me into killing the healer," Gyrfalon's voice was angry, but controlled "And her gentle ministrations with herbs have given me more relief than your numbing burning; that she told me I should hang one so inefficient as you!"

The other voice cut like a whiplash though it scarcely raised above a dry whisper, like the sibilant crackle of the passage of a snake's scales on dry heath.

"Enough! Has not my magic dragged you from the gates of Hell when you have been wounded? You belong to me and to my Dark Master, your own Master!"

"I belong to no-one!" growled Gyrfalon.

There was the scrape of steel that heralded Gyrfalon drawing his sword. Annis and Elissa held hands in the darkness; but that sound that was a sound they understood galvanised them into action and they ran forward into the cavern. Gyrfalon stood, almost at bay, no common thing for the mighty warrior, as the wizard launched a seering bolt of energy at him. The spy, whom Annis now recognised as one of the ostlers, was, the girl noticed, stealthily drawing a sword of his own, his eyes fixed on Gyrfalon's broad back.

"Get the spy!" she hissed to Elissa. The warrior woman sprang forward, glad of an objective she understood, action that did not paralyse her with terror as the thought of fighting magic did. She forced the man to turn, to defend himself.

The wizard, briefly distracted, lost control of a spell and Gyrfalon sprang in; but a sudden wall of energy deflected his blade, that smote upon it with a shower of sparks and a dull 'TANG' sound.

"Fool!" hissed the wizard "Do you not think I am immune to your puny sword blows?"

"That was what I was afraid of," Elissa muttered to herself, as she rained an onslaught of blows on the spy, who was *not* immune to them. "I hope that crazy wench has a better plan that that."

Gyrfalon swung again; this time there were more sparks and something of a buzzing hum as the sword struck the magic shield that seemed to waver. The warlord gave a smile of grim satisfaction.

"We shall see who is the most puny and who tires first," he said; glad that fighting Annis and engaging in passage of arms with

Elissa too that the female warrior's faults be corrected, had made sure he had not let his own stamina diminish in soft castle living.

The wizard was gathering himself for a counter attack.

Meanwhile, Annis had sheathed her sword and found what she was looking for. Gyrfalon was fencing and thrusting, feinting and weaving, watching the magician's fingers ready to thrust for the face of the wizard to disrupt his spell.

Annis moved stealthily with her find, working her way behind the magician.

BONG!

Annis brought the heavy iron crucible that had been heating on the brazier down on the wizard's head. Green sparks flew from it as she let go of the handle and jumped back with alacrity. The wizard had gone down.

Gyrfalon blinked, momentarily frozen.

"What the hell are you doing here?" he demanded harshly "Never mind. Help me cut his head off – and bury it and his body in separate graves."

Annis nodded. Gyrfalon sounded, if not exactly rattled, at least disconcerted. She recognised it. She felt much the same herself.

With her mouth drying and bile rising bitter in her throat, Annis stretched the stringy throat of the unconscious magician for Gyrfalon to sever head from body; and both head and body twitched horribly as he did so and continued to do so after severance was complete. Elissa, having long since finished with her prey, retched as she came over to see what went on.

"Underground and overground, through water and in air," muttered Annis.

"What?" said Gyrfalon, his eyes on the faintly twitching skull in fascinated horror.

"Old superstition; and maybe worth nothing. But it will not harm to bury the head in the bed of the stream and hang up the body for the crows – if they'll touch it."

Gyrfalon nodded.

"Superstition may very well be based on reason; it will not harm to follow it, for that thing like not the idea by its twitches.

"Also," said Annis, "dear God I feel sick … my lord, I pray you to open that horrid mouth; hast gloves on."

Gyrfalon shot her a look; but did so. Annis shook in some salt she had found on a shelf; and lifted her crucifix from around her neck and laid it on the tongue.

The head gave a thin scream and shifted as the flesh shrank, crumbled, and fell away in blackened shards.

The body too was crumbling into dust and Elissa cried out in terror.

Annis sat back heavily, clutching her crucifix to her. Her head swam and her ears rang and roared; and her sight was blurred.

"But I don't faint," she muttered, swaying where she sat.

Gyrfalon unceremoniously thrust her head between her knees.

"Be ill on your own time, girl," he said harshly, shocked and frightened himself. "We have to deal with this thing and your initial suggestion of how to do so still seems good to me."

Elissa was pressed back against the cave wall.

"What did you do, Annis?" she whispered.

Annis raised a white face, her eyes huge and dark in it.

"I think," she said carefully, "it is what my crucifix *un*-did. I think," she shuddered, "that he had been dead already for a very long time, sustained in the semblance of life by spells and rituals the like of which I do not wish in any wise to contemplate. Excuse me," she scrambled to her feet and ran outside to empty her stomach.

The stream was pure and clear; and Annis dipped her crucifix in it before rinsing her mouth in its chill waters, to be sure no taint of evil magic touched it. After all a lich or whatever the necromancer had been needed no water.

There was no reaction to the cross; and she rinsed and spat, and then cautiously drank.

There seemed to be no ill effects.

When Annis returned within she had regained some of her poise.

"I dug a hole in the stream bed" she told Gyrfalon "to purify that thing with running water."

They did so, Gyrfalon holding the dessicated skull from him at arm's length in repugnance; then returning for the body, that he nailed by the wrist bones into the soft rock.

Annis ran to him when it was done and took his hands.

"Has he harmed you?" she demanded.

"No," he said, and firmly disengaged his hands. "To horse; we should return as fast as we may."

The ride back to the castle was accomplished in silence. As they neared the walls Gyrfalon spoke.

"Maybe your God is not so weak as I have thought him."

"Maybe, my lord, you are not aware that he belongs to you too," said Annis quietly.

Gyrfalon snorted.

"You are both disobedient wenches," he changed the subject "Extra sword practice for both of you. You will learn that long handled crucibles are not generally accepted weapon's of war." He put heel to Nightmare's flank's and rode ahead to the castle gates, ignoring Annis' reproachful comment,

"Nor too is magic an accepted weapon of war, and I thought but to fight magic with magic!"

"He ain't listening," said Elissa.

Annis screwed up her face in a horrible grimace and startled the gate guard that she was gurning and sticking out her tongue at the warlord.

"Did that make you feel better, brat?" said Gyrfalon without looking back.

"Yes, thank you my lord," said Annis.

"He can see out of the back of his head?" Elissa whispered.

"He guessed, silly; he know me too well," said Annis.

Gyrfalon grunted something that, were he still not so unsettled, would have been akin to a laugh; for Annis was ever pragmatic.

Chapter 7

Gyrfalon brooded all night on the extraordinary events of the evening. He thought hard about the way Alys's cross had seemed to fill with fire as she cursed him, fire that recalled to him the burning beam which had fallen on him as he dragged his lieutenant from the house where the barbarians had trapped them. It dazzled and provoked the same fear and pain when Falk wore it, in memory of Alys, to taunt him whenever they met and fought, neither able to achieve ascendancy over the other. He considered how Annis looked so like – yet so unlike – his dead betrothed. He acknowledged that the incident had frightened him; not merely the fear of the magic of the undead necromancer, but perhaps fear as well of the power that Annis seemed to wield.

At first light the warlord summoned Annis. She was prompt; she had not slept either, but had spent most of the night praying in the castle chapel. Elissa had got quietly drunk outside the chapel door.

Annis came into Gyrfalon's chamber with her light tread and ran to his chair and knelt beside it burying her face against his leg.

"Please tell me you were scared too, my

lord," she begged, "then I won't feel such an awful coward. We talked about it so calmly while it was happening but I cannot get the horror from in front of mine eyes!"

The heavy lines running down his face softened slightly.

"Oh yes, girl; I was scared," he admitted quietly "Magic is a frightening business to those of us who cannot use it."

She shuddered.

"I suppose there must be white witches, but creatures like that..." she left the sentence unfinished and leaned against him closer. "Some have said I use magic when I heal, but ... I could not imagine using it save when concentrating on helping others."

He touched her head lightly and came close to caressing her pale locks. She was frightened and had come to him for reassurance; and that had been why she had taken his hands the night before. She was not about to threaten him with a power that she even seemed unaware of. She still called him 'my lord'; though she had been free enough with his name when she was so shocked about the adulterated salve. The girl had disobeyed him ...no she had not, he had said he would take no escort; she had not been forbidden exactly. And she had doubtless talked Elissa into following a vow to the letter, to not let her out of her sight or near the troops. Little sophist!

And she had courage and fortitude.

He took her chin in his hand and turned it up to face him.

"It is over, girl," he said firmly. "There is no more need to consider that wizard again; he is no more threat to us."

She smiled up at him tremulously and nodded.

"That command I promise to try my best to obey; and hope that I be able to," she said. "And I suppose that when we have broken our fast – as now I feel able to, from your good comfort to me – it will be time for you to beat me black and blue at sword practice for mine otherwise creative endeavours at obedience."

He laughed.

"Aye, you bad girl," he agreed.

Annis might yet call Gyrfalon 'lord' but he still felt the need to dominate her in sword practice, and pressed her hard. Not that Annis had expected anything else; and she looked upon it as a relatively gentle punishment for following him and disobeying the spirit of his command if not the letter. She decided to try her ruse and fall to one knee ere she was totally exhausted; but Gyrfalon was wise to the trick and effortlessly parried the final upward stroke, disarming her that her sword clattered away from a numbed hand ere he leaped on her to pin her to the ground again.

And he was on his feet again almost immediately, wringing a little cry of surprise and almost disappointment from Annis.

He regarded her thoughtfully; and pulled her almost roughly to her feet.

"Go and wash and change, girl; and I'll show you a different lesson in warcraft. Put on other breeches, and dress warm."

"What will you teach me my lord?" she asked eagerly.

He gave a grim smile.

"Aye, you drink it all in, don't you?" he said "How did I ever manage to call you whey faced? You're no such thing you little white flame! If, as I suspect, your father arrives soon with his forces, I wish to double check that all my defences are secure. We'll ride the outer bailey with a view as to how to attack. You can point out any weak points – if there are any."

"A bit like searching out your virtues – if you have any," said Annis brightly.

"Precisely," his eye glinted appreciatively at her pert answer, and he ruffled her hair.

The black, forbidding keep and bailey had taken on a familiarity that made it almost homely; it was the view Annis saw every time she returned from Mass. A deep ditch crossed by the drawbridge was steep-sided, and rose to a stone glacis beneath the massive walls that had an angle sufficient that the dead angle was reduced. Lest any manage to cross the moat, machicolations ran along the battlements for the deployment of boiling oil or hot pitch or any such offensive rain; and the turrets set at intervals were cantilevered to some extent by corbelling and contained arrow slits covering every part of the wall and reducing the dead angle to nothing. The embrasures atop the walls were deep and well contrived, sloping inward like the arrow notches themselves. The gatehouse itself might be a weak point; as it had been when Gyrfalon had stormed the castle. But it contained two portcullises and murder holes above as well as arrow slits within; that Gyrfalon's men had traversed so quickly that the defenders had not time to make use of their well-devised defences. And immediately within the walls a wall meant that an attacker was forced to turn left or right in a narrow passage, making him vulnerable. This last was newly constructed, Annis thought.

"The funnelling wall is yours, is it not, my lord?" she asked.

Gyrfalon nodded.

"Whilst it be unlikely that the gate be breached since *my* men ought to be well aware of how I did it, I believe in taking no chances," he said.

"And those on the gatehouse roof ready to fire down on the confused mass of men trapped there, and a barrel of pitch at each end of the passage to broach and fire in such an event I suppose?" she asked "That will frighten horses and slow men."

"I'd not thought of barrels of pitch … yes, it takes fewer men to defend than otherwise … and a trough that it flow into to make a wall of flame. Bloodthirsty, aren't you?" he teased.

She shrugged.

"I don't have to like the idea of burning men; but it does make sense; and puts our men at less risk. That's what war is about isn't it, and siege warfare particularly, minimising risk to one's own men and making the game not worth the candle for the opposition?"

He grinned to himself at her choice of the word 'our'.

"So, do you see any weakness?" Gyrfalon asked Annis as they rode from one end of the walls to the other.

She shook her head.

"Not in the structure. The only possible weakness lies in our men. They are, many of them, untried in real battle, being used mostly to skirmishes; though I have to say they're less of a rabble than they were even a few weeks ago. A siege, methinks, is a battle of nerves as much as anything else, on both sides; and it depends in their belief in themselves, and that depends partly on their belief in you, my lord. I think that they believe in you enough not to break; but I'm not sure."

He gave a malevolent chuckle.

"Perchance I should threaten then that *you* will deal with them if they fail me," he said. "They know you for a ruthless one, my vixen."

Annis flushed.

And it were mostly in pleasure that he claimed her as his vixen.

"Ruthless? Yes I suppose I can be," she said, and sighed ruefully. "And that began because I felt there should be object lesson over that rapist. A woman hath a less objective view of the same you see. But on a serious note, my lord, methinks that encouragement would be more helpful than threats. Reminding them that we have plenty of food – thanks in great part to *their* efforts – and a strong castle."

He snorted.

"You encourage them then; I'll threaten. Between us we should strike the right balance."

She laughed.

"By your command, my lord," she said and added, "Do we now take boat to go look round the marsh side? I can collect herbs while we do if we go."

He stared.

"It can't be attacked from that side," he said.

"Indeed? Then as an attacker 'tis where I'd look to effect an entrance. For if 'tis accounted impossible there be a good chance that 'twill not be guarded – nor so well defended in stone."

He stared; and his good eye narrowed.

"Very well," he said, in his dangerously soft tone "And then you shall tell me how such an entrance may be effected."

She nodded.

"If I see one, I shall. It may, as you say, be impossible," she said without loss of composure. "But it were well to make sure, dear lord, that we not fall into the trap of the conventional belief that you have warned me about."

"You quote me back at myself? Thou vixen, thou whelp!" he cried.

She beamed at him.

Seated in the boat, Annis stared up at the sheer, artificial cliff that was the wall of the castle. She grunted.

"Well?" asked Gyrfalon, his composure returned after the brief anger over being flatly contradicted. The girl was right and did her duty to him as her lord as if she actually owed him fealty by her caution.

"No machicolations. Few arrow slits. The embrasures are wider too. Were I a canny warlord I should float down river at night on rafts, clad in dark clothing. I should lash the rafts together and then moor them to stout poles driven into the mud here, that methinks is what I believe is called a dead angle. The mud is but a few feet deep here right under the walls else we could not be poled along but must needs row. Then I should assemble the sections of scaling ladders I had brought and lead my men – unarmoured for silence – over the walls where doubtless few, if any guards patrol. Those best skilled would silently slit the throats of any sentries, being sure to be stealthy to get those silent kills. Then we should barricade the barrack doors and seize the lord of the castle; and let down the drawbridge for our followers."

He stared.

"And you say you have no training in siege-craft?"

"None my lord. But I have imagination and a deal of common sense," she said.

He shook his head.

"Your father is assuredly the biggest fool in Christendom. Had I sired a daughter like you I should treasure her as the best son a man might have. If he thinks he's getting you back, he can think again."

Annis laughed.

"I think that's meant as a compliment – in a backhanded way," she said.

"It was meant as one – in a backhanded way," he returned, laughing at her.

Annis smiled up at him.

The warlord caught his breath.

"I – I shall see to having this wall well guarded," he said, his voice harsh of a sudden. "Your father may be a fool, but he may have competent underlings to whom the same might occur. And I shall have barrels of naphtha positioned to be thrown over to fire any such rafts. And the village geese up on the battlements to give tongue."

Annis nodded.

"Yes; we shall be able to sleep easier knowing that there's less chance of waking up dead," she agreed.

"Foolish child; there be no such chance for you; they want *you* alive," he said.

She regarded him gravely.

"Perchance that be an even better reason for me to wish for strong defences," she said. "That I not feel any risk that I might fall into the hands of my father and his allies that will not use me so doucely as have you. It is good to know that you can keep me safe in your protection. Though," she sighed, "I fear it be at the risk of our men's lives."

"They are soldiers; they know the risks such entails," he spoke harshly. He did not add that Annis' gentle healing probably feel that it was worth taking any risk to keep her – however ruthless she might be capable of being!

The boatman kept his head down and said nothing; but he had plenty to pass on. And that the Lady Annis feared going back to her father beyond the rational fear she ought to feel for Gyrfalon, and to consider that the cruel way the warlord drove her in sword practice was being used doucely meant that they had to fight hard to prevent such a thing befalling her! For Annis was almost universally respected and even now grudgingly loved by the men she had impartially physicked and scolded. She had even treated the ills of those who had at first tried to handle her roughly and it had impressed the rough men. And if they had a gnawing fear of her anger should they transgress, it was mingled with respect that she was no coward!

When they returned to the castle, Gyrfalon ordered Annis to his chamber and produced a pair of beautifully crafted knives in wrist sheathes.
"These are balanced to be thrown; and designed to shake from sheath into the hand," he told her. "Wear them at all times; and I shall teach you how to use them properly. If

we are breached you can defend yourself with them as a last resort; or perchance buy time with the surprise of them to get yourself away."

Annis was delighted and examined the knives with care!

"And an we be breached methinks I'd cut mine hair short and wear baggy tunic and cover myself in the grime of the kitchen if anything had happened to you my lord" said Annis "That I might find a time to take my revenge for you; for I make no doubt the castle will not be lost save over your dead body."

"Possibly not," said Gyrfalon.

"Will you start teaching me now?" asked the girl hopefully.

"Why not?" he said "Art a glutton for punishment."

"I love learning from you," she said simply.

Gyrfalon's own skill with thrown knives was incredible; but Annis had a good eye and did not disgrace herself once she had grasped the basic technique.

"Enough," he said at last "You progress; let not weariness spoil that. And I know at least that you do not freeze in danger as many women do – as your killing of Solly prove, even though you had but little training then."

She shuddered.

"His breath stank," she remarked.

Gyrfalon laughed.

"And were that a good Christian reason to slay him?" he mocked.

She shook her head.

"No; but methinks his intentions towards me justified me using extreme force."

"Had I thought else I had told you at the time," he said. "He gave you room to manoeuvre," he added "What would you do if he had grabbed your throat?" Panther-like he leaped and suited actions to words; but his grip this time was but firm and not so painful as the last time he had so held her; this was an exercise for her ingenuity, no more.

Annis shifted experimentally.

"On anyone but you, my lord, I might try to pull on the little fingers that are generally weak; but I fancy it not always work," she said, trying.

"I have strong fingers for sword work – and knife throwing" said Gyrfalon.

"I cannot reach you with a knee to the crotch" Annis admitted candidly, trying. "You have me held too far away. Methinks, though, most people reach futilely for the hands that hold them; the surprise move would be to reach downwards instead and squeeze hard that which be tender and hope to duck the vomit."

She felt duly with her hand and a blush suffused her face as she encountered a response to her touch above her target of aim.

"Squeeze there, and wilt but drive a man on," said the warlord roughly.

Annis was trembling but forced herself to feel lower to see if she might so reach. She said, trying to sound lighthearted,

"Aye my lord, but perchance on many men, those that need to rape, and so be no real man, I'd not encounter such a, er, flattering or, um, lavish a response to impede mine attempted violence. Here a sharp pinch would, methinks be damaging to any man's ego and equilibrium."

"Indeed. You are quite priceless you know little one," he managed. "Aye, you have the right place to cause most pain. Are you afraid?"

"No," she turned her eyes up to look at him; and quickly looked down again.

"You are trembling."

"Am I? I – I do not want to truly hurt you; perchance that is why."

"Ah, perchance it is. And suppose," he released her throat to capture her wrists, "suppose your hands were not free?"

"Then I must needs kick and bite; or use mine head to try to catch mine opponent on the chin or nose. I wager it dampen the ardour to have a nosebleed or a bloody lip for a tooth stuck in it."

He laughed low.

"Aye, it would; and I note you be kind to my face that you not attempt it. What then if one had got you on your back?" he flung her on the bed and knelt over her.

Her breath came raggedly; but she managed to look up with a mischievous twinkle in her eyes.

"Why, a man must needs be above me in such a situation; and must needs also let go with one hand to loose his nether garments and get at such parts of me as he require; and I think I'd have to do something to put him off his passion, that nutting him be also valid; and biting too."

Lightly she set her teeth to his neck below the helm.

He laughed again.

"Only dogs bite, my dear; and your hair is designed to hold you like a leash," he grabbed her thick plait to pull her head back.

"Why my lord! Unkind of you to call me a bitch!" she returned. He gave a low chuckle.

Hesitantly her free hand came up to rest against his chest and she pulled against the pressure on her plait to look into his face.

There was a loud knock at the door.

Gyrfalon swore and came to his feet away from her, off the bed in one movement.

"Go neaten yourself," he ordered harshly. "You look as dishevelled as a peasant girl well swived in a barn!"

"Speak for yourself," retorted Annis. "You be as awry as the peasant boy doing the swiving."

The knock sounded again and Elissa's voice called,

"My lord?"

Annis slipped round the corner of the chamber to compose herself and the warlord jerked open the door.

"*What*?" he demanded.

Elissa quailed and glanced behind him, half expecting to see Annis hurt or dead if he be in so bad a temper.

"My Lord … I, um, wondered if Annis were here … I had thought I saw her return with you, but I have not seen her…."

Gyrfalon regarded her, and spoke softly, dangerously.

"It were well for you that the girl is with me. Though if she continue to progress so well with thrown knives she will not need you as a protector, but only as a guard."

Annis emerged from around the corner.

"Ah, my lord, must you needs take it out on poor Elissa because I bit you?" she asked, laughing up at him.

"You *bit* him?" queried Elissa, horrified.

"It be safe enough; he not be like to poison me the way Lord Marfey would," said Annis. "He was teaching me to fight barehanded. I was losing. I *hate* losing" said Annis.

Gyrfalon looked at her quizzically.

"Now I thought you were seriously considering yielding to me," he said.

Colour touched Annis cheeks but she answered steadily enough.

"Truly my lord, I think I must always yield to you; but if you teach me to fight an hypothetical battle, why then, I hate losing," she said. "I come Elissa, at your disposal" and she walked out of the room, waiting until she was out of sight around the spiral stair before performing a neat dance step and punching the air.

Elissa regarded her suspiciously.

"What is it with you?" she asked sourly.

"Life is good," said Annis cryptically. "For I have learned something that I were not sure of."

Gyrfalon stared long at the door long after the two women had left. He had not intended to do more than demonstrate potential situations to the girl, suggest ways of breaking holds. It had got out of hand; and it seems as though at times she responded, though her replies were light and facetious. Yet how could that be? He was surely imagining it! She was young, lovely, perfect. And he was marred. It had to be his imagination; unless

147

she had played with him. Women were cruel. She had said so herself.

And yet ….

Annis did not lie … even in her disobedience there was a kind of honour.

The warlord cursed again, pungently; and drew himself a goblet of wine.

It would, he decided, be a bad idea to get into such a situation again. If he had misread, and were then rejected ….

Her knife throwing would take place outside like her sword practice; and if it were erratic, why then, his men must learn to stay out of the way.

And Elissa could teach her some holds and throws.

And so it was for the next few days, that Annis perfected her aim at a target without; and Elissa wrestled with her in the warlord's chamber under his instruction and away from most prying eyes that would leer on two women fighting.

And if such disappointed Annis she tried to show it not. Indeed, she told herself firmly, it was as well; for she was a little apprehensive about what might have happened had not Elissa arrived knocking; and knew deep down that she would have yielded in whatever way the warlord demanded, for her feelings were strange and intense and she was glad of a space of time to come to terms with them. This was arousal and it were a greater force than ever she might have imagined!

And meanwhile she might strive for martial excellence and please Gyrfalon thus; and that she learned for her own satisfaction was subordinate to her desire to please the man she now realised she loved with all her being.

And that he was distant with her was perhaps that he did not wish to acknowledge that he had any feelings for her; if she were not mistaken in all that his face and body said to her. Why that should be Annis was not sure; but decided that it must be something to do with her status as a hostage.

Well doubtless he would get over it.

Chapter 8

Annis had had a busy morning. She had woken feeling sure that something was going to happen; but as nothing seemed to be she had instead put in some work plying her needle on the robe she had all but finished for the warlord. Each stitch in it now was personal; and she hoped he would like it. It was calf length, slit at the sides for ease of movement, and the rich black brocade had a silver thread in the weave in an intertwining spiral pattern that was as exotic and foreign as the fabric itself. She had cut the fur lining larger than the robe, and turned it over the edges of the garment that it show the richness of the fur; and had taken the intricate trim from another garment, knotwork in silver thread on a blood red ground, and was applying that at the edge of the fur where it lay against the brocade, as a separation one from the other. It looked very fine.

She put it aside as Elissa awoke.

The woman warrior looked at her curiously.

"You're such a odd girl," said Elissa ."You do not have to sew, you know."

"I like to sew," said Annis placidly. "It satisfies me. Do you think he will like it?"

"He'd be a fool if he did not," said Elissa

laconically. "And that's another example of your oddness; any other girl confronted by such fine fabrics would sew herself a gown, methinks – not make something for her captor."

"Are you jealous I have not sewn for you?" asked Annis.

"No I'm not; I confess, I have enough woman to me to like the fabrics and if you have time I'd not be displeased to have something to wear for best; that I have a chance to be all woman on mine own terms once in a while ere I get to old to enjoy it. But if you choose to sew for my lord it does not make me jealous. Only confused."

"I suppose I started it in some gratitude to him for being my good rescuer and protector," said Annis.

"You *are* mad" laughed Elissa.

Annis had just sheathed her sword after the day's practice – Gyrfalon had merely disarmed her this time and had not forced her down – when the messenger clattered in, his horse lathered with effort. Annis realised that this was what she had woken up expecting.

One ran to take the bridle of the beast and see to its needs as the messenger all but tumbled off in exhaustion and hurried as best he might to Gyrfalon. As Annis' lesson generally attracted no little interest the man had an audience as he knelt, trembling with fatigue.

"My lord, a great army approaches. There are within it the banners of more than one war leader. The troops number thousands."

Gyrfalon nodded.

"You have done well," he said. "Ale and a hot bath for this man – for Bertric! Foregrim, have one sent to the village to inform them all that the time has come to come within the castle. Check and recheck the supplies of arrows at the defences and all such other appurtenances."

"I will go to the village, my lord," volunteered Annis. "It will save a fighting man going."

He nodded and turned to the messenger.

"Bertic – how long?" he asked.

The man swallowed the mouthful of ale he had readily been given and looked overcome that the warlord knew his name.

"A day – perchance a day and a half," he estimated "I rode mine animal into the ground; I spied them beyond the great forest. It was then first light; and I spied them encamped on the rise before they enter the woods."

Gyrfalon nodded.

"If they are not used to working together we might even have full two days" he said satisfied. "'Twil take them time to mesh the wants, needs and facilities of more than one army; and to deal with frictions between those partisans of one lord over another that be emotionally charged for war that quarrels break out more easily. And even, should we be truly fortunate, a split lead or disputed captain."

He looked forward to discussing such with Annis; who had already saddled Rowan to ride off to the village, that she might quickly circle every part of it calling her news as well as asking the priest to ring the alarm bell. Elissa was not with her; but Annis' comings and goings were so common now that none challenged her. Indeed it was more than all had forgotten that she was a hostage and most saw her as one of their own. Annis rode around quickly, working out in her own mind how a single man might ride in a few hours a distance that might take an army a couple of days. For a single horse required as much care as any in an army. Of course, an army required properly set out camps with pickets, food preparation on a grand scale and usages of courtesy that fighting men not start fighting their own. Inevitably in a large collection of horses, one must need shoeing from time to time, holding up all the rest, where a man alone had more flexibility, and might at need to carry message, risk his horse's feet by evening up all hooves in quickly taking the rest of the shoes off. Bruised feet would heal.

She jumped off Rowan by the church and strode in, giving a hasty genuflection to the altar. The priest was seeing to the candles, but turned as the girl's boots rang on the hard stone floor.

"Father," she greeted him gravely, "armies come. It is time to ring the bells and bring everyone within the bailey."

The priest sighed and crossed himself.

"Will they be safe with that devil, daughter?" he asked.

Annis' eyes flashed but she answered levelly.

"They will be a sight safer under Lord Gyrfalon's protection than from the depredations of a marauding army," she told him dryly. "They are, after all, his people now. To any attacking soldiery they are but prey. Morality tends, after all, to be applied only to one's friends in war," she added cynically. He smiled sadly.

"Alas, too true, daughter Annis. I of course will take my chances without and trust that they will respect a man of the cloth."

Annis snorted.

"With due respect, father, you will *not*. Your flock will be frightened and confused and in more need than ever of spiritual guidance. Would you wish to desert them in their hour of need? For if you would, and come not willingly, I fear I must send a man to bring you in unwillingly."

He flushed.

"I understood that Lord Gyrfalon would have no members of the clergy anywhere near him," he said. "I did not wish to bring retribution on my congregation."

"I will guarantee your safety," said Annis simply.

"Forgive me, but I understood you were a hostage; how come you speak of sending men, or guaranteeing the safety of another?" he was dubious.

"It gets a little more complex than that," shrugged Annis. "Lord Gyrfalon knows that I am a Christian and I think he will respect both my wishes and those of his peasantry and serfs."

The priest nodded, not entirely satisfied, but accepting; and soon the bells rang above the church's thatched roof in a carillon of alarum.

Elissa relaxed in relief as she watched Annis escort the motley band of peasants and serfs and their livestock within the safe, encircling walls. She dreaded the outcome of Lord Gyrfalon finding out that she had lost sight of her charge. Whilst Elissa was fairly certain Annis was daft enough to prefer being

Gyrfalon's hostage to making a bid for freedom, one could never be quite sure with the mad chit. And she had failed to do the warlord's bidding, of not losing sight of the girl.

Annis, unaware of the terror she had caused by not wanting to trouble Elissa, smiled and waved cheerily.

"Help me get them billeted, Elissa and out from being in the way of all this military mayhem," she said.

Elissa nodded as the dryness in her mouth receded, acknowledging to herself that Annis had not frightened her a-purpose.

"The girl doesn't even understand that you're supposed to be scared of Gyrfalon," she growled to herself; and applied herself with rough kindness to hurrying the peasants to where they were supposed to be as Annis comforted weeping, frightened children.

Gyrfalon was too busy to worry himself with Elissa's worries; but he had noticed that Annis had ridden off on her own – and had returned. He contented himself with bellowing a teasing,

"What, froward wench, hast saddled me with a priest and all? I'll have nothing to do with the fellow; if you want him made comfortable, shalt see to it for yourself!"

Annis raised an acknowledging hand.

"I don't think he likes you either, my lord!" she called cheekily.

"Good; let it stay that way!" Gyrfalon shouted back. Annis laughed.

"See?" She said to the priest. "Make yourself at home in the chapel; I've swept it clean long since save where we be storing some of the grain; for want of space to house that and the villagers. They may sit on the sacks after all on Sundays."

"Thank you daughter," said the priest.

As the mayhem decreased, Gyrfalon saw Annis passing, and grabbed her by a wrist and pushed her against a wall roughly.

"When you went out to the village you could have carried on riding, you know; I know you'd not go to your father, but you had time to take a route away from both of us."

She looked surprised.

"Why ever would I do a daft like thing like that?" she asked.

He put his hands on her shoulders and shook her.

"Little fool! Have you forgotten that you are a hostage?" He demanded "At my command?"

"Oh," she said. "Am I so? I had thought you had changed your mind and had said you would keep me … I thought you planned to marry me instead; we spoke of it," she bit her lip and looked down "Perchance I misunderstood."

"That was a hypothetical conversation," he told her roughly. Her shoulders slumped under his hands.

"I see," she spoke to the ground. "So my skills and abilities count for nothing? Your apparent p-pleasure in my company counts for nothing? It cannot be just the gold you crave more than me, for you could just as well demand a dowry. Then it must be that you cannot reconcile yourself to a wife of my Faith; and I cannot change that even if I would. I can swear not to talk about it; indeed I thought not that I spoke so much of it that it might annoy you."

Gyrfalon stared at her. She seemed distressed; truly, genuinely distressed and disappointed. Devastated even. He forced her chin up to gaze in those smoke grey eyes. They held hurt and bewilderment.

"You were serious then?" he asked abruptly "When you said in your teasing fashion that you would marry me?"

She nodded as well as she was able held so tightly controlled by him.

He pulled a wry and self mocking face.

"Of course, compared to your supposed bridegroom, I suppose almost anyone would be preferable – even me," he said bitterly.

She wrenched herself from his grasp, eyes

blazing.

"Oh you impossible *idiot*!" she shouted at him "Put aside thy self pity, Gyrfalon, it becomes you not! You are the mighty warlord Gyrfalon not some April maid smirking vanity at her spotty face in the millpond!" And she stalked off leaving him gaping in confusion at her angered outburst.

Elissa, not far away, as she had vowed not to lose the girl again, cringed slightly and fell into step as Annis slammed through the door into the tower and marched to her room in high dudgeon.

"You shouted at him!" Elissa accused.

"He irritated me," snapped Annis. Elissa blinked. The concept of shouting at Gyrfalon because he had been irritating was a new one on her.

"He isn't the sort of person you ought to shout at," she suggested caustically. Annis sniffed.

"I thought I just did," she said, going on into her chamber and slamming that door too. Elissa blinked, shrugged, and settled down outside the door. Either the crazy chit would get away with it – the way Buto had so often got away with it – or he'd want Elissa to bring the girl to him to punish. Elissa hoped it would not come to that; she would regret it a lot. She was more or less fond of Annis.

Gyrfalon slammed up to and into his own chamber in near as towering a rage as Annis. And when within he engaged in furious thought; and his rage evaporated in other, confused feelings. *Was* he placing too much thought on the scar? Did Annis mean he should behave as though it were not there? Was it even a sign of weakness that he let it affect him? Did she even despise him for such a weakness?

He called for a mirror to be brought to his room; and a minion ran to get one, in some trepidation. The warlord had been relatively douce of late and this argument with the Lady Annis could be bad news for any unfortunate enough to be in the wrong place while the warlord raged. The servant almost passed out in relief and surprised when Gyrfalon barked a word of thanks to him and fled thankfully.

Gyrfalon took off his helmet and studied his face, trying for objectivity rather than using its ravaged appearance to whip him to a frenzy of loathing as he had been wont to do before.

He found its appearance somewhat improved by the salves; and the more repellent of the open, oozing sores had closed and had pink scar tissue to them. He knew cynically that, even as it had looked before Annis' ministrations, there would have been women who would have lain with him; for a price – be that power or wealth – but that was irrelevant.

"That is not what I want," he informed his reflection aloud. Then he pondered. "What do I want?"

The reflection gazed at him and sneered as he twisted his mouth up.

"You fool," he told it. "Physical gratification is not enough for you. You want the love that you imagined that you would find with Alys. You want a woman – you want Annis – to care for you. That is why it matters. Can a woman truly love a man with a dead eye and tatterdemalion features and a damaged soul?"

He resisted the urge to hurl the mirror to the floor as he had often done before; and laid it down gently enough ere he laid himself down upon his bed staring at the ceiling, his view interrupted by the memory of a pair of stormy blue eyes.

The stormy blue eyes in question had cried themselves to sleep but arose determined to reflect nothing but calm. Nothing passed between Annis and Gyrfalon as she applied his morning salve; just a curt nod on his part and the usual gentle ministrations on hers. Annis wandered onto the battlements after breaking her fast to watch for the armies that might hold her fate. As a sharp-eyed watchman called of the flashing of armour in the distance, Gyrfalon found her there. They watched in silence; but somehow it was a companionable silence, not an ominous one. Annis slid a little hand into his; and he squeezed it gently and absently. He half turned to her; but spoke not, for it would have shattered the long moment shared.

And neither of them, caught up in their own feelings, realised the collective sigh of relief that rippled through the ranks that their lord and their little lady no longer quarrelled; and spirits raised.

Dawn of the following day found Gyrfalon and Annis again together on the battlement.

Annis' long hair whipped out behind her in the breeze, dancing like a pale flame springing in an aureole around her head. Its lightness, with her white, set face and the plain unbleached woollen gown she wore that morning were fair contrast to Gyrfalon's black-clad, armoured figure. And though Annis was a cause for the coming conflict, her presence at their lord's side was a comfort to the troops. Their lord's temper had noticeably improved since the girl's arrival; and her herbal skills had also improved the general state of health of the troops. So, Annis was a mascot, albeit an acknowledged ruthless one; and the battle was one to keep her and not to let *them* steal her away. Annis knew nothing of this; she merely felt a deep feeling of regret and guilt that she would be the cause of fighting; and if anger at her father and Lord Marfey that they would plunge their men so blithely into battle without even pretence at negotiation.

"You should call for a parley, my lord," she said.

"Parley?" he almost spat the word. She laid a hand on his arm.

"I will not pester you about my beliefs. If there is no-one else you prefer, to marry me is an ideal solution," she said.

"From whose point of view?"

"Mine. Yours. The men who will not then die over me"

He looked down at her.

"There is no-one that I could wish for more than you. But men will still die. Beside the banner of your father is that of my brother Falk, a version of our one time family banner. And he will only leave when he sees me dead," he paused "I too would like to see him dead," he added.

Annis snorted.

"Is this worthy idiot worth wasting your time and effort on?" she snapped "Let him do the fretting while you do the getting. His line will die and yours will prosper."

He laughed suddenly and the drawn lines of troops without the wall stirred at his harsh mirth; and one slender figure looked up with a frown of concern. Gyrfalon did not notice.

"You always manage to surprise me, Annis. What an earthy little thing you can sometimes be!"

Annis blushed and dropped her eyes.

"I see no point in coy," she murmured.

"No; you are right; it is an irritating trait in a woman," he agreed. "Well, I shall call for a parley anyway, on such terms. Perchance we may at least get rid of your father at least if he might call me son-in-law; for I stand between his lands and the lawless north," he pursed his lips in thought. "Tell me more of the relationship between your father and Marfey. What will *he* do?"

Annis considered, sliding a hand into his gloved fist; and absently he lifted her hand and laid his other over it.

"Marfey would ever run bleating to the church," she said succinctly. "Which, if your brother is here could be what he has already done. I expect that Marfey has bought enough bishops to command the services of Falk; of whom I had heard, isolated as I have been in my father's castle, as a champion to be had only for the most worthy of causes and only as a personal favour. Though if you are involved he might put aside those two conditions I suppose" she added brightly.

Gyrfalon laughed again.

"Your cynicism is refreshing" he remarked "So will he remain?"

"Until or unless his personal safety is threatened," she said dryly "I suppose if we apprise your rabidly righteous brother of his iniquities we might get rid of both as the sanctimonious sibling pursues the dirty little creature."

He chuckled at her descriptions of Falk.

"Well, whatever else I might say of my brother, he does not suffer fools or cowards gladly; and were he aware of Marfey's predilections I could almost guarantee he would be as nauseated as I am. Divide and conquer, hmm?"

She grinned at him.

"Put me up on the parapet, Gyrfalon: then jump up and dangle me off. That way, any shooting at you ensures my death too so you may call for parley in safety."

He raised an eyebrow.

"Are you sure they will be so careful of your life?"

She chuckled.

"I never heard yet it was good politics to kill the hostage you come supposedly to rescue," she commented dryly. "Besides, my lord and betrothed husband – do we not stand together and fall together as husband and wife should?"

"Many women would not take that quite so literally," he said dryly.

She smiled with brittle brightness.

"They say it's not so much the fall that causes the problems as the sudden stop at the bottom."

He ruffled her hair, laughing; pulled off his gloves; and hoisted her up onto the high crenellations. In a moment he was up there behind her, grabbing her wrists and dangling her over. Annis struggled with herself not to look down. Her head swam and she bit the inside of her mouth not to cry out in terror. She concentrated on the comforting feel of Gyrfalon's strong hands at her wrists, his flesh on hers for a surer grip. He rarely removed his gloves and Annis made herself think of the pleasure of his touch that enabled her to school her face into impassivity.

Gyrfalon called,

"This is the Lady Annis for whom you have come. Should I let you have her?" His grip tightened and then he made as though to drop her, laughing. The laughter was a sheer release of mirth that he and Annis fooled them; that she trusted him where no other would. Annis blinked a couple of times, glad he had warned her with the firmer grip before rapidly lowering her ere raising her again. The assembled armies gasped involuntarily.

The firmly impassive look Annis wore was read by them of a girl frozen with terror. Gyrfalon smiled grimly.

"That rather got your attention, didn't it, my brother, Falk?" he called "Well, I want to parley. I don't much care if you be there or not, brother mine, not yet the fat oaf Marfey; I want to parley with Lord Peter Haldane, the girl's father."

There was a flurry in the ranks and the slender graceful figure of the paladin Falk strode forward.

"What is there to parley, Gyrfalon?"

Gyrfalon laughed.

"That is none of your business. Not that such has ever stopped you sticking your nose in. But the longer you waste my time, the tireder mine arms will get. She's no very great weight but even so.... I'm sure you don't want that!"

Falk's mouth tightened.

"Speak then of this parley" he said.

"Tomorrow. Mid morning. In the village church. Oh, and do try to prevent your ruffians from damaging my village too much; you'll upset my reeve."

He hoisted Annis back up with an effortless movement, put an arm about her waist and jumped down with her, lifting her easily with him one armed. She clung to him shaking, her teeth chattering.

"Why, what is this?" Gyrfalon lifted her face, cupping it in both hands, gazing down at the white, set look to it and big dark eyes. "I would not have let you fall, little one; I thought you trusted me?" There was hurt in his one eye.

"I do," she said earnestly. "And I knew you would not drop me; and I know I be stupid but I am terrified of heights. I always have been. Not battlements; or turrets; but climbing or such."

"Then why did you suggest it?" he was incredulous.

"Because it seemed the best way to do it, that would give you some protection," she said simply.

He stared.

"That is true bravery," he was much struck, "to voluntarily do something that you know will petrify you with fear."

She buried her face against him.

"You give me courage by your presence, my lord," she murmured in a muffled sort of way. Then she pulled herself together. "Well, my lord, is it not time to do your face and make you comfortable while your worthy brother suffers pangs of outraged horror and the consequent indigestion that be like to bring?"

He gave a whoop of delighted laughter that had Falk shuddering without.

"You bad girl!" he crowed in delight "So much sanctity as a cause for naught but belly ache….. that will I dwell on with great pleasure!"

Chapter 9

Annis smoothed ointment onto Gyrfalon's face, noting all the little lines of worry that had sprung up since his brother had arrived. He relaxed somewhat under her ministrations, his good eye shut as he lay back in the great oak chair, giving her the perfect trust of being helpless in her presence – though she wore obediently the wrist sheaths and their knives as well he knew – even as she had placed perfect trust in him on the battlements.

Annis smiled wryly and shook her head at him; then leaned forward and dropped a gentle kiss on his maimed eye.

The effect was electric.

Gyrfalon started; and Annis jumped back in consternation.

"My lord? Gyrfalon? Did I hurt you? I am sorry!"

He stared; blinked, and stared again frowning.

"Hurt? No you did not hurt me … It was an odd sensation … like a wound that tightens as it draw together …." he covered his good eye and moved his hand up and down in front of his face, turned to the window; then he rose to his feet as he uncovered the other eye and took her by the shoulders, his face blazing with hope and exultation. "Whatever you did girl – I see light! I can see light and dark!" he told her "Can you do more?"

Annis stared as he sat himself down and looked hopefully expectant. She blushed.

"All I did was this" she said, shyly repeating the kiss.

He gasped again as the odd feeling seized his eye again and gazed at her amazed.

"You kissed it? Why? You could bring yourself to do so?"

Annis flushed scarlet.

"You looked so tired" she managed "I – I wanted to…."

He possessed himself of her hands, and pulled her closer.

"I do not understand it" he marvelled "But it is working … with that second kiss … I see dim shapes!"

"You must not tire it by peering!" she chided "Else you will get headaches; and maybe strain what sight you have regained. I – I do not know how much can be done at once. Curses are outside of normal medical texts you see," she added apologetically.

He came to his feet and looked down at her.

"You are amazing" he said; and bent to brush her lips with his. To his amazement her mouth clung and opened under his; and her little body pressed urgently against him. He slid his arms around her and kissed her fervently, passionately. Annis ran her hands up his back, pulling him closer. When he lifted his face from hers her smoke blue eyes were dark with passion and shining like stars; and though she trembled he knew it was not from fear. He cleared his throat.

"You – you had better go to your room," he told her almost harshly, his voice hoarse. "If you stay I will not answer for my self control. It is better that you leave."

She took a single step back and regarded him steadily.

"Do think entirely of protecting mine honour, Gyrfalon, or is it part of you that is afraid to let yourself go lest I prove as faithless as Alys and run off with your worthy, but boring, brother?" she asked quietly.

He stared.

"He is handsome and dashing," he admitted "Mayhap it has crossed my mind."

Annis came forward again and wrapped her arms around him.

"I am not Alys," she said firmly. "She lost; I have won. I know what I want and I am not such a little fool as she was to lose it."

He could hardly believe it.

"You – you want to stay?" his voice was a whisper, full of deep longing.

She nodded; and raised her face.

"Unless you think it will jeopardize healing you? The maiden pure bit I mean?" she asked anxiously "I'd not want to risk that…."

"I could not care less," he said savagely and swept her up into his arms "I would live with the pain at its worse if you but cared for me!"

"I do care, my love," murmured Annis into his chest.

Somehow they reached the bed; and somehow clothes mysteriously disappeared. Annis surrendered herself to the ecstasy of her lord's hungry embraces until they both slept, spent.

At some point, Elissa had knocked, since Annis was so long; and the knock had not even been heard. The female warrior put her head round the door; and withdrew, hastily, unseen by the lovers on the bed.

"Well how about that!" she muttered to herself; and took herself off to a more comfortable place to sleep.

He could guard the chit quite adequately for himself.

Gyrfalon woke to the sound of the early morning bustle in the courtyard, and lay in happy lassitude for a moment before he awoke enough to be aware of why he was so happy, feeling Annis' little body snuggled up beside him. He looked down at her still sleeping figure with incredulous wonder. No one had instilled in the girl any kind of indoctrination about decorum and restraint in all things for ladies; and she had responded to him instinctively, passionately, joyously and oh so definitely indecorously. Gyrfalon smiled down at her with unwonted gentleness; before he suddenly realised that he was looking at her lovely face with two eyes! Forgetting resolve to leave her to sleep he reached to her white shoulder and shook it gently, calling her name.

"Annis – wake up Annis!"

She grunted, wriggled and opened her eyes to smile adoringly up at him; and then she stared in surprise.

"What do you see?" he asked.

"Your face – why, it is better than ever I could have hoped for with salves!" she gasped.

"And I can see – I see perfectly!" he told her, covering each eye in turn to check.

She grinned a wry grin.

"Well, my love, methinks had I known the proper cure for the same at first I might have been less willing to provide it," she admitted "You are not easy to learn to know."

He laughed.

"But now art pleased to have thus effected my cure?"

"But *now,* my lord," she affected a serious face but her dimple bobbed in and out belying it "But now there might be a few bits of scar left that need more treatment."

He chuckled, and pulled her to him; and the sun rose unheeded.

Some time later came a knock at the door.

"Who is it?" asked Gyrfalon irritably.

"My Lord, it is I, Elissa; to remind you that there is a parley you wished to go to," said Elissa who had told Foregrim that she would run the message to Gyrfalon.

"Damn you, go find Lady Annis a fair gown for it!" called Gyrfalon.

Annis grinned.

"It were not politic to go in yesterday's that you have mussed and crumpled rather" she said "A very hussy I would look and no demure hostage."

"Indeed; for we shall not let your father see that there lies anything between us. It will lower the stakes and we may as well take him for as much as we can."

Annis grinned and nodded and kissed him solemnly.

Elissa came in, averted her eyes and dropped the clean garments. She had chosen Annis' midnight blue gown.

"I'm going now," she said loudly and left.

Annis giggled as she hastily washed and dressed.

"Poor Elissa is scandalised," she said "Hasn't she ever seen naked people before? I thought she was unshockable!"

"'Tis you that shocks her, froward wench," said Gyrfalon. "Ah, you are beautiful!"

"Better not go that road," said Annis. "Hair loose or plaited?"

"Plaited; the better to make you look young so Falk sees why Marfey wants you. That gown is too lovely and sophisticated really; white and virginal might have been better."

Annis giggled.

"Too late for that; and your sheets are a dreadful mess of blood."

"For a girl who rides astride and leaps around so athletically as you that's ridiculous," snorted Gyrfalon. "I suppose it be no surprise that you be contrary. I did not hurt you?" he asked suddenly concerned.

"No, my dear, not at all. Though why you should suddenly care after the amount you bruise me in sword practice I don't know."

"Minx."

"So my lord has said before," she finished plaiting her hair "And we will take the priest."

"Take the priest? Whatever for?" her lover was sceptical.

"If he sees Marfey he may have less objection about marrying us later," she said prosaically. "Besides, a man of the cloth should be able to be trusted if he be witness to the proceedings. It is standard practice. Besides," she added, "I rather think that Brother Michael here is trustworthy. He's an old sweetie."

Gyrfalon snorted.

"Trust you to be able to find good, even in a priest!" he grunted. She put her arms around him.

"Do you mind so very much that I am always optimistic, and look to find the endearing features in people – even when I half expect to be disappointed?" she asked him.

He kissed her briefly, but hard.

"No" he admitted "And another thing ere we leave! We will *not* let on about my face yet either. It may be good to keep my restored sight a secret."

She nodded.

"I do not put it past Marfey at least to have assassins sneak up on your left side," she agreed "And if you and your brother cannot resist the temptation to fight, if he be tactically sound he must needs try to find an opening from a blind spot."

"He is tactically sound," said Gyrfalon. "Remember, it was I who taught him."

The autumn sun was pale and miserable behind a veil of thin cloud that reached damp fingers of clammy cold unable to make up its mind if it were mist or light rain. Damp droplets clung to myriad cobwebs in which fat but disconsolate spiders waited for the emergence of unwary insects. The dampness clung equally tenaciously to eyelashes and hair and insinuated itself insidiously into clothing. Gyrfalon turned up the collar of his cloak and scowled disapprobation at the dismal sky.

"Oh do not look like that, My Lord" teased Annis "The sky weepeth overmuch already – truly if you frighten it any more with such grimaces it will cry in earnest!"

Her sally brought a rueful grin from the warlord.

"Aye, and we go forth from a good secure castle but briefly," he said with some satisfaction. "Falk and his men must needs endure this all day under naught but canvas."

"Oh now you be unkind and gloat. No, do not scowl at me like that; I am too happy to be anything but charitable and cheerful; grant me my little foibles, my lord," she smiled at him sunnily; and he smiled back, suddenly knowing that the weather was irrelevant.

"I am glad you are happy, my lady," ventured Father Michael. "Has Lord Gyrfalon intimated that he will return you to your father?"

"Oh *no*! That were not likely to make me happy!" exclaimed Annis "He has promised me faithfully that he will save me from the foul advances of Lord Marfey to whom my father has promised me in wedlock."

The priest blinked.

"Surely, daughter, it is your duty to submit to the will of your father – a good father does his best to choose a good bridegroom for his daughter!"

"Now you see why I dislike priests," said Gyrfalon. "He assumes your father has your interests at heart and makes assumption that your bridegroom is a good choice."

Annis viewed Father Michael quizzically.

"Yes father; it be plain that you know nothing of either my father or Lord Marfey" she said "My father wants me out from underfoot and Lord Marfey was the highest bidder."

"Is he so bad a potential husband?" Father Michael persevered gently.

"Apart from his physical defects of being some years the wrong side of sixty and being as fat as a flawn, that I might disregard were he a righteous man, he hath a predilection for children," said Annis shortly.

"But that is good; you will want to be a mother surely?" The little priest was a trifle shocked at the age of the bridegroom, but an older man might be assumed to be steady.

And why would she not want children?

"The girl means," said Gyrfalon dryly, "as bed-mates."

The priest stared at him scandalised.

"Are you sure?" he gasped, shocked almost past speech.

Annis nodded grimly.

"I have seen more than enough evidence to sicken me," she told the horrified priest. "And whatever you may think of Lord Gyrfalon, that at least is a crime no man may lay at his door."

"I am inclined to consider rape the action of a weakling," Gyrfalon said coldly. "Especially of a being so much smaller and weaker than oneself."

Those men who were eavesdropping shamelessly shuffled. Rape was part of a mercenary's life. No wonder he had hanged Barthol; the warlord did not tolerate weaklings. That story would go about.

Annis raised an eyebrow at Gyrfalon.

"No sheep either then?" she asked wickedly. The priest choked in horror that she should even know about such things.

"No sheep," Gyrfalon told her, his mouth quivering. "Not by rape nor even by unlawful seduction."

"I am so glad," her eyes danced in a demure face. "Sheep are such silly creatures, I'm sure they'd be easily swayed by flattery!"

He chuckled.

"Be fair, girl, when have I ever employed flattery?"

She grinned.

"There is that…. What other crimes have you *not* committed my lord – lest my father want to know, of course, mine own curiosity being but peripheral?"

He considered theatrically.

"Try some suggestions" he said.

"Mutiny on the high seas?"

"No; but then I have never been on the high seas and have but missed mine opportunity."

"So piracy, barratry and hanging the captain from the yardarm before six o'clock bells are also out?"

"I be afraid so," he admitted "As I am not even sure what all of those doubtless heinous crimes entail – save piracy – I can only say I think I have not committed them; but evidently you have an advanced knowledge of the sea," he gently mocked her.

She grinned.

"One of the travelling storytellers, a one-legged man, claimed to be a sailor once. He would spin yarns for the entertainment of the populace and the enrichment of his own purse. I like a good story."

"Barges don't count, I suppose?" He asked suddenly.

"I don't *think* so" she pondered.

"Oh that's all right then; I have, after all, offered violence to a slaver with a string of barges."

Annis frowned.

"Isn't it almost an act of Holy piety to offer violence to slavers wherever they are?" She queried, her dimple popping in and out as she teased him.

He snorted.

"Thank you, no! Do not accuse me of *that*, girl; it turns my stomach!"

She chuckled at him; and Father Michael was left staring at them open mouthed. Had he misjudged Gyrfalon? He asked himself. After all, the man had shown more consideration to the villagers than many lords were wont to do, more than the previous lord from whom Gyrfalon had wrested the castle. And this bantering talk, if somewhat irreverent, showed nothing of the sadistic, evil tempered creature that Gyrfalon was supposed to be.

The priest was puzzled.

And he would do what he might to stand by Lady Annis and support her, whatever the outcome of the parley.

Elissa too was ready to stand by Annis if she needed her; and had put on a gown over her trousers.

"Will you want me as a female supporter of Lady Annis, my lord?" She asked.

He regarded her thoughtfully.

"Were we holding parley with normal and logical men I should say yes; but as my brother will not even notice that I have arranged a female companion for the girl, and as her father cares for nothing but what he might get out of the situation I think to hold you in reserve, Elissa. You need guard her no longer; if it please you to be her companion after the parley I leave it to you, but of duty you are relieved save if she choose you as a bodyguard in situations when she needs one. When having a woman looking er, demure, who is actually as dangerous as a sack full of vipers might be useful."

Elissa grinned; that was about as close to a compliment as the old man ever came.

She took his point however; for this parley her presence was superfluous and she went to change back into more accustomed garb.

Gyrfalon reflected that in any case, Elissa was prone to outspoken comments; and he wanted to be in control of the situation not to have to deal with some unexpected remark meant to be helpful. It mattered not in one of his captains; but it did for diplomacy.

The castle had a narrow drawbridge that might be lowered to permit the passage of a single horseman to parley and might not then be easily rushed; and this was lowered to allow the castle party out. Gyrfalon strode out – taking horses were superfluous – followed by Annis with Father Michael bringing up the rear. The assembled army peered to catch a closer glimpse both of the feared warlord and of his reputedly beautiful hostage.

Neither disappointed.

Gyrfalon, clad in his customary black, exuded confidence and charisma and scowled at the serried ranks from under his half helm that was appropriately intimidating; and Annis shone in the dull day like a pale sun in his wake, her beauty enhanced by the serene contentment that glowed from her. The way to the church was guarded by a contingent of church knights and their footmen, Falk's personal bodyguard, who ranged along the path they must take. Annis held up her head and scorned to show fear of them for her lover.

"She looks like a little nun," someone muttered.

Of course there is always one with more gall than sense.

A fellow must needs try to be a hero and kill the fearsome warlord and leapt out swinging his sword in a deadly attack.

Gyrfalon's sword was out, parrying, and then moving in one fluid sweep to take off his attacker's head ere the fellow knew he was dead. Gyrfalon shook the blood from his blade, wiped it on the dead man's cloak and beckoned to the nearest captain of men.

"You – is this the usual usage now of church knights for a parley – to use it for treacherous attack?"

The very young knight was shaking with fear – and rage.

"It is not, Lord Gyrfalon," he said "I apologise for the rash action of my man."

"As well you might; his indiscipline speaks not well of the commander," said Gyrfalon "I suggest you report his behaviour and your failure to Lord Falk. He will undertake such discipline as he feels necessary on you and your unit."

"Yes my lord," said the knight tightly. "I shall do so; and I shall not fail too to report your restraint. I thank you for your courtesy."

He hated having to say it, as Gyrfalon could see; but none might have truly blamed Gyrfalon had he struck off the commander's head too.

Gyrfalon nodded curtly.

"Pray inform your other men that if they feel rash, they are not out of range of my bowmen" he said "If any other attack thus treacherously, the truce will be over and all within range will fall dead. And my best archers can reach the church."

"Yes my lord; I shall see that this is known"

said the knight.

If it were true, and he indeed had men capable of such – as was not impossible, taking account of plunging fire – Gyrfalon might have had them all cut down without mercy.

"What is your name, boy?" asked Gyrfalon.

"I am Sir Lyall of Wittensham, Lord Gyrfalon" said the knight.

Gyrfalon nodded.

"You have courage and courtesy, Sir Lyall; I will remember you," he said.

Sir Lyall reflected that such might be a good thing; or a bad one.

He bowed.

The party proceeded into the church.

The delegates of the opposition were already in the church; Annis' father stood beside Lord Marfey and Falk a little way from them. Annis looked surreptitiously at the sword which was one of the bones of contention between these brothers; the silver-chased scabbard had runes of power on it, and the crosspieces of the hilt, also silver, terminated in hawk's heads. The pommel seemed, for the briefest moment, to grow a pupil within its amber depths and scrutinise Annis; or perhaps she imagined it, for it was barely for the blink of an eye that it seemed that way, and might have been a trick of the light.

Gyrfalon strode in, scowled at the altar, nodded to the crucifix and said,

"If you have any nonce, You might keep it raining; it will make mine enemies the more miserable."

Annis walked calmly past him, neatly outflanking her father's reaching hand that she might genuflect to the altar. She knelt and prayed silently; begging for a reconciliation between Gyrfalon and his brother, sensing that the hatred sprang but from one time love, love believed by both to be betrayed. Father Michael too knelt in prayer after a look of incredulous horror at the gross figure of Lord Marfey that even without his perversions could scarcely be seen as a reasonable bridegroom for a beautiful young girl in his opinion. Father Michael's sympathy for Annis grew; and he prayed for guidance and sureness that any decision he might be asked to take be the right one.

"What took you so long getting here?" snapped Peter Haldane.

Gyrfalon looked on him with concealed dislike; and answered quietly.

"Merely a treacherous attack by one of the church troops on the way, Lord Peter. It delayed us slightly."

"What?" cried Falk.

"Oh be not concerned for your honour; the miscreant's commander apologised for his man" said Gyrfalon.

"So you killed him too?"

"Think as you like," said Gyrfalon, shrugging; and turning from the altar to face Falk. Falk and Gyrfalon measured each other up in a long exchanged look. Gyrfalon grinned suddenly; impishly, savagely.

"You *do* look damp, brother," he said with satisfaction.

Falk regarded him levelly.

"You look as wicked as ever," he commented.

"Please, my brother – no compliments so early in the proceedings!" Returned Gyrfalon.

Annis raised her voice.

"If you boys must bicker, can you please do so quietly? I'm busy talking to God and these little interruptions are a trifle off-putting."

Falk blinked in surprise at so imperious a little demand; and Gyrfalon grinned again. Falk missed the tenderness in the grin entirely.

"Yes; behave yourself, Falk," said the warlord in an undertone "When people interrupt her God-bothering she has been known to hit them over the head with a Bible." He had heard of Elissa's religious misadventures. "She's also inclined to half blind the people who irritate her and stick a blade in them," he added.

Falk stared at him. What strange mood was Gyrfalon in? What was he up to? At least he let the girl pray when she wanted to – but who had she hit with a Bible? Or half blinded and stabbed? Surely Gyrfalon would have taken harsh measures had it been him or a close lieutenant? Falk was much bothered.

At least it seemed likely that Gyrfalon had not yet broken the girl's spirit and if some arrangement might be reached to hand her over this day she might escape unharmed bar a serious fright.

Falk was determined to help this lovely, ethereal young girl; whose resemblance to Alys had not escaped him. And he admired the serene way she held herself and her straight, fearless expression and the way she walked past Gyrfalon, ignoring him utterly with all the pride of her birth. To let his brother break this girl's will would be a crime, thought Falk!

Chapter 10

"Hurry and finish your over-long prayers girl and come and stand by me!" snapped Peter Haldane to Annis moving towards the altar, a hand stretched out to grab her arm.

Gyrfalon stood between him and the girl in one of his swift, panther-like movements.

"I would remind you, Lord Peter" he said silkily "That the girl is currently in *my* possession; not yours. Which is why you have come to parley, is it not? She'll pray as long as she feels necessary; the castle isn't going anywhere and I presume nor are the armies without. What matter a few more minutes? What matter an hour? I suggest you demonstrate a little more patience in front of my pious brother lest he think you as impious as me."

"Thank you, Lord Gyrfalon," said Annis levelly. "I am almost ready; but not yet."

Falk was gripping his jaws hard together. What a fool Lord Peter Haldane was to make such a fuss and give Gyrfalon the opportunity to look reasonable by comparison!

Annis finished her own prayers and waited politely for Father Michael to finish his own devotions to offer him her young and now quite strong arm to assist him to rise; and then stalked up the aisle with Father Michael in her wake. She went to stand demurely beside Gyrfalon.

"You look like an icon or a plaster saint," said Gyrfalon rudely.

"*One* of us ought to raise the tone of the proceedings," retorted Annis. "Don't worry; you don't look the least like a saint or a good angel."

He gave a savage grin at that reminder of one of their early exchanges.

Falk smiled at Annis reassuringly.

"Please don't worry, Lady Annis," he said gently "We will soon have you home with your family."

He started at the look she gave him that had a flash of impatient dislike in it; but Annis schooled her features and looked him calmly and levelly in the eye.

"I am told, Lord Falk," she said softly, "that you are a man of honour, integrity, and piety. As I was told by Lord Gyrfalon, who is not inclined to flatter you," – here Gyrfalon snorted and she gave him an old fashioned look – "I am then ready to believe it. I would then recommend you to choose your allies with more care, for accepting visits to the Holy Land as piety rather than church-sanctioned loot grabbing does seem to me to smack of naivety," she finished tartly.

Falk blinked.

"Yes" put in Gyrfalon, smoothly "And

should you examine the young – the *very* young, eight year old or so – peasant girls on Lord Marfey's demesne you might even find that you dislike him even more than you dislike me. I do not number child spoiling amongst *my* faults."

"And on what do base so foul an insinuation?" Falk asked curtly "It seems to me that you wish to slander your captive's bridegroom with the foulest calumny a warped mind can imagine!"

He was trying to be fair; but it was plain that he held Marfey in distaste and was surprised that Lord Peter should arrange a marriage of his daughter to one who appeared senior in years to his prospective father-in-law.

Annis flushed.

"I assure you, Lord Falk, I am neither warped and nor have I imagined this filthy thing," she said with asperity. "I am a healer; and Marfey's lands march with those of my father. Such aberrations leave unmistakeable injuries; and in my experience, nor do children lie about such terrible things that have happened to them if such things be outside what one would expect them to experience. And you cannot say I imagined the eleven year old who died birthing a dead child that made dying deposition that she had been Marfey's to use for the previous three years."

Falk stared in horror.

"Forgive me, Lady Annis; I meant not to insult you. I had thought this was something cooked up by Gyrfalon to frighten you."

"Methinks you also owe Lord Gyrfalon an apology, My Lord Falk" said Annis "Who hath his reputation, but is too innocent to imagine such a horror."

"*Do* you mind not impugning me with words like 'innocent'?" demanded Gyrfalon.

"Not at all, my lord," said Annis demurely.

"I – I do apologise, Gyrfalon," said Falk, unwillingly.

"Well it's a start," muttered Annis cryptically. Falk did not hear her; he had turned to stare accusingly at Marfey. The man flushed and looked angry.

"Who cares about a few peasant brats?" He sneered, shrugging "We are men of noble birth; we are above such mores."

Falk looked at him as though he were something to be raked into the fields.

"I suggest, Lord Peter" he said icily "If you wish to continue to hold me as an ally, that you break any promise of alliance between your unfortunate daughter and that creature. With whom" he added grimly "I will deal in due course."

Peter Haldane was ingratiating in his denials of knowledge of Marfey's activities and Falk listened cynically – his cynicism fuelled by a snort from Annis – as Haldane asked his erstwhile ally to leave.

Marfey scowled.

"And lose my troops? Are you insane, Peter? For one quixotic fool?"

"Who happens to have the support of the archbishop," said Haldane shrewdly.

Marfey snorted.

"Several cardinals – one at least of whom do not despise my tastes, for sharing in them – be worth more than an archbishop. I can command a number of cardinals; my coffers are deep, Peter. And I *want* the girl; though she have grown a little too shapely in the last wasted months," he looked on Annis with such undisguised lust that she took half a step back and stumbled against Gyrfalon's foot. He grabbed her arm to steady her.

"Show not such weakness, girl!" said Gyrfalon roughly, giving her arm a little shake. "He is nothing; you have nothing to fear in him."

Annis pulled herself up and nodded.

Falk ground his teeth. His brother was even cruel to the girl when she was terrified of such a creature as Marfey.

Annis appreciated her lover's stiffening of her courage.

Peter Haldane noticed nothing but gazed helplessly at Falk over Marfey's refusal to leave.

"Lord Falk," he said, "I understand that

you are here because your enemy is mine enemy; that you choose to fight Gyrfalon," he said.

Gyrfalon chuckled evilly at Falk's dilemma.

"Let this add to your education, child," he remarked to Annis "The art of parley involves splitting up your opponents where possible – especially when two of them were not even invited."

"To divide and conquer would make logical tactical sense," said Annis. "If you might strip away the irrelevant ones the talks might move on."

Falk and Father Michael both looked a little shocked.

"One of Gyrfalon's foes is your father, Lady Annis," said Falk gravely "Have you no feelings for him?"

"Plenty," she said coldly. "I met him again for the first time in years about seven months ago when he returned from his sanctified thievery. I disliked him as much on second acquaintance as on the day he left after beating me senseless for asking why he had thrown my mother down the stairs. She took four days to die in agony that I knew not how to relieve. It was why I became a healer. My feelings for my father run to a tall tree and a short rope."

Falk looked horrified, even nauseated. The girl seemed content as Gyrfalon's hostage; and under the circumstances, he could almost see why.

"Then I think the best thing, my lady," he suggested, "is to negotiate having you made a ward of the church."

"A waste," growled Gyrfalon.

"I considered briefly becoming a nun," said Annis conversationally, "but I do not think that I would decorously do good. I do try to be virtuous but I fear I am not nun material. And a ward to the church would be made a novice and they would try to persuade me to enter the church you know. It is not to my liking."

"Quite right," said Gyrfalon. "She's right you know; she'd end up driving the other nuns insane or spend all her time locked in a penitent's cell. She hasn't the temperament. Besides which, despite your unwanted interruptions, my brother, be it not about time to come to the point of my parley with the girl's father? All this byplay is doubtless very interesting but scarcely germane. You and Marfey are superfluous."

"What do you want?" Peter Haldane was ungracious.

"It is very simple," said Gyrfalon. "I do not intend to ask for more than half mine original demand as dowry when I wed your daughter."

"What!" Peter Haldane spluttered in unison with Falk. Gyrfalon smiled thinly.

"I wish to wed her; a ceremony joining man and woman in matrimony. The priest will be able to explain the nature of the matter to you if you find it confusing. Consider the advantages to yourself – father-in-law. I am also a neighbour of yours – and my lands lay between yours and the North. I am the first line of defence between you and the Northmen."

Lord Peter looked both greedy and suspicious.

"For half the money? But if you have the girl, you will need less than that in dowry, surely? She's no great catch for a mighty warlord to be worth such a dowry."

"Methinks an army to keep out the barbarians is not cheap. Of course I could always levy taxes from you or send my men to forage on your land instead….."

Lord Peter bit his lip. Having Gyrfalon's troops loose on his lands was not to be tolerated.

"Done," he agreed quickly. Gyrfalon smiled.

"I thought you would see it my way," he said, catching Annis by her thick plait and pulling her towards him, playfully wrapping it around her neck.

Annis and Gyrfalon exchanged glances; her blue eyes smouldered with promised passion as she lay against his chest; and his nostrils flared. His eyes smiled down at her with love and desire in them. Falk, however, already horrified, saw only Gyrfalon's face; and a look that he interpreted as cruel lust.

"This is iniquitous!" he cried "Unhand that girl – I will take her into mine own protection if she does not wish to return to her father!"

Gyrfalon looked at him coldly.

"I keep saying this, brother; you are irrelevant," he said. "The dispute was between me and my hostage's father; and it is he who is her guardian. As he and I have negotiated terms there is nothing more to be said; all interested parties are happy with the terms."

Falk swung to face Peter Haldane. The lord shrugged.

"She has to marry someone," he said. "It is as good a deal as any I might get and better than most. Thank you for your support, Lord Falk, that has enabled me to get favourable terms; but you are no longer needed. Mine army and that of Lord Marfey will be leaving; since he too has no further interest in the affair."

"Like Hell I will! You promised her to *me*!" cried Marfey. Haldane looked at him with contempt.

"You are a less useful ally than Lord Gyrfalon," he said frigidly. "His reputation as a warrior is superior to yours by far; moreover he is at least still vigorous enough to pursue his martial endeavours. And his promise to repel the barbarians is in his interests too; and therefore believable. You are of no further use to me and nor are your cardinals; most of them at least, save whichever one be as perverted as you, for Lord Falk will surely reveal your actions to higher church authorities."

Gyrfalon chuckled.

"Oh he will, Marfey, believe it. And then he will come after you. What lies between Falk and me will doubtless wait on his desire to catch up with you; I'm likely to live longer than you so he can afford to wait. I'd run if I were you, Marfey. Because if Falk does not get you, I shall. I have a mind to furnish my bride with your head."

"Why my lord Gyrfalon!" exclaimed Annis "Surely not a romantic streak lurking within you that you should give romantic presents? You will turn my head far more than any sheep I wager! Why, you will be offering next to mount his skull as a goblet for a wedding draught!"

He grinned savagely, appreciating the thrust about the sheep.

"Minx," he said.

Falk frowned.

"Lady Annis," he said formally.

She twitched her plait from Gyrfalon's grasp to turn her smoke-blue eyes to look on him queryingly; which gesture might have told Falk, had he not been blinded by hatred that there was no force in the warlord's grip.

"Lord Falk?"

"When he promises you a man's head, you may take it lightly but I assure you, he is not joking; and would present you with the horrid bloody thing in sooth," he said.

"Good," said Annis. "I hate a man that does not keep his promises. Not that he has promised; merely remarked that he was minded to make the gesture for me if you do not get the fellow first. You should listen closely; Lord Gyrfalon is the master of careful wording in any situation."

"Yes; that I am aware, my lady. And I warn you that Gyrfalon is a dangerous man, cruel and unpredictable. I can see why almost anyone seems preferable to Lord Marfey; and even your father. But you need not marry at all if you not wish. I offer you my protection."

Gyrfalon's eyes narrowed.

"As once you offered Alys protection?" He asked, dangerously quietly.

Falk flushed.

"Leave Alys out of this," he snapped "Or is that it? Because Lady Annis looks like Alys you would possess her and punish her instead? Is that what is going on in your warped mind?"

Gyrfalon sneered.

"I am not still ruled by that faithless wench even if you are, brother," he said.

"So I should hope," put in Annis tartly. "Scarcely flattering to the bride if she is not gaining her bridegroom's full attention and faculties!"

Gyrfalon chuckled.

"I would challenge any man *not* to pay you full attention and hope yet to come out of such a dilatory encounter undamaged, you little virago; you take a deal of attention."

Falk gritted his teeth. His understanding of that comment was that his hated brother boasted that he would break the spirit of the girl no matter how much she fought him! The girl was, he thought, trying to be brave and make the best of a bad situation – but she did not know Gyrfalon as he did! Falk in his preconceptions failed to see the way Annis' eyes strayed to Gyrfalon's face; failed to read that the hand Gyrfalon placed on her shoulder was reassuring, not restraining; failed to note that Gyrfalon showed unwonted good humour. He turned to Father Michael.

"Where do you fit in, father?" he asked "Are you Lady Annis' confessor?"

Michael blinked.

"I do serve that function, Lord Falk," he said "But I am priest of this church. She began attending Mass with us soon after she first became a hostage."

Falk stared.

"How the – how come you were permitted, Lady Annis?" he demanded.

Annis smiled demurely.

"I was very reasonable over it," she said

"You were a vixen over it," contradicted Gyrfalon.

"That too," she said.

"Lord Gyrfalon always sent a guard with Lady Annis, whom she only had to reprove once," Father Michael hastened to explain. "And of course now I am within the castle, with all the village, that Lord Gyrfalon brought us within to protect us from the armies."

Falk snorted.

"He probably had some other motive," he said. "But somehow I doubt it was to protect the village. Gyrfalon does not protect; he destroys."

The priest flushed irritably.

"I would ask you, My Lord Falk," he said with dignity, "If you are not speaking purely from prejudice. Lord Gyrfalon has shown his dependants nothing but proper treatment. I have been pleasantly surprised."

Falk looked sceptical.

"He will use anyone, Father," he told Michael. "Beware, for he is the devil himself."

"Funny," murmured Annis to Gyrfalon, "I always imagined the devil must be quite personable else he had not managed to tempt people. And I doubt any might call you personable."

Gyrfalon laughed.

"I concede the point," he said. "To my mind the devil probably wears a cardinal's robe."

Falk scowled and carried on pointedly telling Father Michael,

"You and your flock and the Lady Annis are in the greatest danger. But do not worry; I have church troops with me, and a company of soldiery ready to oppose Gyrfalon at any time. The Lady Annis's father may betray her and abandon her but I shall not."

Gyrfalon gave a dry laugh and a slow hand clap.

"A fine speech, my brother," he said. "But have you checked whether or not the Lady Annis wishes you not to abandon her, or to trust herself to such ill disciplined puppies as break truce?"

Falk flushed at the reminder that one of his men had given such ammunition to Gyrfalon.

"Whatever you have threatened her with that she seems compliant, I know how to serve her interests!" declared Falk.

"Oh this is ridiculous!" exclaimed Annis. "How can you be so thoughtless and wicked as to risk the lives of your men and Lord Gyrfalon's men over one small and insignificant woman who does not require your rather dubious gallantry? I suspect *your* motives, Lord Falk, that you find my superficial resemblance to this Alys fill your thoughts with ideas that are not based at all on logic or indeed Christian charity; but on your own personal wishes."

He looked at her gravely.

"It is true that your resemblance to my murdered wife fills my heart with grief; remembered grief and grief for you. But I assure you that it is the principle of the matter as much as your person, Lady Annis."

"What, you drag the church knights to prevent any marital alliance you personally dislike? You must be very busy" mocked Gyrfalon.

Falk gave him an angry look.

"As you may hear, Lady Annis, Gyrfalon chooses to misinterpret my words," he said.

"Ah? Then perchance, my Lord you will be kind enough to explain to a poor stupid woman that know nothing of the more tortuous workings of a church knight's mind what the principle might be, for in sooth, as Lord Gyrfalon said, so too your words seemed to mean to me," said Annis.

He wasn't as fun to fence with as Gyrfalon; he was far too earnest. It was almost unkind to tease him.

"I mean that it is the principle that I must

oppose the plans and machinations of Gyrfalon, that he must ever need to manipulate those that cross his path. I am quite certain that you do not know what you have got yourself into. You will be rescued, be assured, and Gyrfalon will one day die at mine hands. There is no necessity to sacrifice yourself."

Annis swung round to Gyrfalon.

"Is it *your* fault?" she demanded "Did you perchance drop him on the head when he was a baby?" She added tartly.

Gyrfalon grinned.

"No, he has developed his pigheaded narrow vision all alone; acquit me of any involvement in that," he said.

"You left out rude enough to tell me I'm stupid that I not know what I get myself into," said Annis. "Your brother has no manners, my lord; but as you have none either I suppose that I *might* blame on you."

Gyrfalon chuckled as she turned and stalked out on that parting shot.

"She doesn't like you, brother," he said "Excuse me; I should really catch up with my betrothed in case any of your men offer her insult," and he swung off after Annis.

Falk found his mouth falling open in outrage at such an imputation!

Brother Michael brought up the rear of the castle party, with a half apologetic nod to Falk.

Much against his will, the little priest had seen much to respect in the warlord, and found it difficult to credit stories of a cruel temper. He had, after all, only the evidence of his own senses after the soothing influence of Annis and her salves. And though the warlord had seemed to handle the lady roughly during the parley, Father Michael saw no evidence that she in any way objected. He *had* noted how lightly that the warlord had truly held the girl's plait that she might twitch it from his grasp; he had too noted that Annis had leaned towards Gyrfalon for comfort over Marfey. And though his words had been harsh, his hand on her arm had been steadying and almost caressing. He was a man of worldly understanding and when Annis, her eyes twinkling, made a comment to Gyrfalon about his intent to manipulate her as Falk had suggested that actually brought a touch of colour to the warlord's face he nodded wisely. The little priest only hoped that Annis was not beguiled by a physical attraction that he had thought almost palpable throughout Gyrfalon's handling of her in the parley, and would not find the marriage disastrous.

There was a brief interruption on the way back to the castle; round the side of one of the still-standing peasant huts came a running figure; and Gyrfalon had his sword half out ere he saw it was a young woman, whose face was terrified, dragging with her the sobbing figure of a small boy, scarce breeched, who limped horridly. Some common soldiers were pursuing her, and indeed one of them backhanded the boy out of the way as another grabbed the woman's gown to pull her down. They were laughing in the cruel way common to all but the most disciplined troops when rape is imminent.

The one who had backhanded the boy dropped with Annis' knife in his throat and she sprang to pick the child up. The one holding the woman died at Gyrfalon's hand, and another dropped from one of the warlord's knives. Annis retrieved her knife whilst keeping her arm about the child as the rabble took in the fact that this was a very pretty girl.

"Get back!"

It was the young knight, Sir Lyall, who had come to stand beside Annis.

"These rabble are not, I take it, yours," said Annis.

"No lady; they are not. Methinks they belong to Lord Marfey," he said.

"Ah? Like master, like man," said Annis. "Though they pursue the woman not her child so not quite ... I suspect you'll be rid of them soon. Lord Falk has lethal ambitions for Lord Marfey, and as we be held up here by your siege I expect he'll get him ere Lord Gyrfalon does … little one, what is your name and what goes on? You are a good boy" she added, for the child had dragged a knife from the belt of the man who Annis had slain and stood at bay with it.

"I be Lukat, Mistress; son of Luke the Miller of Staneham" he said "What have died, so ma and me come back to her father's village."

"And these rude men then decided to make what they call sport of her I suppose," said Annis in scorn. "Lord Falk I hear your tread; I trust you will deal with these fellows?"

"Those Gyrfalon has not massacred," said Falk.

"Excuse me, Lord Falk, I claim this one," said Annis mildly. "Lord Gyrfalon insists that I carry knives for mine own protection; he had a bit of indiscipline at first ere his men began to be an army. Well. Lukat, you and your mother shall come within and see your grandsire; who if he was alive before these other rabble turned up is so still; for we've had no deaths since the siege began."

"*You* killed one?" Falk stared.

"He hit the child," said Annis. "'Whoso placeth a stumbling block in the way of a child, it were better that a millstone be tied around his neck and he be dropped in the deepest ocean' … I have no millstones to hand

and the ocean's a long way away so I interpreted that rather freely."

Gyrfalon had cut down several of the rabble; and Foregrim stood, an armoured figure at the sally-port with men behind him, ready to issue out for a rescue. He had heaved the woman roughly to her feet; and beckoned Lyall.

"She will have had a pack; I doubt she had many belongings but they are all she have" he said harshly "Will you bring them here?"

"I will, Lord Gyrfalon," said Lyall. "I am happy to offer the protection of the church Knights to the woman and child."

"Somehow I suspect she'd rather have the comfort of her own family, whom she was seeking," said Gyrfalon. "Is that correct, wife of Luke the Miller?"

She dropped a clumsy curtsey.

"If you please, my lord," she said. "My name be Loveday, my lord."

"The girl Loveday have spoken her preference. You look scarce old enough to have a boy that age."

"I do be almost twenty one, my lord"

"Hmm" said Gyrfalon. "Very well let us be on our way; here is Sir Lyall with your pack that we need delay no longer," and he strode forward as though nothing had occurred.

"Lukat can't go at your pace, my lord," chid Annis.

Gyrfalon sighed, stopped, read what she expected in her smoke-blue eyes and swept up the child in his arms.

"Don't get used to this," he said.

"Oh my lord! It do shame me that you have to carry me! You do be such a wonderful warrior, I wish my foot was not twisted that I might learn to be your man!" said the boy worshipfully; for he knew not who Gyrfalon might be, only that he and his lady had rescued his mother and him.

Gyrfalon laughed.

"Well we shall see what Annis and her salves may do," he said as they entered the castle. "There; off you go and find your grandsire, Lady Annis will see you later."

Falk looked at Sir Lyall, taken aback; then said,

"He let me think he had killed you for one that attacked him."

"He rebuked me," said Lyall "I am to report to you for my negligence. My first meeting with the warlord Gyrfalon is most confusing, my lord. Have he care of his own peasants, think you, regardless of what he do to others?"

"Methinks he plays some deep game," said Falk darkly.

Chapter 11

Annis cast herself into Gyrfalon's arms on their return to the castle and he kissed her roughly.

"At least we get rid of some of the besiegers," she said. "If only your brother had the sense he were born with we might have been left in peace."

"My brother will never be at peace until he has killed me," said Gyrfalon. "There is no other way about it; he and I hate each other too much."

"Pardon the interruption," said Father Michael, "but is not hate next door to love? It is loathing and despising that are its opposite."

Gyrfalon gave a harsh laugh.

"Oh you are quite right, priest; once Falk and I loved each other as brothers should; until he deceitfully stole my betrothed while I was away doing my duty; and when I drew sword on him for his deceit, the silly wench got in the way and she died instead. And that is what lies between us; a faithless woman who encouraged my idiot brother not to tell me that he had feelings for her; and who then destroyed all the rest of our brotherly love by sacrificing herself. There's a bit more; but that is the gist. There was wrong on both sides; but for Falk it was all my fault. And *that* was his mother's fault; my stepmother always insisted that anything I had that my brother wanted, it were to be given to him. I suppose he thought my betrothed might also be ordered thus. Only I have got over her and am happy with Annis; and he still suffers."

"Then, my lord, you might pity him for his unquiet spirit," said Father Michael "And pr – hope," he amended as Gyrfalon started scowling, "that some day you might be reconciled. He is spoken of as a good man who does his utmost; and he *meant* well at the parley, though he were plainly entirely missing the byplay betwixt yourself and Lady Annis for the blindness of his despite."

Gyrfalon stared; then roared with laughter.

"And you a celibate priest picked it up? Why, priest, I do believe that I do not dislike you as much as most; you are no fool. Is reconciliation possible? I know not; but I doubt it. Annis, I suppose you'll be seeing to that young fellow's foot; the tears were of pain, methinks, and anger, not fear."

"He does seem a brave lad," said Annis, interpreting Gyrfalon's words.

Lukat was with his grandfather's family; and his grandfather was Bullard the reeve.

Annis examined the foot.

"He were born scrog footed," volunteered Loveday.

"How much do you want it to be straight, Lukat?" asked Annis.

"More'n anything, Lady," said the boy.

"Even if it hurt you cruelly?"

He nodded.

"It hurt anyway; if it hurt more but I walk straight it be worth it," said the boy.

"Very well; I'll make up an oil to rub it with and pull it straight," said Annis, "and I'll have the tanner see an he might make a heavy sheath for it to hold it straight; that you must then exercise despite the pain to strengthen it. Will you be prepared to do that? It will be held thus" and she pulled the foot towards straightness. The boy winced, but nodded.

"I will," he said. "And will then My Lord teach me to fight like him?"

"What, a glutton for more pain?" said Annis "I have been learning from my lord; and you will get bruises in places you know not that you have places. You can practice for that however as your foot strengthens by weight training to improve the muscles in your arms."

He nodded eagerly.

If Gyrfalon would not train him, Annis determined that she would.

Meanwhile she had a gift for the warlord; and took it to his chamber.

"My lord; I have been sewing on this; it will make a good betrothal gift," she said.

He held up the robe, marvelling at her skills he knew nothing of.

"Annis! I – I do not know what to say….. it is very fine!" he said. "Where did you get the fabrics?"

She laughed.

"Why, my lord, do you not recall that I asked about the chests of clothes the previous lord – several previous lords as I guess – had left and you said I might do as I pleased with them? This is what I pleased. There are other fur coverlets but as I shall not sleep cold and alone those I shall also make into clothing. You do like it?"

"It is the best gift – bar your love and your healing – I have ever been given," he said.

"Try it on," she said "And then I shall have the pleasure of taking it off you."

He laughed and complied; and started at his reflection in the mirror that he had not had taken out.

"I look rather fine," he said.

"You look magnificent," she said. "And now, my lord, methinks it be time to disrobe….."

There was very little further conversation after that.

Much later he said,

"I have nothing to give you as a betrothal gift."

She laughed.

"When you give me freedom, and teach me so much? Say not so my lord! You use your skill in passing on warcraft; and I use my skill with a needle to dress you. A fair exchange, surely?"

"You give me so much; and you are mine!" He said savagely; and started kissing her again.

They loved far into the night and rose tired but yet refreshed.

Meanwhile Peter Haldane prepared to depart; but found that some of his troops elected to stay, swayed by Falk's speech that such was their duty to Lady Annis. Truly they believed that it was her need for aid that must hold them; and they threw in their lot with Falk. Falk's own army had started small but all who felt that there might be a chance to destroy Gyrfalon had joined him. Seizing a rich castle and looting it may have played a part in the motives of at least some of them; as Falk well knew, and deplored, but sighed and accepted. The siege remained.

Marfey had departed once it became clear that Falk planned to hang him as soon as he had proof of the man's perfidies; to which end he had sent a small party to find out. Marfey knew that Falk would find his evidence and much as he failed to understand why a fellow nobleman should make such a fuss about a few peasant brats he knew Falk's implacable reputation and fled, to barricade himself into his own castle.

That Falk had hanged the remainder of those who had attempted to rape the woman Loveday had helped convince him.

Annis sighed that the siege remained; and spoke to Father Michael of banns.

The little priest was still a little dubious; though Annis at least had the permission of her father, that meant no man might blame the priest, only his own conscience.

"You love him truly daughter, and are not swayed by the physical attraction that so magnetic a man must needs exert?" he asked anxiously.

Annis chuckled.

"Why I shall tell him you asked that," she said, "for he was convinced that the scarred face I have been treating render him too hideous to attract a woman's regard! Aye, Father, I love him; faults and all. I should love him for the joy of friendship with him, were our relationship celibate. Though the physical do sway me too," she blushed.

"And so it should within marriage," said Father Michael. "I understand that the impediment be that he is excommunicate?"

"By which Pope?" asked Annis.

Since religious upheaval and corruption had left a sufficiency of factions to raise two credible and one disreputable popes, the argument was cogent; and Father Michael shrugged and read the banns accordingly.

And Annis continued to treat Lukat who ran about painfully but straight in his cuirboilli sheath that the armourer had declared was his job, not the tanner's; all men vying to please Annis. He strengthened his little arms assiduously too and managed to get himself under foot to try to help disarm Gyrfalon when he came off the walls.

"What, thou whelp, dost think art a page at thine age?" roared Gyrfalon, half amused, half irritated.

"I would be if you would have me, lord!" Lukat said, standing up to him.

"*Hah!* Art too small and fubsy as yet; shalt be page to Lady Annis and run her errands!" said Gyrfalon "And if you do well in a year or two shalt then be my page, importunate brat!"

"Thank you my lord!" said Lukat.

"Brat, hast none told thee that shouldst be afraid of the evil warlord Gyrfalon and stay out of his way?" demanded Gyrfalon.

"Oh yes my lord, any amount of people, but I ignored them," said Lukat.

"You – *Hah* ! He ignored them forsooth!

Hast more balls than half my company, little whelp; and more balls for bearing pain in good cheer too," he added. "Very well; hast talked thy way into being my page; and shalt take the odd blow from me if you fail me in any matter, and harsh words many. I am not a douce man."

"No lord; but a douce man were not perhaps so good a warlord," said Lukat.

Gyrfalon laughed and ruffled his hair; and proceeded to mostly ignore the boy save to throw out rough words of instruction from time to time. But he let him be around him and help with simple tasks.

"My lord, you are right indulgent to my grandson" said Reeve Bullard.

"Indulgent? No Bullard, I am intolerant at the brat," said Gyrfalon, "and push him hard. He is a good lad. Methinks one day he will do well."

"Th-thank you my lord," said Bullard who knew indulgence when he saw it but also know better than to contradict Gyrfalon.

The boy Lukat reminded Gyrfalon much of his little brother Falk at the same age; determined despite physical frailness to do all his elder brother did; and of this he spoke to none, even Annis.

She, he suspected, had guessed well enough.

Annis had guessed; and thought it good for her love to take an interest in a lad under his training as well as in her. He continued to push her hard; and one of the most avid spectators was Lukat who cheered them both impartially and learned almost as much by watching as by the relatively gentle bouts Gyrfalon indulged him with two or three times.

At times Annis felt almost guilty of her own happiness as she spent the days ordering the castle, working out, and sewing in Gyrfalon's chamber in the evening discussing many matters, though mostly warcraft and the problem of the northern barbarians. And then there were the lengthening nights spent in happy surrender in her lover's arms.

And yet nothing much happened between the two sides; and within the good harvest provided well enough for all, even being careful to eke out the supplies. If tempers were shorter than usual for the confinement, at least none suffered much from Gyrfalon's uncertain temper that appeared to have healed – unsurprisingly – with his face. Indeed he too seemed to be enjoying himself stalking around in the gown she had sewn, taking a quite boyish delight in instructing Annis in the finer points of siege-craft and military architecture, delighting in her eager interest and intelligent questions. That Lukat often trotted at their heels, with less and less pain to his gait did the lad no harm either; and when he asked questions Gyrfalon cuffed him, but answered them.

Foregrim nodded sagely and expressed the opinion to any who would listen that my lord found as much of the son in my lady as would-be bride. Those who had known the ill-fated Buto agreed. Their lord had given a love not returned to the sullen boy, he had adopted and who never had the interest or ability to learn that Annis had. Unbeknownst to her, she became the soldiers' darling, a mascot, and not just for the healing she gave freely. Her influence on Gyrfalon was welcome; and her presence was felt throughout the whole castle, for her disapproval was accounted to be a great shame on a man and efforts were made to please her. There was even an increase in attendance at Mass by those who had abandoned the church or had never known it; for if Lady Annis worshipped there was felt to be some value in it. Annis smiled approval on the new converts; and put it down to Michael's excellent, down to earth – and brief – sermons. Certainly the priest's practical approach did much to hold the attention of the soldiers who came!

Lukat's attempts to be useful too amused the men; and that he was indulged by Gyrfalon and Annis led to the club-footed lad being treated with more gentleness than he might have otherwise been, sent about his business by kindly word rather than harsh language and a blow. And his brave striving to be a warrior despite his foot won the child some grudging respect; even as it earned Gyrfalon's respect too. And Loveday was but relieved that her son not be a butt for cruel jests as he had been by many in their old village. And when Gyrfalon demanded to know why one of his troops had beaten a villager into unconsciousness that was a matter brought before him, the man replied,

"He never stopped taunting your page, my lord, as would scorn to complain; and I lost my temper."

Gyrfalon nodded.

"Learn to control your temper; no further action".

Still dragged the siege; and the first bright, sharp frost lay on the ground on the day before that designated for the wedding. Annis thought brief pity for those encamped around, especially those near the marsh with its attendant chills and fevers. A mild autumn and early winter had failed to kill all the midges and mosquitoes that carried the disease; though that was unknown to any healer, Annis among them. But even though she pitied those without, it was their choice to be there; and nothing could destroy her happiness in being about to be joined irrevocably to Gyrfalon at a time when she suspected and hoped that she might be in a position to please him yet further with news that he would be bound to welcome.

Annis awoke on the dawn of her wedding day with the hollow-excited feeling in the pit of her stomach; and, being cold, she reached for Gyrfalon. She came fully awake on not feeling him in remembrance that she had spent her last unwed night in her own little turret room by way of preparation; and as sleep eluded her now she got resolutely up in the chill autumnal dawn.

Fog lay across the castle in a chill grey blanket that showed little intention of lifting before the sun's face. Annis pulled a face; then shrugged. The weather was immaterial on her wedding day! She pulled on an ordinary homespun woollen gown to break her fast in and ran lightly to the battlements first, with her heavy cloak pulled securely around her. She knew that Gyrfalon customarily prowled round in the fog and rain, encouraging his men and urging them to greater vigilance. She found him peering into the sea of shifting greys, helmet discarded for better vision and hearing; his sharp eyes picking out glimpses of the enemy as the misty droplets shifted in the light wind before being repulsed by more tendrils of fog seeping up from the marsh. He extended his own cloak around Annis' slight figure for a double layer and she wrinkled up her nose.

"Wet wool and rust" she commented "You are lumpy and smelly to cuddle inside armour, dear one."

"I am also cautious to a fault that I not be a corpse; that would make you a very fine bedfellow, my dear!" he retorted.

She sighed contentedly and laid her head against his chest.

"I wish the idiots would go away" she said "Then it would be just perfect. Why must they insist on wanting to rescue me?"

"Perfect? Smells and all and in November?" He teased "Ah, Annis, now I do know that you do love me, smelly armour and all! But," he added seriously, "it is not really about rescuing you; save for a few idealists. It is me they want; me they want to destroy."

"I suppose I realised that; or for your safety, and that of our men I might have suggested giving myself up into the protection of Falk – who would not, methinks, try to treat me with anything but his clumsy courtesy – for better peace, that I might subsequently slip back to join you. But methinks it were for nothing; so I shall not consider it."

"You are a good pragmatist, my dear," said Gyrfalon "Not letting Christian virtue and self sacrifice – that were a worse sacrifice to me than dying at my brother's hand – stand in the way of realism and common sense. It would not break the siege; it would but break my heart."

She slid her arms around him.

"I will never leave you willingly my dear lord," she said. "I am yours. They cannot take that away from us."

"Aye" the sardonic lines on his face sneered into the fog at the unseen besiegers. "Let them come; I care naught for any of them."

Annis held him closer.

"I wish they hated you not," she said.

He laughed nastily.

"Oh, do not waste sympathy on me," he said "I have been at loggerheads with the church and with Falk so long I could not care less."

"I care," said Annis; but she said it inaudibly into her lover's chest.

Some hours later Annis had changed into her best, deep blue, gown ready for the ceremony; and met with the reeve Bullard, who had agreed to give her away in lieu of her father. Lukat pranced as well as he might in the clothes of a young lordling Annis had found in the chest for he was to be her page and he was tremendously proud of the long tunic of fine white wool embroidered in blue and scarlet thread about neck and hem that he wore over his own best breeches. Elissa had at first refused to be a bridesmaid, in tones of scorn; then rather sheepishly asked if she might change her mind. She wore one of Annis' own gowns, the blue linsey-woolsey and Annis had threaded a filet of ribbon through the warrior's short locks to decorate her head and Elissa had to admit she scarcely recognised herself; and fellow warriors who had been inclined to scoff at the idea of Elissa as a bridesmaid changed their minds and whistled instead. And Elissa found that she did know how to blush, though she thought she had forgotten!

Bullard grinned at Annis sheepishly and offered his arm; and Annis took it, smiling reassuringly. Confidently she walked up the aisle; and though the chapel lacked a bell she was given a resounding if cacophonic carillon of a welcome by the village lads on a variety of pots and pans. Annis bestowed a grateful smile on their unmusical efforts; and reduced the older ones at least to blushing, lock-tugging incoherence.

Father Michael looked at the bride's face; and most of his fears were stilled. When he looked at the bridegroom he knew he was doing the right thing; for Gyrfalon's face had softened at the approach of his bride; and the look in his eyes was one of love. Michael surreptitiously crossed himself and gave thanks; and begged his God to illuminate the mind of the warlord through his love for his young wife. He opened his prayer book and began to read the time honoured words.

Outside the castle, the cacophony, muffled by the enveloping fog, carried faintly to Falk's ears; and soon thereafter the sounds of laughing, music and merrymaking as those soldiers not on duty and the villagers danced and revelled in celebration to the rude music of the village waits. The village managed to field two rebec players, a bagpipe player and a man who played pipe and tabor, banging out the rhythm with enthusiasm and some skill with one hand whilst playing his three-holed pipe with the other, reaching the higher registers by overblowing. The villagers were delighted to rejoice with and for their lord and his new lady and celebrated enthusiastically. The reason for such sounds of revelry puzzled Falk; for he could not conceive of a joyous occasion taking place in the same vicinity as his brother. Yet it were clearly a celebration, for the music that could faintly be heard was of such a nature as to be unmistakeably happy;

and the voices faintly raised seemed merry, not terrified. Falk drew his already sodden cloak closer about himself and sighed, confused.

Not least in his thoughts was the lame lad; that Gyrfalon had carried, so eager was he not to be deprived of the least of his possessions; for so Falk read it. He hoped the warlord ignored the peasant boy and did not make him too much a butt of his ill temper.

He would have been surprised to have seen the lame lad proudly carrying the warlord's sword that he wore not to a wedding and refusing to be relieved of it by some larger person, though it were heavy indeed and tired him.

Gyrfalon finally took it from the boy and declared that it was now his responsibility to care for his bride, not his page's; and Lukat beamed on him.

The newlyweds sat on a dais while the rustic celebrations continued beneath the salt. Gyrfalon had at first demurred at the idea of being on display; but Annis had been adamant.

"It will make little difference to us, my lord," she admonished, "and means so much to them." Gyrfalon had shrugged and agreed to please his bride as she added, "Though of course we cannot feast as such; that would be profligate and improper for us to feast even a little when our people must needs be frugal."

Gyrfalon had grinned at this.

"With all the wildfowl in the marsh?" he had said "Duck roast and watercress with cat-tail pottage will surely do for any feast." Delighted at Annis' confounded look he had explained, "There is a secret water-gate out of the castle hidden in withies and reeds. And I have some good fensmen here!"

Duly then, the fensmen had done the castle proud; and all feasted with duck meat in their pottage, even if the choicest morsels were saved for the high table. And Annis knew that with a secret exit, their people had a better chance of withstanding a long siege. She held her lord's hand lovingly, as she smiled pleasure at the well wishers who approached them to offer their clumsy greetings.

Gyrfalon leaned over.

"And will you permit us to slip away, now?" He asked her. She turned and smiled up at him; and his heart skipped at the adoration in her eyes.

"Yes, my lord and my love," she murmured "We have been properly inspected and approved. Now our presence would be ….inhibiting."

Gyrfalon smiled at his young bride's worldly wise air and earthy instincts that told her that without the presence of the Lord and

Lady the bawdier sides of their vassals would emerge. He rose, taking her by the hand to help her, and they left; and Annis may have assumed a worldly wise air but her cheeks were scarlet as the celebrating peasants shouted out cheerful advice to their overlord.

Alone in Gyrfalon's chamber, the warlord pulled Annis unceremoniously to him.

"And *now* my wife...." he said, almost savagely.

Annis chuckled throatily.

"I can think of a better use for my lord's lips than talking," she said.

Gyrfalon obliged.

Without the castle the sounds of louder singing drifted down to the cold, wet besiegers.

"Bastards, they make celebration on purpose to make us the more miserable" said one foot soldier "To remind us that they have proper walls and roofs; and goodly fires for hot food."

Falk, overhearing that comment, wondered if there be any truth in it; that Gyrfalon had ordered a feast purely to wage warfare on the morale of those without. He would not put it past his brother. And one of the songs drifting down seemed to be declaring at every chorus that 'who can? *Gyrfalon* can, Gyrfalon can and he's a man' or some such. What it was that his brother could do, Falk could not make out; but there seemed to be a great number of verses, and the chorus roared out by all the voices as each verse ended.

The song was rather bawdy and Annis and Gyrfalon chuckled ruefully over some of the suggestions included in it; and then ignored it utterly, following their own inclinations rather than the recommendations of their people.

But Gyrfalon was amazed that he was named in the song; for such songs were sung generally of the popular lords or commanders; and that his people respected him enough to sing such was as moving as it was faintly irksome.

Later – much later – Annis asked drowsily,

"Will we be expected to display the sheets as proof of my virtue, my love?"

Gyrfalon snorted.

"A stupid ceremony. Few country folk bother with marriage 'til the bride's a good few months gone."

Annis blushed rosily.

"Will less time do, Gyrfalon? I – I am not totally sure yet, but….."

She looked up at him; he was gazing down at her, stunned a moment, then he gripped her hand.

"You are with child?"

She nodded.

"I – I think so. I am late with my courses…. I never have been before…."

Gyrfalon grinned suddenly and swept her into his arms.

"Annis – dear one – you must take care!" he exclaimed. Annis laughed happily.

"It is quite a natural phenomenon, dearest. Do not cosset me – promise?"

He laughed.

"Has the irony struck you over asking wicked Lord Gyrfalon not to cosset you?" he said.

She touched his face.

"But I know you," she said softly.

Annis lay happily beside her husband, the muffled sounds of a few hardy and determined revellers drifting intermittently up to their window. Gyrfalon's quiet breathing beside her was comforting; and she reached out a hand to touch his warm, muscular body. He murmured in his sleep and flung an arm across her; and she snuggled up, one tiny hand touching her belly in hope that she might give him a son. A son who would also be Falk's nephew.

Annis sighed.

Would the feud go on for another generation? Would Falk hate their son for his father's sake?

Annis came to a decision.

The feud had to be stopped; and she had to stop it.

Chapter 12

Next morning, Gyrfalon and Annis surveyed the besiegers as had become their wont; the numbers had swelled. Gyrfalon pointed out the pennants of a variety of lords and warriors with dry comment concerning their reputations or prowess. Some were undoubtedly enemies of his; others merely opportunists hoping to gain some loot and a piece of the action.

"Or at least," Gyrfalon added, shrugging, "I do not recall making enemies of them. Lords Baudwine of Amelberg and Berhard of Weinwal are old enemies of mine, so they are honest foes. I see the banner of Arnul of Czernitz who is an eastern marcher lord, whose opportunism is only exceeded by his rapacity. With Melis of Hunisland and Walter of Liutenberg I have no quarrel, and I must suppose that they support my brother. They would not turn out of their comfortable castles for a relative upstart like your father, who has no pretentions to aristocracy beside his marriage to your mother, who was the child of our king's illegitimate half-sister. I was well drilled in heraldry in my youth," he added, as he pointed out the various banners to Annis.

Annis smiled wryly.

"I dare say a few more will not

discommode your mind greatly," she declared "If we have game from the marsh, then they may sit there until they rot. Though it will go hard if we be late with the sowing season *next* year as well as the coming one."

He touched her face.

"You are such a pragmatist, my dear," he said approvingly.

Annis scanned the ranks of the enemy, the colours of the flags and pennants making a brave – if futile – attempt to compete with the lowering grey skies. She picked out Falk's pavilion, his white hawk on a green ground fluttering above it to identify him.

"Aye," she said, answering her lord's approving comment. "I am little given to flower and fancy, I think, and take it all with deplorable equanimity. Yet I think there is only one foe here that moves you, my lord."

"Falk."

It was a statement; it was an insult.

She touched his gloved hand.

"Is our child to grow up to a feud?" she asked wistfully.

He turned and stared. She continued,

"You loved him once; can you find yourself big enough to forgive him? For my part, selfish being that I am, I am grateful to him, for it is I that have you, not Alys."

Gyrfalon blinked, taken aback.

"My dear, you make me happier than Alys

could ever have done," he told her, finally acknowledging it to himself. "Aye, she loved to hear stories of derring do; but I recall that she got squeamish if it involved too much real danger, and wept for the enemy if I had slain any; regardless of circumstances. The idea of teaching her to fight with a sword – of her being capable of lifting one, though she were a sturdier lass to my recollection than you – is laughable. You, with your pragmatism, *you* are a warrior's wife. Alys would have been merely the mother of my sons. Yes; you are right. The anger towards Falk is habitual. I am willing to forgive him that; and forgive Alys too. She has no hold on mine heart or – if I have one – my soul anymore. For my birthright? That is harder to forgive. And yet that was more my father's fault than Falk's; that he let himself be blinded. Falk ran tales to him too; but under the circumstances, and with the way he was brought up it were not so surprising. Of course, the problem then lies that it is unlikely that Falk would ever forgive me; for Alys *or* our father. I am a parricide, remember. For I lost my temper with the old man for believing the rumours without verifying them, and for believing that I had turned against him, also. Which turned me against him. And I have gone out of my way to commit atrocities since to appal Falk as much as for any other reason. Childish really."

There was a note of regret in his voice; the older Gyrfalon examining the angry impulsiveness of the younger, perhaps wishing things different. Annis put her arms about him and smiled serenely.

"Then we shall just have to test the extent of our brother's Christian charity, shall we not!" she declared.

Gyrfalon gave a whoop of delighted laughter; and the besiegers that heard it stirred uneasily.

"My love, that sounds uncommonly like the devil quoting the scriptures to his own ends" he said dryly "Yet somehow I could almost imagine you talking him into it; you are as stubborn as any ass and as persuasive as the devil himself when you've a mind to it!"

Annis smiled up at him and Gyrfalon hugged her to him fiercely.

"Rather a backhanded compliment – as usual, my lord!" she said demurely.

"Know, my love," he said, taking her face in his hands, "that if anything should happen to me, you are to go to Falk. Whatever else he may feel towards me, he will protect you."

"And if he is the one that harms you?" She retorted "Shall I then meekly place myself in his hands and not seek revenge? He obviously feels that it were meet that Alys should cause you so grievous a cursed wound; though I doubt he can understand the depth of the pain and what that do to a man, year in, year out. He must not be surprised, if he harms you, that I would want to harm him back."

"Revenge will not help you and the child stay alive," he said harshly. "Falk can teach our child how to be a warrior. And the Elfsword will at least then stay in the family, not fall into the hands of strangers…..let him not teach our child that I am all bad; and my love, my dear Annis, I pray you will not learn to love him."

Annis shivered

"That I would never do….. though I might take a subtle revenge of making him love me and then rejecting him," she said coolly. "My love, have you had some bad presentiment that you talk thus?"

He shook his head swiftly, seeing the fear in her smoke blue eyes.

"Nay, dearling, merely normal pessimism," he told her "And a warrior must ever have contingency plans."

She slipped a cold hand into his and stared once more on the mass of their foes. Already their ally, the marsh, had carried casualties and she heard the moans of the fevered.

"The marsh heals what the marsh deals," she murmured "You will not let me tend the unfortunates out there, I be sure, my lord, but may I at least despatch a list of herbs that their healers need?"

He blinked.

"Yes" he said "I have no objection; if only because worrying about them make you jumpy as worrying about me shooting them does not. But whether they will heed your words or not I cannot say. They will probably consider it some witch's brew."

"Call for Falk" she suggested "I will write him a note; he may have the native wit to heed it if his brains not be too much afire with hatred."

"Perhaps," said Gyrfalon sceptically.

Gyrfalon leaned forward as Annis fetched parchment and quill.

"*FALK*! Come parley!"

It was not many minutes before Falk appeared.

"You want to discuss terms?" he asked. Gyrfalon snorted.

"My wife pities your fevered soldiers since they are struck down by nature – or the hand of God if you will – rather than by me. She wants to send your physicians a list of locally found herbs to use on your patients."

Falk had gasped audibly when Gyrfalon described Annis as his wife and pursed his lips grimly.

"And why should you permit her to do this, Gyrfalon? Are not the sufferings of honest men as music to your wicked ears?" he asked scathingly.

"My wife shares your religion, brother; she is disposed to be kind to all, even the enemy. Possibly even to cardinals though I wonder if even Annis has her limits. I am inclined to humour her; husbands are supposed to humour their brides."

Falk was suspicious.

He was also taken aback when Annis' face appeared over a crenellation, clutching in her hand a longbow.

"Gyrfalon, you have failed me!" she said crossly.

"Indeed?" Gyrfalon was taken aback.

"You have not instructed me in how to use this wretched thing!" she said. He laughed.

"It takes all a man's life to learn how to use a longbow properly, my dear; shouldst stick to a crossbow as I do. Besides, the deformation caused to the shoulder would be a shame on your perfect figure."

He added that purely to make Falk grind his teeth.

It worked.

Annis shouted down,

"Lord Falk, I think you should stand back" she advised "For I have never fired a bow before and I should hate to miss. Or rather, not to miss, if you see what I mean. I have written a list of herbs and tied it to the arrow;

'tis what they do in bad romances so I hope the writers have it correct, Gyrfalon you are laughing at me!"

"Yes," said Gyrfalon unrepentantly.

Shakily, Annis set her arrow to the string, and drew it back, a little taken aback as the tightly wound list still caught slightly. She fired off an inexpert shot that went sideways more than forward; though it did at least clear the moat.

"Oh dear" said Annis "Where did that go?"

"I see now, brother," called Falk "You have the girl act in good faith, expecting me to collect the note from under the fire of your archers. Nice try, Gyrfalon; but it will not work."

Gyrfalon turned to one of his archers, a burly man head and shoulders taller than the warlord.

"By his feet," he said quietly.

An arrow sang and landed between Falk's feet.

"As you see, brother, I have no need to bring you closer," called Gyrfalon. "You can get your note unharmed. The lady Annis is merely of charitable turn of mind; but then, what woman does not have her faults? She is in other respects an admirable wife, meaning that I have no interest in harming you, for I have better things to do. Oh yes, and she said you should keep your feet dry and your back warm; as her advice keeps my army whole and healthy I make no doubt that you would be wise to listen to her. A good day to you!" he added half mockingly before turning away.

Falk came forward and picked up the arrow, walking back to the siege line almost feeling the arrow he half expected in his back. He could not get over the fact that Lady Annis seemed quite cheery, despite being wed – so Gyrfalon said – to his brother. And she had chid Gyrfalon for not teaching her the longbow; that he had taken in amusement. It was an incomprehensible situation that went on behind the castle walls; and Falk was concerned for the Lady Annis and her brave front. He perused the note carefully, to see whether the Lady Annis had used this as some means of sending a message to him; but it was nothing but a list of herbs in order of efficacy, that might be used to temper the marsh fever. It was written in a feminine, but bold hand with confident flourishes and she had named the herbs in both Latin and by common name. Willow, Salix, was the only one he knew, and she specified a draught of the bark of that. Falk shook his head, perplexed. He took it to a novice monk attached to the church forces.

"Copy this out twice" he instructed "Have those who recognise the herbs collect them from one of the copies; and take the other copy to the Abbey for verification. They are skilled in the healing arts there."

The young cleric nodded and rushed off to comply.

Finding that the nuns declared the cure not only genuine but excellent, Falk consulted with the abbot whose Abbey was his base.

"I do not understand it, Father" he declared, pacing up and down in frustration "What would make Gyrfalon permit such a thing?"

The abbot put his head, birdlike, on one side.

"You say that the Lady Annis bears a striking superficial resemblance to the girl you both loved?"

Falk snorted.

"I loved her; Gyrfalon desired her."

The abbot looked quizzical; for no man might say how another felt, and frustrated love was more like to cause a man to the extremes of behaviour that Gyrfalon had gone to; but he merely said softly,

"Whatever his feelings, if this Annis is like Alys, could it not be merely that he is sufficiently besotted – loving her even – that she can do no wrong for him?" he suggested.

"Heaven help her then when she touches a raw nerve by not being enough like Alys – or too like her," retorted Falk. "It puzzles me that he has not taken her crucifix from her, or convinced her not to wear it. I do take your point, Father Abbot; but I reiterate that Gyrfalon does not love. He possesses."

The abbot suggested,

"As she is a Christian, my son, might it not be that the Good Lord is offering Gyrfalon another chance through her? If they have been wed by Father Michael, I am sure he would have felt that there was good reason. He is a sound priest; and capable of being stubborn. He would die before he betrayed his conscience."

Falk snorted.

"It would take a miracle to make Gyrfalon repent."

The abbot chuckled.

"Our Lord has been known to perform them you know," he said dryly. "Falk, my son, I can see in your face that you think it a miracle beyond the power of God – which if voiced would be perilously close to blasphemy. Is not the possibility worth considering?"

Falk considered the abbot's words.

"It is difficult," he admitted "I have not your degree of faith, I fear, father. Merely my belief in what I know of my brother."

"And did you always hate him so?" asked the clever priest.

Falk shook his head.

"No Father. As a child I hero worshipped him; and followed him around like a puppy."

"So he must have been worthy of some admiration then?"

"I do not know."

He shook his head again.

"I do not know, Father."

When Falk got back to the siege it was to a moment of drama; the men of the attacking armies were laughing at a small figure that capered atop the walls, shrieking shrill imprecations and loosing off ineffective arrows from a small toy longbow. There was a bellow of rage, and the small figure was whisked within, yanked off its precarious perch by a black gloved hand seizing the scruff of his neck.

"Thou cub, thou whelp!" Gyrfalon's voice roared "What would thy mother say an you fell off, thou froward brat? Think you that your foot is recovered enough for a secure footing on those wet slippery stones? It is not! And what if those below not realise you be a child and shoot at you? I should beat you black and blue!"

"But I didn't fall, Lord Gyrfalon!" Came the child's shrill protest "I was keeping their heads down!"

"Brat, they be more like to die laughing at

one of my people falling off!" cried Gyrfalon "If you be so interested in being of real use to the castle shalt spend the next three days emptying all the nightsoil pots into the garderobes and seeing that they be scrubbed! Be off with you!"

"I only wanted to be brave for you my lord!" said Lukat.

"Aye, well, sometimes it be better to live to grow up to be brave then," growled Gyrfalon "If thou canst not behave, I – I'll send you to be my brother's page without!"

"I'll be good my lord," said Lukat earnestly "Only how do I know if I be being bad if something not be forbidden?"

Gyrfalon gave a shout of laughter.

"Try thinking first," he admonished.

Falk listened incredulously; though after the first exchange he had needs to strain his ears.

That had passed in much the same way as many a conversation between himself at a similar age and his big brother, when Gyrfalon had extracted him – as he so often had – from the consequences of his own folly and a spirit greater than his ability.

Hot tears spilled down Falk's face at a bittersweet memory of his childhood.

And even as Gyrfalon had threatened to beat Falk black and blue – and had only sometimes done so – so too he threatened this child – and then sent him on an unpleasant, menial and smelly task. And the boy answered back pertly as though he expected no great punishment for it.

Falk did not know what to think; but he told himself firmly that even if Gyrfalon acted doucely to the boy for the time being because the Lady Annis took an interest in him, it would not be long ere he showed his true colours. It could not be otherwise.

Lukat took the penalty imposed upon him with philosophical acceptance. He would have preferred a beating; that would soon have been over, and he had been used enough to incurring the violence of bigger boys in his previous village. A serious beating from his lord might well have been worse but it would have healed. Three days of messy smelly chores was much worse; which was why Lord Gyrfalon had imposed it. Grown ups were like that; they picked the worst of two punishments as a general rule if there were a choice of such.

Lord Gyrfalon had asked him what he thought the crenellations were for; and explained carefully that they were for the safety of the defenders and not generally for standing on save rarely, to make a point.

And suddenly Lukat had less free time; for

Lord Gyrfalon decreed that a page who hoped to be a squire must acquire literacy, Latin and arithmetic, that he might understand machines of war.

Whatever Gyrfalon ordered was wonderful so far as Lukat was concerned; but he could have wished that a warrior needed less tedious skills than those he was now learning from the priest.

Father Michael had been glad to take a scholar at Gyrfalon's behest; though he warned the warlord he was himself no very great scholar.

"Teach him to read, write, figure and construe enough Latin to start him on the road to understanding how to unravel the rubbish written in diplomatic documents and I'll take over when he's a little older," said Gyrfalon. "When I be less preoccupied than I am at the moment. It may have escaped your notice, priest, but we have a little bit of a war going on out there."

Father Michael smiled shyly; it seemed to him that Gyrfalon's sharp tongue was worse than his bite.

"Why, so I do believe!" he said.

Gyrfalon grinned.

"You aren't so bad, priest" he said.

The siege was not, of course the only thing that preoccupied Gyrfalon; for he was delighting in being married to Annis; to have her sit at his side above the salt acknowledged as his lady by all in the Hall; delighting in the thought that he was to be a father; and delighting in their time together in the private darkness of his chamber, that was chill even for the fire in the grate, and the heavy furs on the bed; that their bodies warmed each other in their loving, and by being together in each other's arms afterwards. Gyrfalon silently vowed that however many children they might have he would do his utmost to show no favouritism; that he would not permit the same troubles to occur as had happened between him and Falk. He tried not to think of the reason why there were so many years between him and Falk; that his own mother had died. For what he would do if he lost Annis, the warlord could not contemplate.

Annis had taken over the duties of lady of the castle with the smooth efficiency with which she undertook everything she understood. She knew about running the everyday needs of a great household; and must only apply common sense to the exigencies of being under siege.

She discussed such aspects with Bullard the reeve, for much concerned the addition of the villagers and their livestock.

"Martinmas is traditional to slaughter," she

said "and so too we must do, for we will not have any spare hay for winter feed; methinks we should slaughter all but the best breeding animals, more than normal, and smoke and salt them down for the winter. Fortunately we have plenty of salt; for I found several barrels of it, permitted to become damp for none having known that it had been stored badly under the previous lord; so we must use wet brine salting not dry. There is good store of firewood that will permit the smoking of the hams; and we shall eat liver and chitterlings for the day or two after the slaughtering."

Bullard nodded.

"There be a pair of plough oxen as I think be worth keeping," he said "Unless we get really low on food; chickens be worth keeping for eggs, methinks my lady, that need not much to keep them up, and the prize sow, who have never farrowed less than thirteen piglings."

Annis nodded.

"I rely on you to segregate those animals we not slaughter, good Bullard," she said. "And to make note of those people whose animals we kill who would normally keep back some, so we may compensate them come the spring….or whenever we get rid of those wretched idiots out there."

"Ar, I'll be glad to get rid of them: why do they still be there if you be married to Lord

Gyrfalon and all arranged by consent with your father, Lady?

Annis gave a wry laugh.

"Somewhere between dislike of my lord and a desire to loot," she said.

"We do have people – you might call them poachers if you were feeling uncharitable – who do know there way about who might slip out of the water-gate and slit a few throats," suggested Bullard.

Annis grinned.

"I have a better idea," she said.

The next day a number of Gyrfalon's enemies woke to the horror of finding a dagger planted in their bed roll beside them; that pinned a note to their pillow in Gyrfalon's forceful hand; for Gyrfalon had laughed and approved Annis' improvement on Bullard's plan. The notes read,

"If this had been a few inches over, you would not have woken to read it. Depart. The next time will not be a warning."

Bullard stood with Gyrfalon and Annis on the walls to watch the sudden departure of quite a number of those to whom Gyrfalon felt it worth sending the warning. This was some dozen as well as those whom he had named to Annis.

"Three have not heeded warning," said the warlord. "A purse of gold for each of them to your men if they manage a neat job of it."

Bullard grinned.

"For a purse of gold they'll make as neat a job as any man might," he said.

"Tell them, leave it a few days; even a week or more" said Gyrfalon "That these lords forget to take their precautions for feeling it were an idle threat."

Bullard nodded.

"Ar; not next dark o' the moon but a few days arter it," he said.

The defenders of the castle also decided to encourage the discomforts of the besiegers by throwing such offal as was not cooked and eaten over the walls when the animals were slaughtered.

Annis muttered that it were like to cause disease; then pulled a rueful face and added,

"I suppose that be the whole idea to keep them unhealthy."

"Quite so my dear" said Gyrfalon. "They could always take the trouble to bury the tripes we throw at them; if they do not they deserve their diseases."

Annis shrugged.

"True enough" she said "And *that* ought to be obvious enough that I not need to issue instructions. Let the frying of the offal be done in the courtyard too; it needs a hot fire but not a long lasting one. Then the smell of good hot food will further demoralise the attackers; and we shall all feast with merrymaking and dancing that be a good way to exercise and keep warm too."

"What, you don't expect me to dance do you?" Gyrfalon said, horrified.

"Why, did you not learn?"

"Of course I learned – not very enthusiastically, but I learned. My father convinced me it would help my footwork with swordplay."

"Why, he was right; and not too late to use it for even more nimbleness that shalt beat me even more black and blue at practice!" cried Annis brightly.

"Minx," said Gyrfalon.

He deigned to dance a little, and with Annis, that his presence encouraged the villagers as they ate fried offal and laughed and sang.

Annis slid away early; for she had something that she felt she must do; and she felt that tonight was the best night for her endeavour when the besiegers were preoccupied by the merriment within the castle.

Chapter 13

Cloaked against the night chills and to avoid recognition, Annis slipped out of the secret marsh gate and into the low skiff of Caleb the waterman. Caleb was a canny hunter but was also what the village folk described as 'a little loight' meaning that he was slightly simple, a big, gentle lad that mourned with genuine grief the ducks and other birds his arrows brought down for necessity's sake. Caleb adored Annis for the curing of some painful boils on his back; and the way she made salves for the injured animals he was wont to nurse. She never made fun of his love of animals as some did and was always ready to show him too some of the simpler cures. Caleb and his brother had come to Gyrfalon's band as preferable to being hanged or maimed by the lord on whose lands they had been caught poaching; and having escaped they had to go somewhere. An outlaw's army seemed at the time as good an option as any; and if Gyrfalon had not been an ideal commander, Caleb's brother had shrugged and said he were no worse than many a Lord sanctioned by the church and given the deference of high degree. Caleb's brother had died fighting somewhere but though the other soldiers called Caleb 'the dummy' they were kind to him in an offhand way for his skills with hunting and his deadly accuracy with a bow. Annis liked Caleb's direct ways and gentle respect for all his fellow creatures; and had asked him to take her secretly to a shore near Falk's tent. She knew Caleb would obey without question; and would use his big fists to protect her if any offered insult.

The skiff bumped gently against hard earth under the cover of a light mist; and Caleb scrambled ashore, tying up the painter to an overhanging blackthorn bush that sheltered it, as did the alder carr, from prying eyes.

"'Tis that way, m'lady" Caleb whispered, displaying the countryman's sureness of direction that lay innate within him. "Should I come with you?"

Annis considered. His size and strength were comforting – but could draw unwanted attention to her. Besides, he might react before it were necessary for respect towards her.

"I will whistle loudly for you if I need you," she decided. "But I will go alone. I have my knives that Lord Gyrfalon has taught me to use so well."

"Take care, lady," his tone was anxious. She smiled at him, touched him briefly on the shoulder and was gone, light footed into the soft grey mist, swallowed as completely, thought Caleb shuddering, as if she were taken by marsh piskies!

Annis was reflecting wryly on the last time she had slipped out of a castle. What profound changes that had wrought on her life! She hoped that this time would have less far-reaching consequences; though hopefully as profound in some respects – at least so far as her husband's happiness and any child's future were concerned. It was different too in many ways; for unlike her midnight flight from her father's keep she had every intention of being back before she was missed; and in case her absence was noticed she had left a note for her husband with her intentions laid out in it. She slid through the mist, like a little shadow, distracting the guard around the tent by tossing a stone into the alder carr where she disturbed roosting marsh birds; and their disturbance distracted the attention of the church knight on guard long enough to slip easily past him.

It was true that she might have asked him to take her to Lord Falk; but Annis preferred her visit to be known to no-one.

Falk had been smelling fried liver and bacon, and listening to merriment in the full knowledge that it was to taunt him and his troops; what amazed him was that there were sounds of what sounded like genuine enough laughter and cheery song, and bucolic dance measures scraped and whistled on rustic instruments that he might have expected Gyrfalon to have banned, or had broken. Gyrfalon permitting merriment, even to lower the morale of his enemy was a new start. Falk returned from his patrol, shaking out the moisture from his cloak that he had picked up from the chill and sodden air and wished that the smell of liver and bacon were not so appetising. The ground under foot of the attackers was too sodden to get more than the most sullen of fires burning; and all the wood around was wet through and almost impossible to light. The besiegers must make do with cold rations; for though some wood had been kept dry, there had not been enough covered by limited canvas to last long. And that would have to be rectified, dry wood brought in, if the army were to survive the winter. It was something Falk contemplated that would have to be arranged; and enough dry wood to get large fires going could then dry out local wood culled from the forest; which was sufficiently depleted to show that Gyrfalon had already prepared well in advance for a siege and had a good store of wood that was unlikely to run low.

Which was almost as depressing to a commander as the more immediate taunts of hot food and music were to the men.

Gyrfalon had something of the upper hand in the war of nerves; and that irritated Falk.

As he entered his tent his warrior's senses told him that he was not alone; and he bethought himself of the warning messages he had heard that some of the lesser followers to his banner had received that had frightened most of them into leaving. Gyrfalon had not troubled to threaten him; perchance he had come himself or sent one to assassinate him instead without warning? Falk tossed back the cloak to prevent it from hampering his movements whilst making it an apparently casual movement.

He did not need to call on the hidden figure to show itself; the shadows quickly disgorged a slight, cloaked figure that put back the hood it wore on seeing that he was alone. Annis' pale hair tumbled back from her face and she regarded him solemnly from midnight eyes too large in her pale face.

"Lady Annis! You have escaped?" he started forward. She shook her head and stamped her little foot.

"*Will* you listen and try not to rouse the whole camp?" she asked waspishly "You brothers share the trait of noisiness if nothing else!"

Falk blinked; and remembered his manners, holding forward a chair for her to be seated. Annis considered; and duly took the chair.

"You had been warmer under canvas had you cut bundles of rushes and laid them under the carpets you use to try to defeat the cold," she remarked dryly. "And cut alder leaves ere they fell to strew within the rushes that deter fleas and other insects that would otherwise lurk within."

Annis hated inefficiency.

"I thank you for the advice. Now, how may I be of assistance, my lady?" asked Falk.

Annis bit her lip.

"I scarce know how to begin," she said ruefully. "I rehearsed in my head all I wanted to say and it all sound trite now I face you. In sooth, what I ask may be too much; but I have to try."

Falk looked confused.

"Nothing is ever too much to help a lady," he responded with automatic courtesy.

Annis pulled a face.

"Promise not ere the request is made," she chided gently. "Besides, what I ask is not merely for myself; but for an innocent."

Falk was yet more confused. She would not describe Gyrfalon thus; who could she mean? The lame child?

"Who then is this innocent, lady? The lame boy?" he asked.

"Oh if anything occur to Gyrfalon I trust

you to take care of him and the other villagers," said Annis firmly. "Or to try; besieging soldiers having the view once they break in that anything within is for their personal use and satisfaction. No; I refer to your nephew," she told him bluntly.

"My ….??!!! But I have no nephew!"

Annis laid her hand on her belly and dropped her eyes, blushing.

"It might of course be a niece," she murmured, "but does that matter?"

Falk exploded.

"By God, has that monster actually forced himself on you?" he cried.

Annis shut her eyes and counted – audibly – to ten.

"Lord Falk," she said firmly, "please get it into your head that, despite his undoubted manifold faults – many of which have improved – and your own prejudice, I find that which is admirable in your brother. 'Tis a match to my liking, for my lord had ever used me with courtesy; indeed I talked my way into his bed ere we were married, which is how I be certain that I am with child."

"Courtesy? Like dangling you over the parapet?"

"Oh, that," her tone was dismissive. "That were mine idea to get your attention; it worked too. And glad was I of his reassuringly firm grip; for heights terrify me and my head swam alarmingly. And I hoped it be worth such discomfort that by parley, lives might be saved that would otherwise be needlessly wasted in war," she sighed regretfully. "Alas, I underestimated the depth of the enmity that lay between you and your brother."

"Do you know why?" he asked bitterly.

She shrugged.

"I know the way my Gyrfalon perceives it; and that he acknowledges himself to be as much at fault as you and your father; for well he knows his hasty temper when slighted or angered."

"The fault was all his," Falk cried angrily.

Annis raised an eyebrow.

"Indeed? You did not then marry his betrothed without any word to him that she had transferred her affections to the younger brother? You apprised him of the understanding that had risen between you and Alys?" she asked "And did you, while he led your father's troops to preserve the safety of your home, do aught but accept the old man's favouritism when he preferred the son present to the one risking his life for those at home? You urged him to send to see if the rumours of Gyrfalon's death or dishonour were indeed true?"

Falk flushed.

"It were better to tell Gyrfalon face to face, I

thought," he said "As to our father's preference, tales had come that Gyrfalon had many times blasphemed and doubted God's will."

She snorted.

"Tell him face to face; aye, by all means; but not to marry the wench until you had done so! That were as venal a piece of chicanery as any I have ever heard – 'oh brother, Alys doesn't want to marry you any more, by the way, she's wed to me this very day.' Sounds fine doesn't it? As to the tales carried to your besotted sire, I say how can you pass judgement when not yourself there in duress and travail considered by your father too hard for you, against a cruel enemy, when there be no words of hope of aid from home to give you comfort?" she asked sternly "It seem a very harsh thing to do to pass judgement without having walked a mile in another man's shoes, when you have no idea of the conditions he be labouring under."

"And can you walk a mile in my shoes?" he asked, stung by some of the truth in her words.

She smiled sadly.

"I think so," she said. "It seems to me that you have always acted meaning best; and are much the victim of circumstance. It seems to me that the worst damage were those who prated to your father with overzealous piety, changing your father's heart and thereby breaking Gyrfalon's. For truly, Lord Falk, I have heard in his voice frustrated love for your father that turned to hate at the old man's seeming despite. Though it were Alys's betrayal of the promise he understood her to have made to him that brought things to a head, I suspect that it was the loss of his father's love and trust that did the real damage and killed a little bit of him inside."

"And you want me to forgive?" his tone was outraged.

"Few have that much Christianity within them," she said simply. "Especially when it is easier to hate blindly than to acknowledge any responsibility in oneself for what happened. I ask you to try to understand the way he sees what happened; and not to carry on the feud to our children."

Falk shook his head.

"And how could I guarantee that, knowing that the children of which you speak will be taught by their father to vilify me?" he demanded.

Annis tutted.

"Gyrfalon has said he forgives all there is to forgive in you; that he accepts you acted in good faith," she said. "And I will see too to bring up our children to try to see both sides," she asseverated seriously.

He sighed, shaking his head in incredulity.

"I find it incredible that you should give yourself willingly to my brother," he said. "I also find it incredible that you feel that he has treated you well. Either he has changed out of all recognition or you have been treated truly barbarously before!"

Annis' dimple peeped out irrepressibly.

"You have forgotten the possibility, Lord Falk," she said demurely, "that I might enjoy a turbulent relationship."

"*Turbulent*?" he exploded "That were an understatement if he hath not changed; and I have to say," he added, trying to be objective, "I would anticipate seeing you more injured in such case." He tried to be calm, wondering if Gyrfalon had indeed succumbed to some kind of infatuation, shooting her a perceptive look.

She smiled.

"Well if it come down to injuries, truly have I drawn blood from my lord as he have not from me," she said. "Though it was accidental; but he approved of the principal and I bound the wound straightway. He teaches me swordplay," she added.

Falk shook his head.

"Truly, I do not understand you," he said.

"That is not required; my husband does understand me and that makes me content," she said "You ask if he have changed; when first I knew him he was hot of temper and not tolerant; as might any man be, be he ne'er so douce by nature when in constant pain. I have treated his face that within days of my ministrations the pain reduced; and in consequence so did his temper. That I know have only coloured the last ten years or so; that there lie other things between you that led to the cursed wound. But even so, I beg you to consider my words. Must I kneel as a supplicant? I have never knelt to any but God before but for mine husband – my lover – and my child I will do so if you demand it."

She rose in graceful movement from the chair and made to bend the knee; but Falk forestalled her with a rapid gesture.

"I will consider," he said, his tone harsh; the voice suddenly almost like Gyrfalon's, Annis thought, as he fought back remembered griefs. "And I will not pursue a feud unto another generation, that I do swear, unless I am myself sought out under arms by your son. But as to peace with Gyrfalon, I fear that surely cannot be. Indeed, Lady Annis, I urge and beg you to take this opportunity to leave Gyrfalon and bring up your child in Christian freedom."

Annis sighed impatiently.

"It is my duty and my pleasure to return to my dear lord and husband," she said firmly. "I have come as a herald, not for or at knowledge of my lord but on his behalf and that of his heir naytheless; and though not a formal herald I shall take it most discourteous of you, my lord, if you lay rude hands upon my person to prevent my departure. Which action I should militate against strenuously; that I warn you."

Falk grimaced bitterly.

"You give me little choice but to comply, my lady," he said grimly. "I am aware of the rules concerning heralds; and whilst one might say that you are not in official capacity and hence do not count, I will accept that you place yourself in my hands under belief that the rules pertain unto your person. I pray for your safety and hope you do not regret your rash action in returning to the arms of the devil you have wed."

Annis looked down her nose in a gesture Gyrfalon would have known well; and swept from the tent, leaving Falk much to ponder.

He knelt in prayer for guidance; for if Gyrfalon *had* changed for the Lady Annis' ministrations, he did not know even so if he might find enough within him to forgive his brother.

Meanwhile Annis must find her way back to Caleb in the monotonous mist; getting past the guards to Falk's tent were easier going out than in and she grinned to herself thinking that she should let him know that they were less vigilant than they might have been. She hoped she had struck the right direction; and was glad to see the shape of the blackthorn that she had remarked as a landmark looming softly through the mist. She whistled softly, and Caleb replied; and Annis heaved a sigh of relief.

Gyrfalon was striding up and down when Annis returned, the revels having mostly ceased and Gyrfalon having sought his own chamber and his wife; to find only the letter she had left.

"Annis!"

It was a cry of relief and near a groan of pain as he swept her into his arms; then immediately pushed her away and, grabbing her shoulders, shook her wrathfully.

"What was I supposed to do when I found you gone? How dare you worry me like that?" he cried in anguish "I feared you might not be able to return!"

Annis smiled up at him and reached out a tiny hand to touch his face, utterly unperturbed by his shaking of her.

"Dearest, I *had* to go and talk to your idiot brother," she said calmly. "You must surely see that – for as well as you to worry about, I have our babe. And he has promised at least that he will not fight any offspring of ours."

Gyrfalon frowned.

"A concession I suppose," he grunted "But

such a risk to take!"

Annis made a rude noise.

"I took Caleb. He's your best fensman and a staunch defender. I knew I had naught to fear from Falk himself; he being mostly harmless so long as you talk fast about honour and duty; and I took care to be seen by none other."

"I suppose it serves no purpose to shout at you, my lady," Gyrfalon growled at her "For you go your own way regardless."

"Is it not that independence of spirit that attracted you to me?" she asked, simply.

"Do not throw mine own folly in my face, wench!" he roared; but she knew he was now but playacting his rage and peeped demurely at him from under her lashes.

"Doth my lord wish then to chastise me for my disobedience?" she asked, her dimple popping in and out.

"Assuredly!" he bellowed; and swept her up into his arms. Annis settled an arm about his neck and sighed contentedly. He gave a faintly malicious grin.

"Truly, my lady, it were as well that you did not prefer Falk to me; for I doubt if anyone but I could school you, that you be not in the least douce, nor are you tractable in the slightest!"

"Infamous," she retorted, sticking her tongue out at him. "And moreover the pot doth call the kettle black!"

He laughed and bore her away to their deep, warm bed, willing for her to show him again the depth of her love and desire. And as he slept at last, Annis gently stroked his hair and wept for the foolishness of the sire that had scarred her lover's soul more deeply than ever the girl Alys had added to the scarring of his face.

Meanwhile Falk had another visitor.

"Excuse my, my Lord, this blind woman asked for you" said Sir Lyall, who was escorting The Woman.

"Thank you Lyall" said Falk "She is known to me." The Sibyl was an old friend, versed in the ancient magic of prophecy, for Falk did not reject magic as unchristian.

When Lyall had left, the Sibyl asked,

"Is Gyrfalon dead, Lord Falk? I am unable to feel his hatred for you any longer."

Falk stared.

"No, he lives still; it is his castle that I besiege here; and I was alerted to his presence for he seized a hostage, a young girl. Whom I find incomprehensible," he shook his head, "for she cleaves to him and has willingly wed him! Her father is at best a boor and at worst a murderer; and he had arranged for her a marriage to a man I despise utterly. Even more – aye, Gyrfalon was right on that – even more than Gyrfalon himself."

"Is this a man named Marfey?" asked the seeress.

Falk nodded.

"You have seen something of him?" he asked.

"I have" she replied "And that is why I have come to warn you. This Marfey sends an assassin to try to kill you; one who bears a poisoned blade. You must take care, Lord Falk."

"Thank you; I shall do so," said Falk grimly. "And a rare occurrence to have one that hates me more than Gyrfalon does! Sibyl, is it possible that Gyrfalon could change?"

She frowned.

"I would need to look deep into a carefully prepared bowl of pure water to find that out, my lord; I can only tell you what I feel from having attuned myself to you for your protection, that I feel no hate for you from him. It seems to me that something has happened that has dispelled it."

"Well, it may be so; but I dare say it be only temporary," said Falk cynically. "That poor girl! She is completely in his power; he treats her with indulgence because she resembles Alys, but the moment she does something too like or too unalike Alys I have no doubt but that he will rage against her and all will be back to normal. Marfey, however, I can do something about; and I can alert the church troops that guard me that he sends an assassin."

Falk hoped the assassin was not so clever at avoiding his troops as Annis had been!

He had not asked how she had got into his tent unobserved; and that unnerved him, that she had been able so to do. Still, perchance he should just tell the knights to be doubly vigilant; and be on his guard himself too. This was a nuisance, to have the pervert ready to strike first while he was tied up with Gyrfalon; and he contemplated leaving the siege for a few days with some picked troops to deal with Marfey.

He would wait the day round to be sure that Gyrfalon had not punished Annis cruelly for creeping out to see him unbeknownst to her husband; for Falk was half inclined to think that Gyrfalon would equate such an act with Alys's meetings with him, Falk, while Gyrfalon was away at the wars. And he awaited with trepidation what might thus befall to the fragile looking girl.

She said that Gyrfalon taught her swordplay?

Ridiculous! She was too frail to hold a sword; it was surely his way of humiliating her and causing her pain and exhaustion! Falk knew well the way Gyrfalon trained; having been himself on the receiving end. It was inconceivable that so delicate a girl could match Gyrfalon's stringent standards! The poor girl must have been truly starved of affection and attention before, in her father's castle, that she take such as being a better degree of attention as might be interpreted as affection!

Falk slept uneasily with much on his mind.

Gyrfalon and Annis slept deeply and peacefully in each other's arms; and if Annis worried about how she might bring her husband and his brother together, at least she no longer worried about their unborn child.

She had every faith that she could work on Falk, given a chance to do so, until he capitulated and realised that he and Gyrfalon should return to an old love such as brothers should share.

And she thought scorn on Alys for a coward that would not let Gyrfalon know that she had feelings for his brother and who was so devious as to get an upright type like Falk to agree to a marriage before letting the older brother know how things stood!

The last determined revellers also slept the sleep of the just – and in the case of some, the sleep of the intoxicated – while those without shivered and dozed the doze of the cold, wet and miserable.

Chapter 14

Annis rose next morning searching for a nettle and St John's wort salve to ease the itching from insect bites she had sustained travelling through the marsh.

"Wretched mosquitoes ought to have died off in the cold," she grumbled, as she slapped the cooling salve unto her swollen wrists "It must be sheltered down there that enough survive the frosts to still be biting."

"Aren't they your God's creatures with a right to life?" Teased Gyrfalon. She grunted.

"All things have their season. Most insects die in the winter. It's nature; and nature is a part of God's law," she said, a trifle waspishly. Unlike her usual sunny self, Annis felt bad tempered; her head ached and everything seemed too much trouble.

Gyrfalon remarked on his wife's lethargy at their customary sword practice; where she did little to defend herself even.

"You are not concentrating," he chided gently. Annis sat down on the edge of the horse trough and her midnight eyes filled with tears.

"I *can't*," she said, bewildered. Gyrfalon looked at her sharply. Her eyes were bright with tears – and more; and there was a hectic flush to her normally pale cheeks. He laid a hand on her forehead. Its heat was a shock.

"You have the fever from that fool trip through the marsh," he said harshly. "You should be in bed."

Annis raised her face wearily to him.

"I'm not sure I can even get there," she said dully "My legs hurt so and I don't think they'll hold me."

Gyrfalon picked her up tenderly. Indeed she seemed to have worsened in the last few minutes; and by the time he had carried her to their bed and undressed her she was scarcely conscious. Fragmentary, disjointed phrases came to her lips, including an oft repeated concern that a herb Gyrfalon had no knowledge of should not be used to ease the fever as it was an abortifacient. Gyrfalon gazed down at her helplessly. He knew not what herbs to use, not how to prepare them; for Annis always made fresh doses for the men who had a touch of the ague. And the man Kai who helped her out had not learned enough; and was like enough to panic without the gentle guidance of his mentor.

Annis tossed fretfully and Gyrfalon clenched his fists in frustration. He could see that she was really very ill – maybe ill enough to die. And he did not know what to do.

There was a tug on his cloak. He swung round to the scared face of Lukat.

"Oh my lord, can I help?" said the child.

Gyrfalon was about to deny curtly when he recalled something else Annis recommended for the fevered.

"Yes lad; shalt draw cold water and bathe her face with it to take out the heat in her head," he told the child "I think that be what is correct."

"Oh yes my lord, that I can!" said the child, joyful to be able to help. "She will get better, won't she, lord?"

Gyrfalon looked at him seriously.

"I don't know, boy," he said gruffly, "but if there be anything on earth I may do to make her well, I will do it."

It was hesitantly that Gyrfalon entered the castle chapel, much surprising Father Michael, who was engaged in trimming candles to make them last as economically as possible with a good steady flame. The warlord spoke first.

"I need to speak with your Principal," he said, peremptorily, "but I'm not sure how to set about it. Annis is ill."

The little priest was seized by a variety of emotions, primarily shock – at the surprise that Gyrfalon should wish to pray to God and at this sudden illness of the gentle yet iron willed young girl who had wrought so many changes. He crossed himself over the fear for her; and said,

"It's quite simple, my lord. If you kneel before the altar and just say – or even think – what you want to say to Him, God will hear you; and he will hear all you want to say even an you cannot formulate it in words," he added kindly.

Gyrfalon nodded; and strode on. Kneeling went against the grain, but he feared so for Annis, too for the loss of the happiness he had just found; knew that he could not bear to lose her.

Long he knelt, trying to bring some coherence to his thoughts; then rose in one fluid movement and strode out, a muttered word of thanks to Father Michael as he went.

That he managed such a courtesy in his distress made Michael smile in pleasure at the warlord's increased courtesy to his underlings of late.

Annis would be sadly missed an she did not survive.

Michael also knelt and prayed, for his lady and for her lord.

Gyrfalon knew what he had to do; it had come to him as he knelt, and whether it was because of a divine suggestion or whether it was because his thoughts calmed in the quiet chapel Gyrfalon did not know; and he was not prepared to speculate.

He strode to the battlements and jumped up on them, contemptuous of the danger, scornfully knocking aside an almost spent arrow fired by and opportunistic archer.

"*FALK!*" he bellowed.

Falk was quick to respond; fearing that a flood of vituperation would be the herald that Lady Annis lay dead from Gyrfalon's wrath over her visit to him.

"What do you want?" demanded Falk suspiciously "Where is the Lady Annis? Did you lose your temper with her, damn you?"

Gyrfalon gave him a pitying look.

"My worthy, but tedious brother. How well my Annis described you thus. I do not intend to bandy words with you like this before all the world. I want to talk to you, my brother – alone. Here in the castle."

"You must think me stupid if you think I would come within and trust any guarantees of safety that you give," said Falk in scorn.

Gyrfalon sighed wearily.

"No Falk; stupid is one thing I have never thought you. I am….asking ….. you to come into the castle. It is…. A family matter. I can send out my page, the boy Lukat, as a hostage if you will; into the care of Sir Lyall," he added. "If Sir Lyall can manage him."

Falk was more puzzled than ever before.

This was not the manner – save the last sharp remark – that he expected of Gyrfalon. There was something almost akin to defeat about his brother; and his tone was diplomatic, almost unwillingly so, the reluctance seeming to argue against it being some trick.

Then something struck Falk.

Gyrfalon had forgotten to put on the helm he rarely wore within the castle to address him; and Falk blinked in amazement as he realised that he was seeing his brother's face whole and un-maimed! He could not contain an ejaculation of surprise.

"Gyrfalon – your face!"

The warlord's hand went to the side of his face. He pulled a wry grimace.

"Ah. Yes. It seems I forgot to don mine helmet," he said dryly. "Well, no matter that you know; I care not. Will you come?"

Falk pursed his lips. There were mutters around him at Gyrfalon's colossal cheek in so asking, hostage or no; for they had no doubt that the warlord would care little of any hostage. But Falk came to a decision.

"I require no hostage in exchange; open the sally-port. I come."

Gyrfalon nodded briefly and sprang from the wall lightly; and as Falk walked towards the castle the smaller drawbridge dropped and the little gate in the great iron bound main gate opened.

Gyrfalon greeted Falk tersely.

"Annis is ill," he said without preamble.

"Ill?" it was almost an accusation, as though Falk thought 'ill' to be a euphemism for harm inflicted; as indeed the younger man was half inclined to wonder. Gyrfalon ignored the imputation.

"Marsh fever," he explained laconically. "Through too well developed a sense of responsibility that she must needs visit you … she is feared in her delirium that one of the herbs she uses commonly is also an abortifacient; that matter not on my men or yours since none of them need fear such effects. But in any case, I do not know enough to medic her," he stopped and caught Falk's gaze with two good but anguished eyes. "I need your help," he said simply.

"And you think that I will give it?"

"To whom does a man in desperation turn if not to his brother? Besides, it is not for me, it is for her. She is the reason, or at least she is the excuse, for your presence here, that without her you had not been. What do you want me to do? Beg? I can do that if I have to. What is pride next to her life?"

Falk stared.

"You have changed, brother," he said slowly. Gyrfalon shook his head.

"No, not substantially. It is merely that I

have put aside much of mine anger and taken up the concept that life be something to be enjoyed, not endured. Freedom from pain has a marvellous effect on a man's capacity for good humour," he gave a brief, harsh, mirthless laugh.

"I can scarcely believe it," marvelled Falk, staring at his brother's face. "I take it that the Lady Annis has wrought this miracle with her healing arts; yet I understood it were incurable."

"Not solely her healing arts," Gyrfalon's voice was low, intense. "The wound was cursed. It was her love that set me free of the last of the pain, brother, and gave me back mine eye; and perchance her prayers. She has a remarkably good communication with the Almighty. I ... do not. That is why I ask you – beg you – to take her to the nuns. They understand herb lore. And they too must surely be able to invoke your God with prayers that have more effect than mine."

Falk stared, open mouthed, momentarily lost for words. Then he said,

"Let me see her".

Gyrfalon nodded; and presently Falk gazed down on the restless, delirious little lady. The assiduous Lukat, who was refusing to cede his place to a hovering Elissa, pulled a face at him and Gyrfalon absently tweaked his ear in admonition.

"Gyrfalon – Gyrfalon!" Annis called; and he was at her side, holding her hand, smoothing the pale hair from her hot brow.

"I am here," he said softly.

Her hot little hand clung to him, aware of his presence vaguely through the fever dreams.

"Don't go away," she begged.

"Not for a little while" he promised "But I must see to our people; you must not fret. And I must send *you* away to be healed."

There was a storm of crying at this; and he shushed her gently.

"You will go with Falk; he will take care of you." he assured her. She pulled a face.

"Don't want to go with Falk," she sounded childishly petulant. "Falk doesn't like you. He's silly."

"It's not important whether he likes me or not," Gyrfalon said; but the monetary lucidity had gone, and she started tossing again.

Lukat pulled on his cloak.

"Do you *trust* this Falk fellow?" He asked in a loud whisper.

Gyrfalon knelt and took his shoulders.

"Falk and I have quarrelled over something a long time ago," he said, "that, both feeling wronged, we have been unable to agree about because neither of us wants to say sorry for something we not think our own fault; for we cannot talk about whose fault it might be without fighting. But he is a man of honour and I trust him utterly to care for Lady Annis as carefully as if she were his own sister, not just his sister-in-law. As I would trust him to care for you if anything were to happen to me; that he is one you might always go to, my boy, even though I tease you that I make you his page as punishment. That were for the cold and wet outside."

Lukat considered.

"When Lady Annis is better, I will med'y'ate between you until you've found out whose fault it really was. Granpa says, most things are six of one and half a dozen of the other in the village."

Gyrfalon pulled a wry face at Falk.

"Much wisdom from the mouth of a child," he said dryly. "His grandfather is my reeve and reckoned wise at settling disputes."

There was a tap at the door.

"Come" called Gyrfalon with some impatience. Father Michael entered hesitantly.

"Lord Gyrfalon, I thought to say a Mass for the recovery of the Lady Annis," he said. Gyrfalon nodded.

"I will attend presently. She will be going to the Abbey for healing. Perchance you would care to add prayers for a safe journey?"

Father Michael nodded. Falk said quietly,

"I have not said I would take her".

Gyrfalon's eyes blazed.

"Then if you will not, I will, and be damned to you. And if your damned troops kill me and hence her, it will be on your head and I hope you will be able to live with yourself!"

"Coward," said Lukat. "Bet the quarrel was all your fault an' you too cowardly to say sorry."

"My Lord Falk!" said Father Michael, shocked.

"Poltroon," said Elissa. "So much for your fancy words about how the Lady Annis was all your care; that prove a lie then I see. I'll ride out with you my lord. And so would any of us make sally and die holding up the attackers that you get her to safety."

Falk stared.

He had always found the loyalty to his brother was such that feared to cross him; but the tone of this woman was such that was assured of the troops' genuine loyalty, even love, for Gyrfalon! And the boy – that he should be so partisan towards Gyrfalon was astounding!

"I had not," said Falk, "said that I would not take her; I merely resented the assumption that I would."

"It is not a time in which I can think in courtesy and save your tender feelings, my brother," snapped Gyrfalon *"Will* you take her?"

"Yes; I will. And first I would attend this Mass if I may."

Gyrfalon shrugged.

"Certainly. It will make a pleasant change for you, after all, you only have Bishops with you who know only how to pray to the god of Wealth and his angels Bribery, Corruption and Self-Righteousness."

Falk ignored the insult; it was, after all, too much of a wonder to find his brother ready to attend Mass to quibble over what he feared were at lest half-accurate jibes.

Father Michael's service was simple and moving; and Falk, surprised enough at the number of rough soldiers of the sort that looked as though they would torture their mothers to death, laughing, that attended, was even more surprised at the number openly and unashamedly crying over their little lady's sickness. A big simple-looking man approached Gyrfalon after the mass, twisting his hands together in an agony of distress.

"Lord, were it my fault?" he asked.

Gyrfalon laid a hand on the big man's shoulder.

"Nay, Caleb, 'twas none of your doing. You kept her safe from other dangers. She insisted on going and gave you your orders;

and can any of us deny her anything when she's a mind to it, hmm? Have not my harshest words and threats to her – until I learned to give in gracefully – been ignored when she's a mind to it? You cannot deny your Lady when she orders you. You have done no wrong. Do not worry; my brother will take her to the nuns; they will care for her."

The big man gave him a shy half smile and a nod; and left reassured; and Gyrfalon strode away so that the tears held back through the Mass could flow unchecked in private.

"I never thought to see you weep," Falk touched his brother's arm.

"It does not do to let the men see, to let them know how much I fear for her; if I show an optimistic face they will worry less," said Gyrfalon. "She would not want me to let them down."

Falk marvelled.

"I wish to go to make arrangements to be away for a few days," he said, "and reassure my people that I am not dead and dismembered. I will return for the Lady Annis. Though I would wish not to expose her to the curious gaze of all."

Gyrfalon turned to face his brother.

"Caleb shall bring her by water to your tent, the way she came last night," he said. "He and I will prove sufficient. Then you can ride with her under darkness. And take my helm; I have had the eye-covering I added removed, the helm is elven and magical, it is the part of the legacy our father forgot."

"I did not know it was elven, but the workmanship ...."

"It gives the power of Eyes of the Hawk on command; which was useless to me, for I could but feel it pulling at the useless eye, it was agony." He gave a wry smile. "Who knows but that the elven magic might have had some positive effect on the curse; but it gave me too much pain to think of that. However, it also warns you of sneak attacks from behind, which has saved my life more than once, and may save yours."

Falk nodded.

"I thank you, and I will be glad if Caleb will bring it. But come not yourself," he advised. "And advise Caleb that I am also expecting an assassin sent by Marfey with poisoned blade lest he run into him. But it were not well if you too caught the fever, for it would bode ill for your people without your direction to them."

"Are you not supposed to wish for such?" asked Gyrfalon ironically. Falk shrugged.

"Perchance I should; but it is mine advice anyway as brother to brother; for what it is worth."

Automatically, Gyrfalon reached out a hand to put on his brother's shoulder.

"And, my brother, you must see that it is not to scorn you – for I do not – that I must refuse your advice," he said. "But 'tis for the love of Annis; she is confused and delirious; my presence may calm her and prevent accident or discovery in the marsh."

Falk nodded unwillingly.

"Then I pray you take care," he said.

It was Gyrfalon's sharp eyes and warrior senses that realised that a figure lurked at Falk's tent when he arrived there with Annis in his arms; Falk having sent his guard on patrol for the purpose.

The warlord passed his wife swiftly to Caleb and pounced in almost one and the same movement as the figure froze in immobility in the shadows. Vice-like hands immobilised the intruder's arms and squeezed hard to make the figure cry out and drop the blade it carried.

Gyrfalon held the figure by its upper arms and marched it into Falk's tent.

"Knife's round the back, brother," he said laconically. "I think this is your assassin; and I thought you might like him alive. Not necessarily undamaged; but alive. I believe I broke a bone or two in his hand."

Annis was sobbing again and Gyrfalon thrust the assassin face down on the floor to leave him to Falk as he relieved Caleb of the slight figure of Annis to comfort her.

Falk grabbed the intruder and searched him ruthlessly, Gyrfalon signing to Caleb to lend aid holding the fellow; and soon the assassin was trussed up securely. Falk retrieved the knife from without.

"Something dark and sticky on the blade," he said grimly.

"Just mud where it was dropped," cried the assassin. "I was just passing and this big ape of yours jumped me! Why couldn't he mind his own business?"

Falk wavered.

Gyrfalon took the knife from his brother and smiled gently at the intruder.

"Then that being so, you won't mind the faintest of scratches on your body with this self same knife, will you?" he said, ripping open the fellow's tunic.

"Oh please, no!" screeched the assassin.

"Why not? If it is but mud, 'twill do you no harm," said Gyrfalon. "If it be poison on the other hand … Hsssh, Annis, do not interrupt, I am busy menacing this fellow … if it is poison then you should worry. For you would only have one brief chance to wound Falk; he cannot be killed in normal combat they say, for there is only one in the land that is a match to him …. One wound. One chance. It must be virulent."

"I pray you! It is death in seconds!" babbled the man "And a second dose to kill the Warlord Gyrfalon, who is that man of whom you speak that is Lord Falk's match … be merciful, my lord, I am but a hireling!"

"Well, it is not for me to say," said Gyrfalon "You are my brother's prisoner; though an he wish, since you have my death too in your orders, he may hand you over to me when he has finished with you; if he not hang you outright. Falk?"

Falk frowned.

The prisoner, catching on that only one man could call Falk 'brother' and suggested having him handed over, passed out.

"Funny. I seem to have that effect on some people" murmured Gyrfalon. "Do you want me to take him away and hold him? I will hand him back to you – no further damaged but possible well frightened – when you return."

Falk nodded.

"If you will, brother; I would question him further. I trust your word not to torture him."

Gyrfalon chuckled.

"I do *not* promise not to threaten to. I'm not in a good mood right now; I could use some light amusement to take my mind off Annis' illness."

Falk looked at him; then shrugged.

"I suppose it be inevitable," he said.

"Come, Lady Annis; we must away."

Annis clung to Gyrfalon and tried not to let him hand her up to Falk when he had mounted; but her husband was inexorable.

"I do not order you much, Annis," he said, "but this is an order. Go with Falk; and get well."

She let go of him, sobbing; and Gyrfalon dropped a quick light kiss on her brow; and watched Falk out of sight as he rode with his precious bundle.

Annis never had any recollection of that wild ride through the night, close under Falk's cloak, protected from the chill, miserable rain; nor did she remember arriving at the Abbey where Falk peremptorily informed the sisters that as their patient was with child he feared their choice of herbs might be curtailed. She was aware but vaguely of cool sheets and cool hands and fought the bitter draught she was given; and was reassured by a matter-of-fact voice and practical tone that told her it held no tansy; and Annis swallowed obediently.

Falk spoke to the Abbess.

"It is fantastic to contemplate," he said, "but that girl might just be the saving of the soul of Gyrfalon – and through it a reduction in the danger to ordinary folks unlucky enough to cross his path" and he explained the situation quickly.

Mother Superior frowned.

"This Peter Haldane that is the girl's father – we know of him. He is no true Christian. Let me find you something to read."

She rummaged in a chest and handed Falk a parchment written in a firm young hand; a hand that he recognised in greater maturity as the one that had written the list of herbs. There was less certainty to the formation of this younger letter; but it was equally forceful. It ran.

"*Please to give this man the remainder of the monies I have promised him. You will find the sum in Sister Agatha's marsupium where I have placed it. You will find that she have reached an age of confusion and will be happier among her own sisters. Signed this day, the last of May, Annis Haldane.*" The date was some eight years previously; Annis would have been just eight years old.

Falk frowned puzzlement and the Mother Superior explained.

"Sister Agatha was tutor to the child, Annis Haldane. At some point she began to slip into senility. The man who brought us back to us here, an itinerant story teller, told me privily that Peter Haldane had noticed the old woman's confusion and had declared that he would not feed an idiot – and ordered her out of the castle that she return to the Abbey. Alone, mark you, regardless of her age and infirmity. The child Annis arranged at least that she have an escort who also had an ass that he was willing to let Sister Agatha ride."

Falk exclaimed over this.

"Did he not expect to be found out and censured?"

Mother Superior snorted.

"None knew of her confused state. Perchance he thought some other traveller would take pity on her; or perchance – and unchristian as it is of me, I believe this more – he did not even care if she went to her death. But he is a wicked man. In her lucid moments Agatha rambles about her time with the child sometimes, and his cruelty to her, and to the girl's mother; and since hearing of the death of Lady Emblem I have had good reason to suppose the man may have caused her death."

"I have heard that too – and from Annis herself who witnessed him throwing her mother down the stairs," said Falk. "It is not difficult to see that with such a father and with the repellent beast he wished her to marry, even Gyrfalon must have seemed an improvement. He has never, for all his faults, played the hypocrite. But it seems that there is real love there."

She sniffed.

"Well, we shall see," she said dryly "But I

remember *you* cautioning us not to be too trusting; and I hope this is not merely a desire to believe the best since he *is* your brother."

Falk gave a rueful laugh.

"Between Annis ticking me off for being prejudiced against her husband and you telling me I trust him too much I am not sure what to think," he said. "But I have never seen my brother so … so ready to ask for aid. For he is normally self sufficient; and ever was even when we were close. I think I believe him, and I know I hope."

Chapter 15

Gyrfalon cleaned all the poison off the assassin's blade and replaced it with artistically painted grease and dirt to look similar. He had promised Falk that no harm should come to their prisoner after all.

He proceeded to truss the fellow up with an ingenious system of pulleys so that if the man moved too much the knife would descend and pierce his bared chest.

It was one way of keeping him still with relatively little need to watch him.

Gyrfalon then proceeded to explain that he was in a bad mood and that he was contemplating all the ways that might constitute not harming him very much before Falk had him back. He suggested partial flaying, emasculation, and cutting off toes one at a time to start with and left the swooning prisoner contemplating such barbarities.

"You should menace him with Lukat," growled Elissa who had suffered the boy's demands that she reassure him that Lady Annis would be all right "That child is torture unmitigated."

Gyrfalon laughed and ruffled Lukat's hair.

"We'll make a warlord of him yet, then," he said.

Falk returned the next day and Gyrfalon relieved himself of his prisoner via the sally-port.

The assassin was ready to speak if only Lord Falk promised he not be given back to Lord Gyrfalon who was a veritable monster as everyone said, and please would they only hang him and not make him swallow germinating seeds so an appletree grew right out of his belly like that monstrous child suggested.

Lukat had put in a few of his own suggestions to keep the assassin unhappy once he found out that he had intended killing Gyrfalon too.

Falk did not bother to point out that the stomach acids were likely to kill any germinating seeds and wondered where Lukat got his ideas from; then recalled that a child with an infirmity might well have contemplated ways of punishing bullies that had a greater level of imagination for being relatively immobile, with time to sit and think.

Long days Annis lay unconscious in the meantime, long past the resolving of the matter of the assassin; and the nuns treated her and prayed. Then one night that had become wilder and wilder brought a peremptory knock at the Abbey door.

A sister unbarred the door; any traveller on

such a night would doubtless need succour.

Without was a black garbed figure, snow sprinkles and with a rough bandage about one arm.

"*Gyrfalon!*" the sister who answered the door took an involuntary step of terror away from the warlord.

"I took liberties with your stable and your oats for the comfort of mine horse. You have no quarrel with a dumb beast at least," he said tersely. "I come for news of my wife. I will understand if you not let me in to see her. But tell me how she is."

Little Sister Barbara looked up into the tortured eyes – two, whole eyes as Lord Falk had said! And then she stepped aside.

"Come in Lord Gyrfalon," she said, her voice steadier "We do not turn away genuine travellers. And before we go any further," she added firmly, "let me see that arm."

Never was Sister Barbara so surprised in her life.

The warlord gave a wry chuckle.

"Girl, you sound just like Annis," he said appreciatively. He did not add, though he thought it, that Annis would never have displayed her fear to an enemy at first; the only time he had seen Annis recoil was before Marfey, and that was revulsion more than fear he thought.

The nun showed, at least, no disposition to

fear consequences; and that told some news at least about Annis. But still he kept his own agenda. He said,

"You may look at mine arm when I have seen my wife. It has kept this past three hours and will keep another quarter."

His expression was grim and uncompromising; and Sister Barbara acquiesced. Gyrfalon could hear in his own head Annis' firm tone telling him that if it had already waited three hours the sooner she saw it the better; but Annis was made of sterner stuff than the little sister who led him obediently to Annis' chamber.

The girl looked even tinier than usual in the middle of a big infirmary bed. She no longer tossed but she muttered in the midst of strange dreams.

"She is approaching the crisis," whispered Sister Barbara as Gyrfalon knelt beside the bed, cradling one tiny hand in his. "When it comes, the fever will break – one way or the other."

He looked up sharply.

"You mean she still might die, even yet, even with herb lore and care?"

Anguish betrayed his voice, and he cleared his throat irritably. Scared, Sister Barbara nodded and swallowed several times.

"Can she hear me?" asked Gyrfalon.

Barbara nodded.

"She seems to hear well enough; Sister Pauline makes her mind, and tells her to take her medicine. I'm supposed to wake Pauline when she comes to the crisis so she can take over and do all she might."

"Well if this Pauline can make her mind, she must be the first person ever to do so," said Gyrfalon dryly, after nodding acknowledgement. He addressed Annis.

"Annis; hear me. Now you listen to me, you little virago, it's going to get tough soon. But you're no quitter, are you? You'll fight, do you hear? You come back to me, my little vixen, or….." he tailed off and added softly, more to himself than to Annis. "Or I do not know what I will do. What would be the good of following you if they will not let me into your Heaven?"

Soft-hearted Barbara's heart was wrung; but stern Pauline's voice on the threshold of the chamber said uncompromisingly,

"So he's here, is he?"

Gyrfalon looked round.

"Should I be flattered to be identified so easily merely by a pronoun?" He asked sardonically. "Yes, I am here. I was intending to leave as soon as I had submitted," he bowed ironically to Sister Barbara, "to the sister's insistent ministrations. But if Annis is approaching a crisis….. well then I would ask to stay."

"There is nothing you can do" Sister Pauline informed him crisply.

"Wrong, sister; I can call her" he said coldly "She is in the habit – when it do not inconvenience her – of mostly falling in with my wishes. It might help."

Pauline snorted.

"Agatha always says what a nice little thing she be and how full of common sense. She must have taken leave of her senses to cleave to you."

Gyrfalon's eyes flashed and he compressed his lips.

"'Tis yet so her choice made freely," he made himself speak quietly, "and as such, sister, none of your business."

Sister Barbara reflected that only a wicked warlord would dare to speak to the formidable Sister Pauline like that! She asked timidly,

"Should I see to Lord Gyrfalon's arm now, Sister Pauline?"

Pauline glanced at the rough bandage.

"You may as well," she said indifferently. "We are a house of healing after all. It would be embarrassing for even a sinner to bleed to death within our walls."

"Tell me, sister," asked Gyrfalon, curiously, "were you trained by Sister Agatha of whom I have heard Annis speak?"

"I was indeed," said Pauline "What of it?"

"That explains a lot," he said nodding. "Well, I have seen Annis," he addressed Barbara as Pauline blinked puzzlement over his query about Agatha – his first minor victory over her – and gave a brief grim smile to the younger nun "And you wished to poke at mine arm."

Barbara flushed.

"If it is wounded," she said faintly.

"I know, comfrey, bugle, woundwort, calendula, St John's wort and I forget the rest" he untied the kerchief that had served as a bandage. "And first you will have to dig out the arrowhead. I snapped it for convenience riding; it would not push right through, I tried. The wretched thing is lodged on the bone. It is a standard arrow, not barbed else I had bled more and might not be sitting up now to have conversation. Annis would have it out in a painful trice; but she is very good."

Barbara quailed; and Pauline stepped forward, examining the wound.

"You know the salves, girl," she snapped to the younger nun. "As he said; and a draught of willow bark to avoid fever from it. That it be a painkiller too I care less about. Also bring me a sharp knife and boiling water to cleanse it; Thyme oil to clean the wound; clean linen; and my needle and gut to sew it," she looked hard at Gyrfalon "This will hurt" she said.

He laughed grimly.

"How very kind of you, sister, to keep most of the satisfaction you must be feeling out of your voice," he mocked gently. "Pain I know about; I do not fear it. Delirium from fever because it becomes infected, that I do fear."

"Hmmph," Pauline snorted; and armed with a sterile knife began the gruesome job of cutting out the arrowhead. He grunted once as she pulled it free and dropped it in the bowl held by a rather pale Sister Barbara.

"Cheer up, child" he gasped at the young nun "'Twas not you that had the arrow in you!"

"Do *not* faint now, Barbara," chided Pauline "It is almost over; this will sting."

Gyrfalon jumped involuntarily and swore as Pauline flooded the wound with thyme oil.

"Why, Lord Gyrfalon, you said you feared infection more than you feared pain," she said sweetly.

"Indeed I did," he forced command of his voice, "and I thank you and commend your skill in surgery; I have not seen Annis perform the same more deftly," he added. "Your bedside manner is less to be desired."

She laughed dryly.

"You are a less exacting patient than I expected; and I commend you for scatological rather than blasphemous utterances. And now I must display my skill as a seamstress," she told him. He nodded; and endured. After, she wrapped the wound again in the clean linen Barbara had brought.

"The stitches must come out in a few days else they will fester," she told him. He nodded.

"If I am not able to come here I can do that for myself," he said "Now I must check my horse ere sitting with Annis. Have you any idea how long it will be to the crisis?"

Pauline considered.

"There is a calm period that will build rapidly to a storm. Already her muttering increases; it will only be a few hours."

He nodded.

"I will then take rest in your refectory for an hour after I have seen to Nightmare," he said. "It were well for me to be fresh for her at the time she needs most to hear my voice," and he strode out, leaving Pauline half seething at his peremptory manner. Yet if he sparred with Annis as she healed his ravaged face with the same – albeit black – humour as he had sparred with her, Pauline could see how the high spirited girl described by Agatha might have been attracted to him. There was that about him that appealed to an intelligent woman often bereft of worthy conversation. Yet his manner had altered since the times when no holy woman was safe from kidnap; and Pauline crossed herself and thanked God for Annis, praying fervently that if the girl died the warlord would not take his grief out on all of them.

When Pauline came to fetch Gyrfalon from the refectory she found it empty; but heard his voice in the chapel. Quickly she stepped over, wondering what he was at.

Gyrfalon was standing before the altar, gazing up at the crucifix. He was speaking.

"You know what I ask. And I know well enough You will not do it for me. But she is an angel, as You know; and our child has had no chance to sin. And so I ask....."

The voice was low, intense, tortured; and Pauline withdrew quickly and quietly, then made a deliberate effort to make a noise in the refectory.

Gyrfalon emerged from the chapel. His warrior's senses had warned him of her presence; but it had been immaterial. Still, he appreciated her tact.

"Is it time?" his eyes, dark and unfathomable locked with the nun's eyes. She nodded. He gathered himself and strode to Annis' chamber.

The young girl's muttering had increased and again she tossed her head back and forth with increasing violence. Sister Barbara was bathing her brow and moistening her lips frequently.

"Speak to her all you like if you will but stay out of my way," Sister Pauline instructed Gyrfalon tartly. He nodded briefly; and strode round to the far side of the bed where he might sit conveniently without impeding the nursing sisters.

Annis was calling Gyrfalon's name; and he took her hot little hand and raised it to his lips.

"I am here, Annis," he reassured her, "and I shall talk to you constantly so that you know it. What to say I am not so sure," he paused, then inspiration struck him. "It is my voice that you recognise that soothes you, my dear one; so what I say does not greatly matter. So I shall tell you some of the scrapes Falk and I got into when we were still friends in those days when girls were strange beings that it would be foolish to quarrel over," he squeezed her hand gently "And if your God is kind I will perhaps be able to tell them again to our child. Our children even, maybe"

And so he talked, until his voice started to hoarsen, speaking of the everyday adventures that two high spirited boys, albeit of such disparate ages, could get into; how often times he had answered back his stepmother when she chid him over his disreputable appearance to give the boy Falk time to neaten up, so that he not be forbidden to play again with his half brother; and even Sister Pauline raised an eyebrow at such a foolish parent.

"Poor little Falk," Gyrfalon sighed, "she would have wrapped him in cotton and imprisoned him in the cradle, methinks, if she could; and because of that early weakness father cosseted the poor brat especially after his mother died, until you could see him just dying to break out in mischief; and when he did, of course it was always my fault. I suppose that were one reason I minded less being sent off to lead the troops in the north for father; that I was not there to blame when he was at that most high spirited age. And yet it was *she* who died of the sickness while our weakly little sprite pulled through, despite sneaking out of bed to go sail his new boat on the pond."

"What became of that boat? It was a beauty."

Falk had entered the room unnoticed by his brother; and Gyrfalon answered automatically.

"Don't you remember? Father burned it after you fell in the pond," and then he started round, "Falk?" he exclaimed.

Falk shrugged.

"I came for news," he explained. "I have a friend who is a seeress, and she told me it were close to a crisis and that I might wish to be at your side."

"I am glad of you," said Gyrfalon softly.

"And here you are, telling Annis of our – or my – misspent youth? I had forgotten that father burned the boat. I suppose I did not want to remember how I resented it at the time. Then he bought me a pony to make amends."

Gyrfalon laughed dryly.

"A placid little beast, overfed and amiable; a veritable cushion to sit on! And when you could sit straight, you thought yourself a great rider and I had to thrash you for trying to mount my first warhorse."

"And needfully; I thoroughly deserved your belt end across my backside!" Falk acquiesced ruefully. "You always had a taste for half wild terrors. Your current one tried to bite me in the stable here."

"He was probably just hungry," said Gyrfalon. "I like an independent spirit; and it thrills me that I can master a horse with such by personality and mutual understanding. My horses are like me and I'd take it as an insult if any called me docile."

"I can believe that; but I doubt that'll ever happen," Falk's tone was dry. Then, "Gyrfalon she is quiet!"

Gyrfalon was on his feet, looking down at his bride, anxiety – terror – in every line of his taut body. But the little breasts rose and fell slowly, evenly; and her eyelids lay still, their dark lashes a smudge across the white cheeks.

"She will live?" His voice was harsh as he queried Sister Pauline.

The nun nodded.

"The fever has broken. You might raise her while I change the pillowslip. It is sodden from sweat."

Tears coursed unbidden – and indeed unnoticed by him – down the warlord's cheeks. Tenderly and easily he lifted the girl in his arms and he cradled her to him.

"You may as well strip all the linen," he suggested gruffly. "She is no burden."

Pauline pursed her lips; then nodded. Annis made a contented noise in her sleep and snuggled in her husband's arms. Falk looked on amazed and delighted.

The last time he had seen such a tender expression on his brother's face was after that incident with the boat when everyone had feared that Falk would die.

When Annis was laid in clean fresh sheets, lavender scented and sweet as was the clean nightgown Gyrfalon had himself put on her, Falk laid a hand on his brother's shoulder.

"I am going to give thanks in the chapel," he said "Will you join me?"

Gyrfalon nodded.

"He is due all my thanks," he said, "as are you. Well, I reassured Annis speaking of telling stories to our child; but I suppose there is a price to pay; there always is," he sighed. "I would have liked to have seen our child grow up."

"What do you mean?" demanded a mystified Falk.

"Well I presume that you will want to hie me back to some church authority in chains; that God will expect a life for a life."

Falk blinked.

"You look upon your prayers for her wellbeing as a kind of bargain?" He asked incredulously.

"I do not expect something for nothing. Though….though I would ask that you give me time with her before you take me to answer for mine actions," said Gyrfalon.

Falk shook his head.

"The God I serve is not vindictive; nor impractical. Now that you have returned to Him, He rejoices. As do I. It is hard to forgive the deaths of our father and of Alys; but I am trying to at least understand as Annis asked me to. And, frankly, you are the best hope for civilisation against the northern barbarians."

Roughly Gyrfalon embraced his brother.

"I have missed our friendship," he said savagely, "and I appreciate what you do. I also appreciate your cynicism about my possible use to the church at repelling invaders; over which I don't doubt you'll talk very fast. You always were very good at talking very fast and getting us out of a thrashing from father. But truly, Falk, is it enough? The Hierarchy want my head on a plate."

Falk shrugged.

"They can go on wanting. If they want *my* services they can leave my brother alone."

"Heh! That should bring them whining to your orders," said Gyrfalon cynically. "You pick up the pieces of everything that scares them. Which is mostly me, but not entirely," he added meditatively.

"Besides, as I shall point out, the scriptures tells us that the Lord takes infinite pains over straying sheep….."

Gyrfalon interrupted.

"Please! Not a sheep. They are ridiculous creatures. If you must have a farmyard analogy, pick a bull. Or a goose. Geese are more intelligent than many give them credit for and are quite vicious and excellent watch animals. We didn't kill the geese at Martinmas that I might have them on the marsh wall in case of sneak attack; and my sentries reported an attack that never materialised because they gave tongue quickly."

"Geese? My captains would have it that you had some unholy beast like a cockatrice up there. Geese! Well that be something to keep that cocky fellow Therry in order with!" he chuckled.

"Heh, and were it not for Annis I'd have gone with received wisdom that it were impregnable. You floated rafts down and moored in the dead angle with scaling ladders in sections I suppose?"

"Yes. She suggested that? Gyrfalon the girl is a prodigy!"

"She – you remark on her resemblance to Alys, but Falk, I swear she has ever reminded me more of you as a youth than of Alys. Her thirst for knowledge; her spirit, her stubborn refusal to give in. How could I not love her, a feminine version of the person I have always loved best in the world?"

Falk put a hand on his brother's arm and strove to get his voice back.

"Well; I am glad. And I notice that she too is cynical about the hierarchy of the church. And on that, I am inclined to believe that as you have said often enough there is too much corruption at a higher level; as with that cardinal that shares his predilections with Marfey. Together we might perchance fight that corruption! I love the church and would see her purified and purged of its more venal members. And I shall of course be withdrawing mine army from your gates as soon as possible."

Gyrfalon's face brightened.

"In time for the spring planting? That will please Reeve Bullard and the peasants. We had calculated to go on short rations a long time yet. Then we might have a true feast at

Christmas!"

Falk smiled and his face lightened.

"You see, my brother? Your first thought is for your peasants!"

"I have ever cared for my dependants," Gyrfalon said stiffly, "if less for hirelings."

Falk touched him on the arm.

"Aye," he said softly.

Amicably they went on to the chapel; and glad was Gyrfalon to give thanks. For the first time in many years his heart filled with joy, not dread, in the sanctified atmosphere and he felt filled with energy to rebuild the village and add to the fortifications against the northern barbarians. He told Falk,

"I am looking forward to showing Annis how to construct watch posts utilising the minimum numbers of men without compromising either their safety of that or the main keep for posting men outside."

Falk raised an eyebrow.

"Well, you said she has a thirst for knowledge; it is extraordinary but then she's not a very ordinary sort of girl."

"Remember that with her steward's help she held her father's castle when he was on crusade; she is very able. For a long while I thought it were a shame she was not born a boy. Had she been a boy, not a girl, methinks I should have adopted her as my son."

Falk laughed.

"I wager you be happier that she be a girl now, that you had opportunity to wed her; that brings you wife and son both."

"Aye; I am. Though I was considering adopting her even so when she came up with the idea of marrying me."

"It was her idea?" Falk was taken aback.

Gyrfalon grinned.

"She bullied me firmly from the moment I took her hostage; and had me wrapped firmly round her delicate little finger quicker than I can tell it," he smiled gently "She is as gentle as a songbird and as hard and tough as steel," he said "And I shall never trammel her into a woman's traditional role. She is, as she specified as a condition she expected from a husband, my partner – in all things."

Falk clapped him on the shoulder; and did not voice aloud his though 'and your salvation'.

Chapter 16

Gyrfalon left Annis sleeping peacefully and rode home in something of a reverie. So deep in thought was he that he was almost caught off guard by the cry,

"Stand and deliver!"

Half off guard he might be; but Gyrfalon was a warrior; a warrior born that was also trained to an incredible level. Indeed his sword was out of its scabbard and starting to swing without even thinking before he registered the not only was the voice youthful, but so was the skinny body of his would be assailant.

What Gyrfalon saw in the pale light of the waning moon was an ill-nourished lad of perhaps twelve summers old with tousled dark blonde hair and dark eyes too big and hungry in a pale face, holding a rusty old sword as though it were some farm implement.

What the boy saw was not the lonely traveller he had hoped for but a fearsome warrior whose eyes blazed into life as the sword came preternaturally fast from its scabbard and swung towards him. With a gasp of fear at the practised ease with which that blade was drawn and swung in one movement the boy fell back, then turned and fled as Gyrfalon, with consummate skill, stopped the blow that would have cut the boy in half before it even touched his hair. The boy glanced over his shoulder at the warrior and promptly tripped over a tree root.

Gyrfalon sheathed his sword and dismounted, striding forward. The boy's breath was sobbing as the warlord dropped to one knee beside him.

"Aren't you a little young for this game?" Gyrfalon asked, his voice half amused "And don't you think you should learn to use a sword as a weapon, not as something for cutting the hay with?"

The boy stared up at him, dully miserable, waiting for the blow to come, either fist or blade. Then his eyed widened, staring behind Gyrfalon.

The warlord half turned, and saw in time before he enacted violence the small human missile that landed on his back.

"Leave my brother alone!" demanded the treble voice before small teeth attempted to fasten into his shoulder.

"Wilt break thy teeth on mine armour, little one, if you continue thus," said Gyrfalon mildly.

Armoured as he was, Gyrfalon had no difficulty dislodging his tiny assailant.

And gasped.

The little girl could almost have been Annis

at a similar age; about the same age as Lukat.

"Oh please, lord, don't hurt my sister!" the boy was scrambling to his feet, tugging at the warlord's cloak.

Gyrfalon held the child at arm's length.

"Why, my good lad, it seems that both of you attempted an attack first!" He said, good humouredly. With Annis on the road to recovery, and Falk reconciled to him, little could destroy the warlord's good mood. "Attacking without provocation at that."

"Bad man, you attacked my brother!" the little girl cried. Gyrfalon shook his head.

"Oh no, my moppet," he said, "your brother drew a blade on me; and had the sense to realise he was outclassed. And fortunate he be that I am a good enough swordsman to pull short a blow that had I carried on acting on instinct instead of realising him a child would have taken his head off. He fell as he did the sensible thing and fled, through doing the unsensible thing of not keeping his mind on what he was doing. I went to him, girl, curious that so young a lad should seek so risky an occupation as being a footpad. A rather inept footpad. It seems that he had you to feed that he be so desperate. Is that it lad?"

The boy answered sullenly,

"That's it, my lord. And I bain't selling her to slavers not no how. Reeve warned us about them looking; and I have to feed her somehow."

"Well you did right to keep away from slavers," agreed Gyrfalon. "I've had dealings with a few myself. I don't believe many of them survived. Is not Peter Haldane prepared to finance his own get though?"

The boy gave a brief, but pungent description of his thoughts on Peter Haldane; in which Gyrfalon gathered that his guess that the man had forced his attentions on their mother around the time he killed his own wife was correct. He said conversationally,

"His legitimate daughter hates him too, you know."

The boy stared.

"How do you know that?" he demanded pugnaciously.

"Because she's my wife."

The boy paled even further.

"Then that means you are ...." he tailed off.

Gyrfalon grinned wolfishly.

"That means I am Gyrfalon," he finished for the lad. "And you and your sister are thus my kin. My wife would not take it kindly if I left you to starve. I presume you are orphans?"

The little girl spoke up.

"Brigands killed Ma and Pa. We were in the woods. J- Joachim looks after me. What do you mean, we're your kin? I never saw you before!"

"You have a big sister whom you have not yet met," Gyrfalon explained "And you will not yet; she is ill and the nuns care for her. I have been to see her. So that makes me your biggest brother; and a sight better equipped to care for you than an untrained stripling. You will both therefore come with me and I will see to your needs."

"But..." Joachim began. Gyrfalon quelled him with a look.

"You may earn your keep," he said sternly. "You are old enough to be a senior page learning to be a squire; and you *will* learn not to disgrace the weapon you hold. You, angel-child," he addressed the little girl, "Will run errands for Annis when she is home; learn sword if it by thy bent, and such arts of herblore as she sees fit to teach thee."

"Her name is Sylvia," muttered Joachim.

"Sylvia? A wood nymph? Almost appropriate," said the warlord dryly. "I will hold her ahead of me if you can ride behind. Try not to fall off my crupper."

The boy Joachim clung to the rear of the saddle casting many darkling looks at the warlord's unresponsive back while Sylvia prattled freely about both of them; until she fell asleep. Gyrfalon listened with half an ear, sorting out the relevant from the rest. He could see why slavers might try to persuade the reeve of their hamlet to sell them two good looking orphans – especially Sylvia – and thought well of the man to have gone to the children to warn them to depart.

Annis might like to make a project of hunting down these slavers, he mused, and it would give her real practice at her fighting arts without being in any real risk.

"Joachim, the slaver does not know it yet, but he is a dead man," Gyrfalon remarked conversationally over his shoulder.

"L- lord?"

"He thought to harm my kin. I do not take that lightly," explained Gyrfalon grimly.

Joachim was left wondering whether being the warlord's kin was good – or bad!

The siege not yet being lifted, Gyrfalon rode upriver and embarked the broad raft where the patient Caleb waited. Nightmare made his usual protesting snort but obeyed the heel that urged him onto the unpredictable and wobbling land that his master used for moving without hooves in so unsettling a fashion. Caleb made ready to cast off; and looking on the children gasped.

"My Lord, have them nuns magicked our lady into a mere babe?" he asked in hushed, superstitious awe.

Gyrfalon smiled and laid a hand on the

shoulder of the simple-minded man in reassurance.

"Nay, Caleb, fear not; 'tis the Lady Annis' little sister I have here – and her ... brother."

"Be she awright now?" Caleb asked. Gyrfalon interpreted – correctly – the 'she' to mean Annis, whom Caleb adored.

"She is on the road to recovery at last," he said. Caleb grinned all over his face.

"Then the Good Lord be praised!" he said.

Gyrfalon nodded, wordlessly, aware of the scrutiny of the big eyed Joachim as they drifted down the river silently towards the river gate in the grey predawn.

The sleeping Sylvia was put to bed in Annis' old tower room; and though her older sibling hid yawns of exhaustion so close to dawn Gyrfalon beckoned him peremptorily to his own chamber. The youth stood in trepidation as Gyrfalon doffed cloak and armour with a sigh of relief, massaging his bandaged arm; then swung round suddenly on the youngster.

"And now, my child, why not tell me your real name?" he demanded.

A gasp, a hand raised to the mouth showed the shaft of insight had gone home; but dark eyes were defiant.

"I do not understand, Lord Gyrfalon."

Gyrfalon frowned.

"The need for the deceit I understand; it were a good protection. You have drilled the child well to use a male name, to call you her brother – did you take the identity of a dead brother, killed with your parents, that she almost forget which you truly be?"

The stripling flushed; and Gyrfalon nodded.

"Yes I thought so. It seemed strange that a boy might be walking with his sister in the woods when the brigands came, not be helping on the holding. And then Sylvia told me that the reeve had worried how slavers were looking always for pretty little girls," he shot a look at the youngster. "Not pretty children. And I would guess you are older than the twelve or so I took you for at first; old enough to be at risk from any licentious type, not just the perverts that like children. Now, do not cry," he added exasperated as tears started suddenly upon the girl's lashes. "You are in no danger of such from me. And nor will I permit it from my men. But I would know the truth if I am to be your guardian."

The girl scrubbed her eyes with the back of her hand in a boyish gesture.

"I'm not normally weepy," she said. "I'm just so tired and we're both so hungry…..I am Jehanne," she admitted, seeing that deception was useless. "It is as you have so cleverly guessed. Besides, boys have better lives."

Gyrfalon grinned.

"Your – let us call you her step sister – would disagree," he said laconically "She tells me that girls have it best because they can learn to fight and ride like a man and yet to choose to wear pretty gowns and embroider fal-lals. Yet a man might not so easily undertake female pastimes."

Jehanne flushed.

"And as a girl what will I be permitted to do?" she asked scornfully "I am no real kin of yours; I am here on sufferance. I will be permitted to sew for and feed your filthy army and I suppose you'll expect me to warm their beds for them too!"

Gyrfalon took her chin, almost brutally; and his eyes glittered angrily.

"Did you not hear me say I would not permit my men to offer you insult?" His tone was dangerously soft. "Clean they may not be, for being under siege conditions; but they are not filthy *nor* are they ill disciplined. And have I not accepted you as my kin – as Annis most assuredly will? And did I not tell you, my girl, that you might serve as my squire and learn feats of arms? I like your spirit in speaking up but before God, I like not your lack of common sense and your failure to listen! If you not listen when acting as squire, wilt get blows for it, that I warn you!"

She held his gaze briefly then dropped her eyes.

"I – I thought that as you had said I should be your squire before you knew it would not count" she muttered.

"Aye; I did not *know*; but I had my suspicions almost from the first. If you have talent 'tis of no moment to me if you be boy or girl. If you have no talent, it were foolish to pursue the craft anyway and so I shall tell you when hast had time to find out."

He released her.

"I am sorry," she said.

"Next time think harder that you not have to be sorry after," he said. "Now get you to your chamber with your sister and sleep out your sleep. Shalt both join me above the salt for the noon meal; for I doubt you'll wake afore then. Wait," he went over to the bowl of fruit he kept in his chamber and tossed her an apple "Eat that afore you sleep to keep thy belly from growling and to prepare it for a proper meal later. Whether you be clad as boy or girl be your choice; some of my wife's clothes are in the chest there, both breeches and gowns that may fit you."

Jehanne ran stumbling from the room, grateful for the apple, and the rough kindness, but tears of exhaustion and humiliation that she had made a fool of herself flowing down her face.

She devoured the apple hungrily before lying down beside Sylvia; and sober reflection gave her the realisation that she and her sister might have found hope with the harsh tongued warlord; and even a real chance of happiness.

In the Abbey, Annis woke before dawn as the Matins bell tolled its summons. Sister Pauline sat by her side sewing by candlelight on shifts for poor children.

"Hello?" said Annis.

"Awake are you?" Pauline laid aside her work. Annis frowned thoughtfully.

"I know your voice. You gave me medicine."

"Yes. You are a bad patient."

"I think I did not realise I was with nuns who knew what they were doing; I was afraid for my baby," it was an apology for being difficult; and Pauline smiled her grim smile.

"Yes, you made that quite clear; your baby is fine."

"Sister, how came I here?" Annis was puzzled.

"You don't recall? No, you were in a bad state when Lord Falk rode in with you."

"*Falk?*" Annis blinked "Dear God has the castle fallen? Mine husband ..." she made to rise. Pauline pushed her back.

"Your husband is in fine fettle and he and Lord Falk have both been to see how you do," Pauline was watching narrowly the young girl's face; and saw it suffused with relief, and love and joy.

"Then I *did* hear Gyrfalon's voice? … I have had such strange dreams that it all seems mixed in and I know not what is truth and what is not … he came here? Through the lines of besiegers? Oh he should not! He put himself at too much risk!" She sat up again. Pauline pushed her back again reflecting that at least the troublesome patients generally healed well.

"Lord Gyrfalon got through well enough," said Pauline; hesitated and added honestly, "he did sustain a small wound, but I have myself dressed it and I understand that as he and Lord Falk are now reconciled the siege is to be lifted."

"He let you dress it? That's good, he wasn't in too cussed a mood," commented Annis. "And he and Falk reconciled? How came that to pass? It seems almost miraculous!"

Pauline smiled a half smile.

"There are those who think that Gyrfalon's changed attitude is little short of miraculous," she said dryly "But it came about, as I understand, that he asked Lord Falk for aid for you; and they started talking."

"Then I be glad I was ill that it bring about such," said Annis. "I prayed for reconciliation; I suppose if I want miracles I have to pay the piper for being the means. Though I think my Gyrfalon have not changed so very much," she added. "He hates hypocrisy and suffers fools not at all. But he have come to recognise the hastiness in himself that has led to actions he regrets. But once these feuds start, and you be accused of certain behaviour you get rather locked into those behaviour patterns, don't you, in the attitude that you may as well be hung for a sheep as a lamb." She frowned "He wouldn't like being likened to sheep or lamb; as well be hung for a wolf as a dog perhaps would be a better phrase."

Pauline raised an eyebrow.

"And to what do you attribute his improvement in temperament?" she asked.

"I would say, if it be not immodest, that freedom from constant pain must have helped. Had he only permitted the abbess here to aid him when he kidnapped her instead of taking a contrary fit as he do at times he might have been happy sooner. Perchance she did not shout at him and call him names as I did."

Pauline blinked.

"You shouted at him and called him names?" She could hardly believe it.

Annis giggled.

"He only took exception to one; when I told

him that as an effective rescuer he was almost a good angel ... his face was priceless! And so he let me try, expecting me to fail, and then he got quite happy because I knew what I was doing. And of course being free from the clutches of that awful magician helped some too methinks."

Pauline had not heard that story; so Annis told it in a way that made light of her own contribution. Pauline drew her own conclusions.

Annis brightened as a thought struck her.

"An Falk be intending to lift the siege, only Gyrfalon's most militant enemies will hang stubbornly on; and perchance he will be able to come again and see me more easily," she said.

Pauline patted the girl's hand.

"I am sure he will come and see you," she reassured Annis. "He is not a man to care for any risk anyway."

Annis frowned.

"He had better not take too many risks or I shall have to tell him off," she said firmly. "His disregard for his own safety in coming before displeases me."

"Yet it may have helped save your life. Be not ungrateful; you clung to the sound of his voice in the crisis" said Pauline, wondering to herself that she was defending the actions of the warlord.

Annis felt her eyes fill.

"Ah, he is so good to me," she whispered. "You are right, Sister; I will not carp at him for his concern. I must have worried him greatly. I wish I had not put him through that; I sought only good by risking the marsh to speak to Falk."

Pauline knew little of what she meant but said,

"And good has come of it. Has not your husband returned to God and come to friendship again with his brother? There, child, do not cry; you are still weak. You should try to sleep."

The cup she gave Annis had a bitter taste; and with a protest on her lips at the drug, the girl slept again, good healing sleep.

Sylvia awoke refreshed and promptly woke Jehanne once she had had a peer out of the turret's window.

"We're in a castle, Je – Joachim!" she said excitedly.

Jehanne rubbed her still sleepy eyes.

"Yes, it's lord Gyrfalon's castle," she said "And we do not have to pretend now, sweetheart, about my name; he knows."

The child's mouth made a scared 'O' and Jehanne hugged her.

"It's going to be all right," she reassured her little sister, praying that it might indeed be so. "Well, let us get dressed and go explore our new home, shall we?"

An examination of the chests uncovered a tunic that would do as a gown for Sylvia; and Jehanne, after a moment's hesitation, chose breeches and a tunic for herself.

And so they came to the battlements where Gyrfalon stood, watching Falk's men pack up camp. Not all the enemy were going; for Gyrfalon had too many enemies to give up siege on him on the say so of one warrior, however famous or favoured by the church that one warrior might be. Some of those who remained had been those who had ignored the warning; some had come since. That night, those who had not heeded the warning would die; and the rest receive a warning. Gyrfalon kept his promises.

The warlord turned and favoured the youngsters with a half smile. Lukat, at his side, gave them a searching and direct look.

"You should have slept on," Gyrfalon commented.

"Sylvia woke and needed me," said Jehanne.

He nodded.

"You remain Joachim?"

She shook her head.

"N- no. But – but I like the breeches."

"You mean you would like to use your true name and make no issue of your garb?"

She nodded, grateful for the understanding.

"You can work out with me if you like," said Lukat. "My lord says you have no training at all, so I can start your instruction."

"Scubby brat, 'twas *not* what I said," said Gyrfalon. "I said she might work out with you; and I shall oversee the instruction of the both of you; and Sylvia too if she wish to be my page and learn swordplay."

Sylvia considered.

"If I learn, I don't have to use it if I not want but it might be handy," she said.

"As practical as Annis too," approved Gyrfalon. "Art of an age with Lukat here, Sylvia; he shall be your companion and show you around in his leisure hours; and the two of you will take lessons with him under Father Michael; whether art to be page and squire or ladies of the castle shalt need instruction. Lessons in warcraft shalt have from me."

"Please, what is happening out there?" asked Jehanne.

"My brother, Falk, is dispersing the church troops and mercenaries. I suspect he may set them against that nasty villain Lord Marfey; who did, after all, attempt to have my brother assassinated. The most temperate of men finds that irritating."

Jehanne shuddered.

"I've heard rumours about this Marfey,"

she said.

"Well, I doubt even rumour tells the worst of him. Anyway, they go; only my most diehard enemies remain and without the binding influence of the church and Falk, those I cannot kill will soon fall to bickering," he grinned a lupine grin, "and with a few spurious peasants spreading rumour and malificent calumnies of treachery between camps they'll hopefully fall to fighting between themselves rather than me, and we may sit back and enjoy the show until 'tis time to sally out and defeat them in detail."

Jehanne frowned as she digested this.

"That do seem to be good sense rather than spend your own troops," she said.

"Good; we may make a warrior of you yet" he said. Sylvia tugged his cloak.

"Do you *have* to fight and kill them?" she asked "Can't you make them go away another way?"

With a swift movement he lifted her so he could speak face to face.

"Angel child, your sister Annis would ask the same question. And I say the same; sometimes it isn't possible. I try a trick to frighten some commanders; and kill those that would not be frightened, that may make their men go away; and that will kill the least possible if it works. But as your sister Jehanne understand, *my* job is to see that *my* people do not get killed. Others should care for their people; and they did not have to come and attack me, you know."

Blue eyes – lighter than Annis' midnight smoky eyes – regarded him solemnly.

"I s'pose so" she said dubiously. "It's not nice."

He gave a harsh laugh.

"A lot of things aren't nice, Sylvia. Lukat will tell you that the men who tried to hurt him and his mother ere we got them to safety in the castle aren't nice; he has no sentimental feelings for them, have you sprout?"

"Only the ones that were polite like Lord Falk and Sir Lyall," said Lukat.

"What do I call you?" asked Sylvia.

"You call me Gyrfalon; for I am your goodbrother."

"And what do I call you?" asked Jehanne.

"The same; I care nothing for titles in any case. Shalt call me 'my lord' in company when you serve me as squire. Or page, at first methinks. Annis says 'my lord' but she has her way of saying it….." he tailed off, picturing Annis beside him, her face demure and her eyes roguish. And gave thanks again that so she would do again, that she lived.

Jehanne nodded.

"As Pa was used sometimes to call Ma 'Goodwife'" she nodded. She sniffed loudly. "Cold wind up here" she remarked.

Gyrfalon passed her a kerchief without comment.

Through the day the massed troops dispersed, trudging away in the cold winter's air, their bright banners and tents replaced by churned dirty-looking muddy ground. The reeve Bullard exclaimed in horror at what had happened to the village; but Gyrfalon laughed.

"Why, man, think of all that free manure! We shall plough in the piles of shit they have left and raise fine crops on it and rebuild the huts better than before too, and have a good rich little village!" He did not add, as he thought, that the blood and flesh of those who had died in the harsh camp would add even better to the nourishment of the soil. But he caught Bullard's eye; and each knew that the other had had the thought. And Gyrfalon thought better of the reeve that he was a realist.

"It's an ill wind, my lord, that blows nobody any good," ventured the reeve.

"Aye, man, it is," Gyrfalon agreed. "And you may pass the word also that by next harvest the keep will have an heir. Now that my lady is out of danger from the fever 'tis not inappropriate to pass on that message."

Bullard grinned.

"Congratulations, my lord!" he cried "Will our little lady be coming home soon?"

Gyrfalon nodded.

"I hope so; but I will not risk her travelling before she is fit enough. I hope to have her here for Christmas. Now, Bullard, I expect you to organise a celebration for all over the raising of the siege and mine own good news."

Bullard stammered pleased acquiescence and hurried to set such things into motion. Gyrfalon remained at the battlement, watching his brother's lithe figure expedite the departure of stragglers. At last, Falk approached the castle and gave a whistle – a signal used long ago between the brothers to get each other's attention. Gyrfalon whistled back the curious lilting call and waved a laconic hand; then descended the gatehouse stair to meet Falk at the sallyport.

"Want to get your horse and go visiting?" Suggested Falk. "I can even arrange an escort of church knights an you like."

Gyrfalon snorted.

"Is there anyone in the land can stand against the pair of us united?" he asked.

Falk grinned.

"Probably not," he admitted.

Chapter 17

Despite startled and disapproving exclamations of the sister sitting with her, Annis flew out of bed straight into Gyrfalon's strong arms.

Close he held her, tight to his chest, burying his face in her pale hair. Then he lifted her and deposited her firmly back on the palliasse.

"She's supposed to stay, there isn't she, sister?" he said ironically to the nun "I wish you joy; she rarely does what I tell her, but perhaps Sister Pauline might get further; she's a more fearsome personality than I."

The little nun twittered in confusion at such comments from the feared warlord, uncertain if he insulted Pauline or what.

"He compliments Pauline," said Annis, dryly possessing herself firmly of her husband's hand and clinging to it, her eyes devouring his face as he gazed into hers. There was no need for words between them; and Falk beckoned to the nun to leave the lovers alone.

Later, while Annis ate, and the brothers declined to dine on the frugal repast of the nuns in the refectory but rather sat with her, Gyrfalon told her and his brother of the two children who had accosted him. Falk listened, half amazed that his brother should have shown the pair such gentleness; acknowledging Gyrfalon's desire to act as his adored Annis would have him do. Annis nodded, and pulled a face.

"I fear I do have a number of half siblings" she said "One is a captain in father's guard, a mean bully like him. I expect we'll have to go to war with that one when my father dies for my birthright of the lands. He never forgave mother for producing only one live babe and that a puling girl, and flaunted his male bastards before her and me. Such girls as were his get he made nothing of, so I know nothing of them. Indeed, I fancy he does not know the extent of his get; he's not the most careful of men. One day, he'll catch a disease and it'll turn black and drop off."

Falk exclaimed in some shock at this callous and revolting thought from a young girl calmly eating bread and sausage; and Gyrfalon laughed out loud.

"Falk, your face is just priceless!" he chuckled "Remember, mine Annis is a healer; and knows her husbandry too. She's an earthy little thing for all that she looks like a saint on an icon."

Annis was revolted.

"No-one has ever suggested I look pi-faced and sanctified before!" she protested "And I swear half of them look constipated too. And nor has mine husband ever complained that I be so distant and unkissable as such!"

Gyrfalon's eyes met hers yearningly; and she blushed, smiling at him.

"I take it back," he murmured, "even though you did once call me your good angel, you pert virago."

"Rankles that still? I shall have to make it up to you," she said.

Falk cleared his throat ostentatiously. Somehow the highly charged atmosphere seemed to him to be wrong in an Abbey.

"What are you planning to do with the children you found?" he asked, changing the subject back, rather pointedly.

"Look after them," said Gyrfalon simply. "What the hell else am I supposed to do?"

Annis frowned in thought.

"A little girl so young we can raise easily; she shall play too with Lukat. Jehanne, methinks needs gentle handling from what you have said. I will teach her basics in swordplay with Elissa's help; but your style of teaching, my lord, may prove too much for her fragile ego, bereaved and scared as she has been."

Gyrfalon snorted.

"I pushed you, my love, to see how far I could push. You are unique and thrived on it; that made me proud of you."

"You push all that you want to see

succeed" she contradicted "You push Lukat, who loves it for you do not baby him; and I wager you pushed Falk too."

Falk nodded.

"He did."

Annis continued,

"Once she has the basics it were better, methinks, that she squire someone more patient than thee, my love. Besides, dear lord, I am jealous of mine own position at your side as squire. I suggest there be none better to teach her tha other kin – which is to say, Falk."

Falk blinked and his jaw dropped.

"But …." He managed.

"You need a squire, dear brother," said Annis firmly. "It behoves you to take one as befits you position of church champion. Who better to serve you than one who has – albeit tenuous – familial connections?"

Falk could muster no cogent argument against that, though he attempted to expostulate. Annis cut through his protests.

"Good, that's settled," she said. "You must lodge with us a while to get to know the child. It were unfair to pack her off to a stranger as though she were not wanted. And of course if you take dislike to each other, we shall have to rethink. And you and Gyrfalon too need to get to know each other again and do the sort of things brothers do together that involve getting tired, wet and muddy and explaining how big the one was that got away. Isn't that so?"

Falk was suddenly beginning to gain insight into the point at which Annis took over his brother's life. She had simply decided that Gyrfalon was hers; and his poor brother had not stood a chance! He exchanged a rueful look with Gyrfalon.

"Managing woman, my wife," said the warlord. "Life is generally far easier if you fall in with her plans. My men are terrified of her I assure you; and I am thoroughly henpecked."

He was laughing as he said this, and Annis took his hand firmly that she might gaze adoringly up at him.

"It seems to be a henpecking that agrees with you brother," laughed Falk ruefully.

Gyrfalon visited the Abbey every other day while Annis regained her strength and renewed her friendship with old sister Agatha; who to her surprise was still alive. How much the old nun understood or remembered of recent events was debateable; but she recognised Annis, though she insisted on addressing her as though she was a small child. Annis cared not; she was grateful that Agatha had reached a safe sanctuary and had been safe these past years.

After a week, Annis pronounced herself fit

to leave on Gyrfalon's next visit; and stuck firmly to her decision in the face of Sister Pauline's opposition. That worthy's argument about risk to the baby was considered briefly; but set aside.

"For," as Annis said, "'tis the worry of being from home will harm him more than a ride. The Good Lord gave women well padded behinds to save their unborn infants that much jiggling on horseback."

To argue to the contrary seemed almost blasphemous; and Pauline gave up. The girl was stubborn enough to survive in any case and so the Sister said, to Annis' amusement.

"You noticed," said Gyrfalon dryly, who was staying well out of the argument.

Pauline scowled at him. The little nun who had been so scandalised that Gyrfalon had said Pauline was more fearsome than he had reported to Pauline, to that Sister's amusement; but it seemed appropriate to scowl.

"Almost – not quite, but almost – I pity you lord Gyrfalon," she said sternly.

Gyrfalon grinned. He was starting to understand Pauline and knew she but teased.

"Remind me never to take you hostage Pauline," he said. "You might not be boring as a hostage, but I wager you've a tongue sharp enough to cut a man's gizzards out at twenty paces."

"Why thank you Lord Gyrfalon," said Pauline.

Back at the castle, Sylvia and Jehanne had settled into a routine. Gyrfalon had employed Loveday, Lukat's mother, to see to the little girl's physical needs and to free Jehanne to enjoy the last remnants of her girlhood without having to be mother to a small girl. Sylvia was happy enough; she and Lukat had become firm friends, for the boy was determined to protect his Lady's little sister and Sylvia was impressed enough by Lukat's knowledge of the castle and position at Gyrfalon's heels to accept his protection. They squabbled and played together like brother and sister.

Gyrfalon had schooled himself to be patient in his instruction of Jehanne; teaching her too the basics of etiquette to suit her new estate in life, as well as the basics in castle management. He oversaw Elissa's basic instruction in swordplay, that he made comment on and called for answers to questions afterwards. He had made a shrewd guess as to Annis' purpose in suggesting that Jehanne squire Falk and wanted to oversee the girl's progress that she not get to Falk with bad habits that his brother would hesitate to be harsh in correcting. In the evenings, Gyrfalon made a point of telling both girls – and Lukat who sat at Gyrfalon's feet to hear stories – highly embroidered tales of his and Falk's childhood exploits, to make Falk a figure of more substance to the girl even before he came to stay. And briefly he filled Jehanne in on the background of the feud when she asked, confused, how come they had fought but were now friends again.

Jehanne herself was enjoying life. She spared many a guilty moment to go to the chapel to pray for the souls of her parents and her brother; and still she grieved. Yet life was good – and she was young. And it both grieved and pleased her that she could see that it would not be long before Sylvia saw Gyrfalon as much her father as their own; and realer in some ways as the memory faded of their parents in the little girl's mind. And of course, their father was not even Sylvia's real father by birth. Well, Lord Gyrfalon seemed to be a good father figure to Sylvia. Jehanne looked forward to meeting his wife – Sylvia's sister – with some considerable trepidation. Suppose this Lady Annis, who seemed to be held in great awe by the soldiery, wanted Jehanne thrown out as no blood kin?

Jehanne said nothing of her fears to Gyrfalon; but she drank in every day to have good memories if the worst come to the worst.

Annis' return home was unexpected, having made so firm and instant a decision, but the news that their lady rode with Gyrfalon roused cheers throughout the castle and everyone who might gathered in the courtyard to see her come in.

As Nightmare clattered onto the courtyard cobbles making light of his extra burden, Jehanne gasped at the little figure secure in the warlord's arms. Why, she was so little and frail looking – Annis seemed almost transparent since her illness – and so like Sylvia! And how plain it was how much that fearsome Lord Gyrfalon adored her; and the men too, many of whom wept openly in joy, knelt to her, and crossed themselves. If so adored a person decided against Jehanne, she would have her way.

Jehanne did not need to worry.

Annis slid to the ground with Gyrfalon's aid and came straight to her, taking her hands.

"You must be Jehanne! How nice to have a sister nearly mine own age to chat to!" she said "Elissa and I have only some things in common though she is a dear friend," she turned to reach out to touch Elissa's arm. "Oh, Kai, there you are, have you been making the common salves I taught you?" She said to another who wanted to see and touch her, as he nodded "Caleb! I am glad you never took the fever, my lord relies on you so much!"

There were others, all greeted by name, and the tiny girl almost knocked over by Lukat's exuberant greeting. Jehanne steadied her with an arm and Annis smiled thanks. Jehanne could see why she was so loved; she knew every man's name and all about him and asked after ailments and family.

Gyrfalon intervened.

"Lady Annis is still not well," he said "She is glad to see all you reprobates – though I'm not sure why – now let her get to her chamber."

There was affectionate laughter at his insults and the press of men cleared from Annis who still held Jehanne's arm.

"Ah, nice to breathe again," said Annis "Your pardon, Jehanne; I had to greet people. Sisters understand things like that. Isn't it nice that we look different, we won't get odious comparisons. It don't matter with little Sylvia of course as there's enough years between me and her; but you and I will have to make sure she has a good sense of worth for herself and not let people make her into a small edition of me, mustn't we?"

Jehanne blinked.

"Y-yes" she agreed "B-but I'm not really your sister. I'm her half sister," she explained herself.

"Close enough," said Annis, airily. "Anyway, I be sure we can be close enough friends to be as sisters, can't we?"

"I - maybe. I hope so," Jehanne was cautious. Annis laughed.

"Well, we shall see," she smiled apologetically "I'm still feeling weak; will you lend me your arm to get to bed?"

"Willingly!" said Jehanne, obliging. Her arm was strong from helping on her parents' smallholding that she had little trouble hefting a sword.

Gyrfalon started forward; but checked himself. It was important that Annis establish a rivalry free friendship with Jehanne and she was using this means to do so. He heaved Lukat up by the scruff and informed him that they had a horse to see to; and in the stables told the lad that it were unfair to prevent the sisters who had never met having a chance to be private; even as he, Lukat, had met his grandfather before Annis had seen to his foot that first day. Lukat considered that; and nodded acquiescence. Besides, it was good to be talked to man to man by his lord; and he drew himself up to his full height in pride.

Annis knew she had to overcome Jehanne's feelings of inferiority and insecurity; and chatted on about the things that would need to be done on the farmsteads and in the village to repair the ravages of war. And Jehanne was able to respond knowledgeably and was grateful.

Annis did not need to pretend to need the younger girl's strong arm by the time they reached the chamber she shared with Gyrfalon; she was sweating and shaking with fatigue.

"He could have carried you," said Jehanne.

"He could; but he knows me well enough that I wanted time with my new sisters; and that I be too stubborn to let a staircase defeat me," said Annis. "I am glad however that I be wed now and have not a further two flights to mine old room, that is now yours. There, help me onto the bed. Sylvia, my sweet, why don't you pour us all a goblet of water from the carafe on the table?" she smiled as the child rushed to comply. "Then you can tell me all the story of how you came to be here, without leaving out the important bits that men never remember!"

They sat above the salt for the evening meal as a family; Gyrfalon on the great armed chair as lord, and had his big chair from his chamber brought down as added support for his young bride, pale still, but erect in bearing. To his right sat Falk; and on Annis' left was Jehanne, quiet and a little ill at ease in her still newly exalted position. Sylvia and Lukat ate earlier and had been put to bed already. The rest of the high table was made up of Bullard the reeve – for the village being largely destroyed the villagers still lived within the castle until the building of new houses might begin – Father Michael, Elissa, Foregrim the Captain over all; and Wulfric, Falk's personal bodyguard, suspicious of Gyrfalon, but willing to trust where Falk led.

Annis laid down her knife and looked around the table.

"And now," she said quietly, "We must needs discuss what is to be done about the slavers that would have taken Jehanne and Sylvia and who doubtless prey on others; for I consider it would be a good Christmas gift to all children to deal with them permanently."

Father Michael crossed himself.

"I fear that none but a violent solution will end their pernicious depredations," he said regretfully. Gyrfalon grinned.

"You see why I like this priest, brother?" He remarked to Falk "He has a good grasp of reality and does not wrap things up in sanctimony and clean linen."

"Do not tease the poor man," chided Annis. Michael flushed and smiled.

"I do not mind, Lady Annis. And Lord Gyrfalon is right; it is not Christian charity and humility to hide from the truth."

"Well that's a first; approval from a representative of the church," laughed Gyrfalon.

"They didn't get us," ventured Jehanne.

"No child: but they might have done," said Falk gravely. "And there are other children. If we can clean up this region it will be a very good start."

"It will also," added Gyrfalon grimly, "be a start to march with some of your vaunted church knights on Marfey's lands and evict him."

"Evict? That don't sound anything like permanent enough," protested Annis. "The only word I can think of suitable that sounds anything similar is eviscerate."

Gyrfalon chuckled.

"Bloodthirsty minx. Hang then; I care not. If the knights are too nice to do the job, if they evict him the peasants will. Or eviscerate him. One thing – or another."

Annis grinned.

"I *like* the way you think, my lord," she said happily.

"It is too late to plan for Marfey," interposed Falk dryly. "I already dispatched men to hunt down and hang the man before he reached one of his bought and paid for cardinals."

"Truly, brother, my wife and I accept the spirit of your belated wedding gift," said Gyrfalon, his eyes twinkling.

"I wasn't planning on having his head brought to the Lady Annis on a plate, however," said Falk firmly "She may not be squeamish over such things but I am."

"I think you're supposed to boil all the flesh off and mount with silver," said Annis. "I'm a little hazy about the details but I've read about goblets made of skulls. I should think Marfey's whole being would be too poisonous to drink out of anyway ... Sorry Falk" as Falk made protesting noises. "It would not be so pretty an object methinks."

"Fellow's no real challenge anyway," put in Foregrim, unmoved by his lady's occasionally bloodthirsty tendencies "Even church knights ought to be able to manage that fat oaf easily. The slavers you want to move against, my lady, are another proposition. They are always on the move; and the places where they customarily stop are full of people either bribed or terrorised into compliance."

Annis shrugged.

"They can in that case be outbribed and out terrorised," she said coldly. "Gyrfalon has a certain reputation; let us use it. And as church knights are sworn to poverty, they will be happy to turn a portion of Marfey's coffers over to the relief of distressed victims like his own."

"My lady," said Falk, astounded, "did anyone ever tell you how manipulative you can be?"

"Why yes, my brother, mine own dear

husband tells me constantly!" she told him brightly.

"He's right; you are a minx," Falk had to laugh.

"We might set a trap," said Jehanne, then coloured and dropped her eyes as the others turned to look at her.

"Continue, little sister," Gyrfalon encouraged. "I believe I see what you are thinking, but go on."

"What I thought was, that if their spies caught sight of Sylvia and me … but I'd be afraid to risk her…."

"But at a distance, where size were not as evident, I have the same hair," said Annis, happily. An you were seen with Sylvia she could straight way be taken up on horse by one of our people hard enough to take care of her and cut down any slavers – Elissa say – and ride to safety; and I'd join you instead and lead them to a hiding place we set up that they would see a figure with the hair. I am smaller than you anyway so that too would add verisimilitude….."

Gyrfalon's knuckles had whitened on the edge of the table; and with a conscious effort he released their grip. His voice did not shake; and Falk, who had noticed his brother's battle with himself admired Gyrfalon the more for that; admired a man that had learned to love well enough not to smother.

"And while you waited for the rest of us to spring the ambush, any that got ahead of themselves would find not two frightened children but a brave lass and a very competent swordswoman," Gyrfalon said, apparently calmly.

Annis sighed with relief.

"I wondered if you were going to veto it, dear heart," she said, smiling at him. He crooked a finger under her chin.

"I never win an argument with you, my wife. But you *will* promise me something," his voice was steel; and willingly she nodded. Some tones of voice were unassailable. "You will not risk our child," he said. She nodded again.

"We are only a little diversion to keep them occupied for you and Falk to have fun with," she acknowledged. "See, I can be an obedient and dutiful wife!"

"When it suits you," he growled, smiling at her.

Falk said,

"But we shall not catch the leader – only foot soldiers sent to do the dirty work."

"They'll talk," said Annis firmly.

"I will not countenance the use of torture," his voice was firm, his face stubborn.

Annis raised her eyebrows.

"Torture? Who needs such crudity?" she said scornfully "With potions I can loosen their tongues yet leave them quite unharmed for the hangman."

Falk blinked.

"Truly? Then why do not heads of states use such methods?"

Annis chuckled.

"I suspect that they have expensive physicians of proper learning and more Latin than good sense; who have learned only such cures as be laid down in the classics. Such I learned from Sister Agatha – to some degree; but the nuns also use herbalism like unto that used by village wise women. And village wise women use more than the nuns, and you have to unravel from their cures the magic that may or may not work to get the truth, though our village wise woman was the daughter of a gypsy with good lore from yet another source. And the visiting sailor storyteller had tales of the cures of the Orient where ways are strange. By examining different ways I have learned the more and have more exotic lore at my disposal than a self satisfied little man in a robe with a degree from a university."

Falk looked at her anew.

"Then you probably know more than many twice or thrice your age," he acknowledged "You should write it down."

"Some I have started to; I thought to do more as I got unwieldy in my pregnancy that it were something useful I could do. And I pass on knowledge too to those who are interested. I hope Sylvia may like to learn; Jehanne have not an interest," she smiled. "So we need not worry about finding the leaders or any place there be slaves held that we might free them, for our prisoners will beg to tell us every detail of their revolting little lives."

Gyrfalon grinned.

"My dear, I'm only surprised that you fled your father's castle instead of poisoning your father."

She regarded him gravely.

"It crossed my mind," she said seriously. "But I could not bring myself to use the gifts God gave men to bring harm – and sink to his level. He killed my mother because she angered him and she was inconvenient. I was angry with him and I found him an inconvenience and I wanted not to act like him. This however is different. It may inconvenience the slavers I drug; and I care not how much they suffer; and it will help to save others."

"Vixen, I recall you threatened – so delicately – to temporarily inconvenience me," said Gyrfalon.

"Not at all, my lord; it was not a threat. It was merely a promise of what could happen if I were made miserable," she said demurely.

"What?" Asked Falk, curious despite himself.

"Purgatives," exclaimed Gyrfalon succinctly "Doubtless at both ends if she were feeling particularly vindictive."

"Oh," Falk half wished he hadn't asked!

Annis just grinned!

Chapter 18

Jehanne held Sylvia's hand firmly as she slipped into their old hut. It was already looking the worse for wear, some of the thatch slipping away and letting the rain, snow and hail in. She waited inside with her little sister, making a bundle to make it seem as though she had come back for some goods. And one thing indeed she meant to keep; their parents' bed quilt, made of scraps of all kinds of fabric from clothes made and odd scraps bartered for from the tinker who would exchange fancier cloths he had got for good linen scraps to sell to paper makers. Jehanne waited long enough that someone might have noticed; then as they left she let the door bang as though by accident; and glanced nervously about before dragging Sylvia at a run towards the forest. Fortunately Sylvia had liked the idea of playing a game to catch the bad men and willingly followed her sister's lead. Jehanne and Gyrfalon had been privily to see the local reeve, who had been terrified of the warlord, but glad the children had a place where they were at least better protected than with slavers; and on hearing Lord Gyrfalon's desire to catch the slavers had been willing to tip them off that the girls had been seen around, that watchers be set.

Elissa waited out of sight to take the little girl up in front of her; and Annis emerged from her hiding place amongst the dry bracken beside Jehanne. She nodded to Elissa; and the woman warrior rode off with the little girl, whose part had been enough to excite without scaring her.

"We must needs let any following see glimpses of mine hair," said Annis. "One comes; I hear his footsteps. He is no countryman, he crashes through the brake like a billy goat after nannies and puffs and blows like leaky bellows."

Jehanne swallowed and nodded; Annis' levity helped overcome the dry terror in her throat and the tight knot of fear in her bowels. Reassuringly, Annis took the younger girl's hand and they ran into the forest. Annis' fine golden tresses streamed out behind her, enough to tantalise and draw any follower on to the lair they had carefully built the day before. It was in the middle of a huge gorse thicket on the edge of a clearing; a thicket old enough that the centre had died, leaving a ring. They had cut a tunnel into it and built a roof, thatched carefully so that a tall man looking could see it; as children might not be expected to realise. From this roof escaped a thin spiral of blue smoke supposedly coming from their cookfire. Gyrfalon's men were hidden about the forest; the warlord himself and his brother were in the gorse lair waiting to spring the trap. Gyrfalon had made a dry comment about the narrow entrance; and Annis had shrugged.

"Two children would scarce be like to make an opening bigger than it had to be. And you have armour, my lord," she declared unsympathetically.

Falk chuckled reminiscently.

"Gyrfalon, do you remember, we used to play at castles in these gorse fortresses? We would take turn to defend and attack and sustained awful scratches that we heeded not; or we would pretend that we held it against imaginary besiegers without... I recall I caused a fearful to-do because I fell asleep in one and no-one could find me; I'd gone to play on mine own because you had lessons."

"I remember," said Gyrfalon grimly "Your mother accused me of doing away with you or hiding you and demanded that I be beaten until I revealed where you were."

"Father never did, surely?" Falk was aghast.

"I think he considered it; even with the word of the priest who taught me Latin that I had been with him, and he had seen you tell me to hurry up with my lessons ere I began ... and then suddenly you appeared and demanded your evening meal because you were hungry" said Gyrfalon "I never quite made up my mind if I were just relieved to see you safe or wanted to give you the best spanking of your life for worrying me."

"I'm sorry," said Falk contritely. Gyrfalon shrugged.

"Boys," he said succinctly. "And probably girls too," he added reflectively. "As no doubt I shall find out when mine own children give me grey hairs by doing the sorts of things you and I did."

Falk laughed and linked his arm into his brother's.

"It was my mother, wasn't it?" He said quietly "She started turning father against you, didn't she? Because she felt jealous on my behalf, having a big boy not many years younger than her who was a rival to her own child.

"Aye; I'm afraid so," he said. "But you may abuse a man's sire, his wife and his children but I have heard it said you should never say a word against his mother or his horse."

Falk laughed.

"Idiot," he said. "I – I do not recall her well enough to have deep memories. I loved her; of course I did. But even as a small child it angered me that sometimes she was unfair to my brother" he sighed deeply "We have neither of us behaved totally well; but circumstances were not always helpful."

"We have each other now," said Gyrfalon

"And the world may never recover from it."

They grinned at each other; and suddenly looked more alike than either realised!

The two brothers were waiting in comradely silence as the two girls scrambled in through the entrance.

"We've a hunter behind us," reported Annis. "He isn't what you might term efficient."

"Good," said Gyrfalon. "Let's hope he reports back to someone to claim his reward."

Annis buckled on her sword in anticipation. The lair was deceptively rough; but left plenty of room for fighting.

It was but an hour's wait before sounds of grunting, swearing and the shaking of branches heralded an intruder; and Falk and Gyrfalon stepped to the sides of the entrance quietly that they might remain unnoticed if, as they suspected there was more than one intruder.

The first unkempt head poked through. Jehanne gave a little involuntary gasp.

"Har, har, we has you wenches now!" chuckled the slaver "Cmon Lem, they'm both in here," he heaved himself out of the tunnel and advanced on the girls. His companion, a fatter man, came slower and cursing; and Gyrfalon clenched his fists in impatience: for both must in for the trap to be sprung and none left to flee and warn their superiors. The first started to reach out a hand towards Annis; and his face was lascivious.

"Well, older'n I thought....very nice too," he said.

Annis whipped out her sword; and her would-be assailant started laughing.

"Fight me would you, liddle girl?" he said. ""D'ye see that, Lem? The liddle girlie has a swordie! Well, I'll not mark you up, but just disarm you!" He drew his own sword; and suddenly he was hard pressed for Annis advanced on him with determined tread and skilful economical movements and he found he had no breath to laugh any more! Gyrfalon had half an eye on her approvingly; and Falk watched astounded. He had not yet seen their practise bouts; for they had been too busy setting up this play to catch the slavers.

At last the second head appeared – it was but seconds after Annis drew blade but it seemed an eternity to Gyrfalon and Falk.

A hand on either side seized the villain by the scruff of his neck to drag him howling at the violence done to his person by the gorse as they did so. The other fists of his assailants hit him simultaneously on the sides of his head and he lost all further interest in the proceedings.

"We have swordies too," said Gyrfalon

coldly, nodding Jehanne to help deal with the man Lem as he strode, panther like to lay his own cold steel over the first man's shoulder against his neck.

The man whinnied in sudden terror.

"I cede him to you to play with my lord," said Annis sweetly, saluting her husband.

The fight was short and ugly and as Annis remarked to Jehanne of no instructive value since a swordsman battering an idiot was scarcely edifying.

Gyrfalon used the flat of his blade and the pommel to reduce the man to a gasping pile on the ground rather than follow his instincts to carve the man into little pieces.

He did make sure to hit him in as many painful places as he could however.

Soon both were tied.

Annis approached the prisoners with a stoppered flask. The fatter one had recovered his wits enough to groan by now.

"Be so good as to hold their nostrils closed, brother Falk," Annis said briskly. Falk gave her a startled look; but complied, nipping the nose of the first man. His breathing restricted he was forced to open his mouth; and Annis poured a measure of her brew into it. He must perforce swallow or drown; and swallow he did, spluttering at the bitter draft. The performance was repeated on the other rogue, despite his voluble protests and attempts to gag. Annis explained,

"'Tis a method used with small children who refuse medicine. It causes no harm but has the desired result. It will be a few minutes before the drug has the desired effect. When their pupils dilate we can question them for then the effect will have become sufficiently profound."

"What's in it?" asked Falk curiously.

"Very small amounts of Henbane and Belladonna" she replied "Very dangerous if you don't know what you're doing. The preparation is crucial. Fortunately for them – although when we hang them they may disagree – I do know what I am doing."

"Indeed!" said Falk, amazed once again by his tiny and implacable sister-in-law.

It was not long before the two precious villains were in a stupored state. Annis spoke in a soothing voice.

"Not very fair of your boss to leave you to be captured and take all the blame for him" she said conversationally.

They grunted in vague assent.

"Now, where was it you said you'd meet him with the girls?"

One of the men shook his head in a dazed manner as though to clear his turgid thoughts.

"Di' we say?" he queried dully.

"Of course. You wanted to tell me," said Annis "But I just want to check I had it right."

He nodded owlishly.

"At the river.... By the sign of the Green Goose. Mine host is a good friend or ours" he achieved a sleepy leer "He often puts up li'l guests ai y'know what I mean."

"I know what you mean," said Annis softly "And where are the slaves kept if they are not in the inn?"

"Oh, on ve barge.... There be a landing stage upstream f'om ve inn...." His lids drooped.

"You may both sleep now if you like," said Annis. "I'm sure you're tired."

Drugged and suggestible their heads lolled.

Falk was shaking his head in amazement.

"You are one very dangerous young woman," he said.

She shrugged.

"It's taken you this long to work that out? I am your brother's true match. And if you ask me. 'tis a good thing, for we need dangerous people to act against scum like this," she added crisply.

"My wife!" Gyrfalon dropped an arm around her shoulder, pride in his voice "There's not another in the world like her, Falk," he gave a lupine grin "A bit tough on you, but there it is. She saw me first."

Annis grinned up at him.

"My lord is understandably biased. It may be that a man as virtuous as Lord Falk might find himself at a loss were there another such virago as you usually name me such as myself."

"Good," said Gyrfalon, savagely, kissing her.

Mine host at the sign of the Green Goose was very happy with the lucrative arrangement he had with the hard faced slaver. Olav Hardmann, the said slaver, was a competent warrior whose career as a mercenary had been damaged by the loss of his right lower arm; where now he sported a hook. That and the scarred, villainous looking visage he sported helped to cast terror into the hearts of the slaves he took, especially the children. Hardmann specialised in children; he might sample his own wares amongst the older girls but the children he kept frightened but innocent.

His high paying customers, some of them churchmen, paid highly for that.

Neither the fat greasy innkeeper not the hard bodied slaver were prepared, as they sat in the inn drinking and discussing business, for what happened next.

The most beautiful young girl Hardmann

had ever seen walked in the door. Her hair was so pale as to be almost silver; her skin was as white as snow. Her eyes, dark in her pale face, made her even lovelier than the infant of similar looks from the village of Avenford he had ordered the capture of. She must be an older sister. If she had come to beg for the brat....Hardmann leered. The child was not yet in his possession but he did not doubt that she would be; and he would enjoy the favours of this one as payment to release the child; and then keep both of them to sell.

"Well, well, my pretty! What can I so for you?" he chuckled.

Annis viewed him thoughtfully. She could guess pretty much the thoughts that were going through his heard; his face was not pretty but because it was scarred he did not trouble to hide his thoughts from it thinking none would notice.

She smiled a little smile.

"You can die," she said, in a dispassionate tone.

Hardmann flung back his head and started to laugh. It was a laugh that ended on a horrible gurgle as Annis' little throwing knife caught him full in the throat.

His men, who had been preparing to watch the fun, jumped up. Most of them promptly fell down with knives and arrows and crossbow bolts sprouting from their necks and shoulder blades as Gyrfalon, Falk and their band stood up outside the windows and loosed their missiles.

"I like your double crossbow," said Elissa to Wulfric. "I don't fire a bow account of not having learned from an early age like a boy."

"I'll see about building you one" said Ranulf. "If we're going to work together it makes sense to have Lord Gyrfalon's favourite captains as effective as possible."

"Cheers" said Elissa, eying him covertly and speculatively.

Meanwhile the brothers leaped lightly through the casements into the inn, cutting down with efficiency and ruthlessness any that remained.

"*ANNIS*! You robbed me of my prey!" roared Gyrfalon.

"'Twas my sister he sought to steal!" retorted the girl "And the way he looked at me meant he was planning on taking me too! I claim first right!" She grinned suddenly "Besides, it were too tempting a target to pass up!"

Gyrfalon grunted.

"And what of this pig?" he asked, heaving up the landlord from behind the bar where he had thrown himself. "What will my lady have me do with him?"

"You insult good swine, my lord, by comparing them to so venal and contemptible a creature," said Annis. "He hath a prosperous enough house here that he did not need to supplement his profits helping with the trafficking of children. He was on good terms with the slaver as far as I could see. Hang him."

Gyrfalon's men nodded approval; this was their ruthless lady who was gentle at need and as hard as nails when she had to be. The couple of church knights along with Falk looked faintly askance and glanced at their captain, Falk.

Falk nodded.

"You are right, Lady Annis; we have no choice. An example must be made that those who aid slavers are tarred with the same brush.

Gyrfalon thrust the squealing man towards two of his men.

"See it done," he said.

They took the struggling, pleading, sobbing captive without.

Annis went over to the slaver and opened the scrip he wore.

"Looting, sister mine?" Falk enquired surprised.

"Looking for anything that may help us find some of his customers," she said grimly. "It occurs to me that maybe I was too hasty in killing him ere we had questioned him thoroughly."

"Runs in the family," said Gyrfalon laconically. "Hastiness I mean. Anything in there my virago?"

Annis nodded.

"A rewarding number of letters ... some of them seem to be requests of quite particular types .... Falk of you goodness, if you know any *honest* high ranking churchmen you should show some of these to them. I have here two bishops, a cardinal and a prior to date in addition to many merchants in the city. And if he have a chest in a chamber above stairs I wager we may find more there."

Falk made a noise of disgust.

"Iniquitous!" he said.

"Aye; but power can corrupt; and more often, methinks, the corrupt seek power to indulge their corruption," said Annis. "The slaves will be upstream no doubt as our loathsome informant said. And Falk, ere thou exercise the famous family hastiness and your own naïve zeal, and thou returnest them willy-nilly to the bosoms of their family *do* check that it were not their families sold them in the first place."

Falk was shocked; but nodded. Somehow he could see Peter Haldane selling Annis into slavery if the price was good enough. He had after all been prepared to effectively sell her in marriage to the best or most useful bidder. And girl children were, to many a peasant useless, unable to do as hard work as a boy on the land and requiring a dowry into the bargain. It made sense that the less sensitive might just see the selling of unwanted daughters as reasonable as well as profitable.

Annis and Jehanne soothed the frightened slave children and began the painstaking task of discovering their origins and how they came to be in slavery; so that those who had been kidnapped might be returned home.

"You'll not offer homes to any, I suppose, brother?" Falk asked Gyrfalon.

Gyrfalon grunted.

"Do I look like a nun able to deal with excess brats? Kin is different," he said nodding to Jehanne, who smiled shyly at him for that comment. "If any have useful skills like spinning or herb lore I can find them a home. Otherwise let the nuns train them as good maidservants."

"Does not Annis need a maid?" Falk suggested slyly.

The warlord snorted amusement.

"Not she! She's extremely capable, never know what to do with one, who'd end up bone idle for having no tasks to do! A nursery maid in the future, that is different. And I've one in mind anyway, Lukat's mother. Besides, what will we do with some puling wench when we go on campaign against the northmen next campaign season?"

Falk stared.

"You're never taking the Lady Annis on campaign!" he said in horror.

Gyrfalon grinned wolfishly.

"No? I'd not dare break that to her. Would you?"

Falk blinked.

"Lady Annis? My sister? Can he be serious?"

Annis chuckled.

"He'd better be."

"And who will hold the castle?"

She grinned.

"Jehanne will have been well trained by them; unless she comes too; certainly she will be capable of so doing with Foregrim's help. I'd been holding my father's castle since I was younger than she. Else Foregrim will do so; he's getting too old to go on campaign."

Falk sighed.

"You are extraordinary, Annis," he said. "I wonder, if you had been in Alys's situation, you might not have ridden forth to find an erstwhile betrothed and tell him that you no longer wished to wed him."

Annis looked surprised.

"Assuredly I should!" she said "To write were cowardly; though still better than sending no word. To leave it overlong were dishonest. In honour, I could not see that anyone could do anything else without making a cheat and liar of themselves. Of course I should have ridden north in Alys's shoes. But I understand," she added kindly. "From such as I have heard from My Lord Gyrfalon that the Lady Alys had the misfortune to be rather wet and not over-endowed with intellect." Falk flushed angrily and opened his mouth; then determinedly shut it with a snap.

"I never said so," said Gyrfalon mildly. "Indeed I never thought so at the time."

"But you described her actions my lord," said Annis, "and she seems to mostly have hidden or run until forced to bay with another to protect like a roe deer with her fawn. Sorry, my brother, but I think that had she lived you would have tired of her lack of spirit and been hung up on guilt for the reason of it."

"We shall never know," Falk's face was set and grim.

Gyrfalon put a hand on his shoulder.

"You know – or perchance you do not – that I am truly sorry for the hurting of you," he said harshly "She split us before; and you were the one that brought her into conversation. Let her not split us again from beyond the grave; let her rest in peace and we live in peace."

Falk bowed his head.

"You are right," he said. "She is gone; it is time to live for the future; to build a better world for my nephews and nieces yet to come." He looked rueful. "One time we fought, and you fell into a dark chasm, and I though I had killed you. I do not know how you survived, but I am glad you did. My life was empty. I missed even the hatred between us; without you, though I could work for the church nothing had any great meaning any more."

"And now, let any that cross us beware; and let us go on a spree of cleansing!" grinned Gyrfalon.

The brothers embraced.

And so the party returned to the castle in time for a Christmas celebration that was unrivalled in its joy and comradeship as brothers celebrated together; and the children enjoyed the excitement of the season.

And the villagers rejoiced that their lord and lady had the support of the church and might too expect help from the same in a campaign against the northmen when the barbarians ventured south; and Gyrfalon and Falk planned tactics with the odd opinion from Annis and wide eyed wondering attention of Jehanne that they might inflict such losses on the northmen in one campaign as to frighten them from returning for many long years.

Printed in Poland
by Amazon Fulfillment
Poland Sp. z o.o., Wrocław